June Tate was born in Southampton in the 1930s and spent the early years of her childhood in the Cotswolds before returning to Southampton after the start of the Second World War. After leaving school she became a hairdresser and spent several years working on cruise ships, first on the *Queen Mary* and then on the *Mauritania*, meeting many Hollywood film stars and V.I.P.s on her travels. After her marriage to an airline pilot, she lived in Sussex and Hampshire before moving to Estoril in Portugal.

June Tate, who has two adult daughters, now lives in Sussex.

Also By June Tate

Riches of the Heart
No One Promised Me Tomorrow
For the Love of a Soldier

Better Days

June Tate

headline

First published in 2001
by HEADLINE BOOK PUBLISHING

First published in paperback in 2002
by HEADLINE BOOK PUBLISHING

A HEADLINE paperback

7

ISBN 0 7472 6324 8

Typeset by
Letterpart Limited, Reigate, Surrey

Printed and bound in Great Britain by
Clays Ltd, St Ives plc

HEADLINE BOOK PUBLISHING
A division of Hodder Headline
338 Euston Road
LONDON NW1 3BH

www.headline.co.uk
www.hodderheadline.com

To Beverly, my elder daughter who shares my sense of humour and soothes my soul.
And in memory of my darling husband, Alan.

ACKNOWLEDGEMENTS

As a crew member on an ocean liner, you live an extraordinary life in cramped quarters. The hours are long and the work is hard, the passengers demanding – yet I would not have missed the experience.

Friendship is a precious thing and I would like to thank my old shipmates, Sylvia Brooks, Annette Nichols, Thelma Hardacre and Pam Webb for the friendship that has endured over so many years.

My gratitude to Frank Hayward for his research into La Cosa Nostra on my behalf. Your help was invaluable.

My thanks to my neighbours, Becky and Andy Wigsall for their love and kindness.

And finally, to my younger daughter, Maxine, who is a great DIY woman, and my rock.

Prologue

The small child ran up the gangway of the *Edinburgh Castle*, clinging tightly to her father's hand, dragging him behind her.

'Gemma! For goodness sake,' he cried. 'I'll break my neck at this rate. Slow down!'

But she was too excited to listen. Breathless, they both arrived at the top and stepped on board, turning to wait for Eve, Gemma's mother, who was following behind, walking as sedately as she could on the uneven surface.

'Mummy! Hurry up,' pleaded the child. At five years old, she hadn't yet learned the art of patience. She jumped up and down, her blonde curls bouncing, until Eve joined them.

For Jack Barrett, this was a proud moment. He was the coxswain of this fine vessel and was anxious to show his family where he spent all his working days. He led them to the bridge.

Standing in the wheelhouse he picked Gemma up and let her hold the helm. She turned it first one way and then the other. Peering out over the brow of the ship she said, 'We aren't moving!'

1

He chuckled. 'Of course not, you goose. We're in port, so the engines aren't working.'

Eve stood beside him, awed by the size of the ship, fazed by the unfamiliarity of her surroundings. 'What's it like in a rough sea?' she asked apprehensively.

He gazed fondly at her. 'Exciting. It gives me such a sense of power, battling against the elements and when it is calm, the view is quite beautiful. The sea is fascinating.' He gave a wry smile. 'She's a bit like a woman,' he said. 'Tempestuous at times, at others, beguiling.'

Eve turned to look at the handsome figure of her husband. He was tall, with broad shoulders and slim hips; muscles rippled beneath his shirt, and his blue eyes twinkled when he laughed, but were ice cold when he was angry. He grinned at her. 'She's like you, Eve. She can be a handful at times.'

She laughed, knowing it to be true. She had a fiery temper, but Jack knew just how to handle her. He either ignored her, or if he felt she had gone too far, he told her to stop her nonsense in such a manner that she didn't dare defy him.

'Come on,' he said, 'I'll show you around the rest of the ship.'

It was an education to both Eve and Gemma. The staterooms were panelled in the finest wood. The furniture was solid and elegant. Richly patterned carpets covered the floors of the huge rooms, each one far bigger than the whole of their council house with its two up and two down and small bathroom.

They visited the swimming pools. The one outside on the deck was empty at this moment, much to Gemma's great disappointment. Then Jack took them to see the First-Class cabins, which were luxurious with their twin beds, polished furniture and expensive drapes.

Eve looked around in awe. 'These passengers must be very wealthy to travel in such style,' she said.

'You should see the way they dress up in the evenings,' said Jack. 'The women in their fine gowns, loaded with jewellery.'

Eve twisted the small insignificant engagement ring on her finger and wondered what it must be like to wear diamonds.

As they walked around the decks looking up at the lifeboats hanging from the davits, Gemma, eyes wide with wonderment, asked, 'Daddy, do you think I could work on a ship one day like you do?'

He ruffled her hair. 'Well, you couldn't work on the bridge like me, but you could be a stewardess.'

She looked puzzled. 'What do they do?'

'Look after the passengers in their cabins. Serve them breakfast if they don't want to go to the dining room, make the beds, see to their clothes. Look after all their needs.'

'Will I get to see all those wonderful places you tell me about?'

'Of course. When the ship gets into a port, the crew are allowed to go ashore.'

She gazed up at him and declared, 'When I grow up, that's what I want to do.' That was the day her dream was born.

Chapter One

Sixteen years later

Gemma turned up the collar of her coat and pulled down the woollen hat over her blonde hair against the cold wind blowing in from the Solent, as she made her way to work, singing as she walked 'April in Paris'. I don't know about April in Paris, she grimaced. It's got to be a bloody sight better than November in Southampton! But at least this part of the country had been spared the flash floods of August 1952, when half the town of Lynmouth in Devon had been swept away.

She stopped as she heard the throaty roar of an ocean liner, echoing from the docks as the ship prepared to sail. The sound always gave her a frisson of excitement. She remembered with fondness the time she saw over the *Edinburgh Castle* with her father. Her childish dream of going to sea herself was as strong as ever.

The war years had been traumatic for everyone in Southampton. The town had suffered badly during the Blitz, when the German bombers came night after night causing devastation and destruction.

Gemma remembered the fear she shared with her

5

mother as they hid beneath the stairs during the air raids, listening to the bombs falling all around them. Jack was away during this time serving in the Merchant Navy on a minesweeper, leaving the two females to cope alone, like many others.

But as the years had passed, the relationship between her parents began to disintegrate. Her mother had become a bitter woman, always complaining about being lonely. Jack and she rowed more and more and Gemma longed for the happy times. The better days.

She pushed these thoughts to the back of her mind and walked on. This was no time to feel sad. Today was her twenty-first birthday, a day for celebration, after all. Officially she was a woman – able to stand on her own two feet. Old enough to vote and answerable to the law for her actions. It made her feel really important.

She glanced at her watch as she approached the staff entrance of the store where she worked in the costume jewellery department. She must hurry. Old man Granger, the floor manager, could get very snotty if you weren't behind your counter at ten to nine, ready for the first customer. Unfortunately, Gemma with her independent nature often fell foul of his temper. It was a cross she had to bear. Him – and her mother.

She took off her coat and hung it up, stuffing her hat and her handbag into her locker. Then she quickly ran a comb through her hair and smoothed down her black skirt, checking that the seams of her stockings were straight. Looking in the mirror, she adjusted the collar of her pristine white blouse and buttoned up her black cardigan. First thing in the morning, the premises were cold until the heaters had been on for a time. Ready at last, she opened the door which led to the interior of the shop and hurried across to her counter.

Her friend Eunice, as dark as Gemma was fair, grinned at her and started softly to sing, 'Happy Birthday to you'.

Gemma smiled back but muttered, 'You'd better not let the old man hear you.'

Pulling a face Eunice said, 'That miserable old bugger hasn't got a birthday.'

'Don't be daft, everyone has one,' Gemma argued.

'Not him. He came in a box of knicker elastic.'

They both doubled up with laughter, trying to smother the sounds of their merriment.

'What's so funny?'

Gemma looked round guiltily at Hazel, another assistant who had just arrived, cursing the lateness of the buses.

'Nothing,' answered Gemma, knowing that Hazel was jealous of her and would use any means of getting her into trouble. She had been furious when Gemma had persuaded Mr Granger to allow them to wear some of the costume jewellery whilst they worked. As Gemma had explained, 'If the customers can see how attractive the items look when they are actually worn, it might increase the sales.'

After some thought, he had agreed, and the takings had risen, but he had been adamant that all the pieces they wore must be returned before they left the store, or their jobs would be in jeopardy.

Hazel had grumbled incessantly. 'If I forget, I could lose my job because of your high and mighty ideas.'

Gemma pinned on to her cardigan an exquisite diamanté and pearl brooch and glared at the other girl. 'Oh,

7

for goodness sake, stop whining. You're only mad because you didn't think of the idea first!'

Today was Wednesday, half day closing. There was a buzz of excitement as the girls went to the staffroom to collect their coats, as some of them were going home with Gemma to a small lunchtime party her mother was giving to celebrate her coming of age.

There was much chatting and giggling as the small band made their way to Duke Street. As they approached the front door, Gemma felt her stomach tighten with apprehension. She prayed fervently that Eve wouldn't make a spectacle of herself.

On the door was pinned a silver key with *Twenty-One* written on it. Gemma put her own key in the door, opened it and stepped inside the front room.

Eve Barrett walked towards them. 'Come in everyone,' she said with a welcoming smile. She was a striking-looking woman of medium height, slim with almost jet-black hair, parted in the centre, softly waved to frame her face before being caught up in a chignon at the nape of her neck.

Eunice smiled at her. 'Hello, Mrs Barrett,' she said. 'Every time I see you I'm amazed just how like the Duchess of Windsor you are.'

Eve beamed with delight. 'So everyone tells me.'

The girls crowded inside the front room and settled down on the three-piece suite, covered in uncut moquette, that was now badly worn. The few brass ornaments shone, however, bringing a modicum of brightness to the gloom. The council houses were built back to back and so close together in the narrow street that sunlight seldom penetrated. At the far end of the room, a gate-legged table was set out with a clean cloth; thick white china plates, their chipped edges concealed by paper doilies, offered dainty sandwiches, sausage rolls and small vol-au-vents. Tomatoes were cut in water-lily shapes and radishes trimmed to resemble small roses. In the centre of the table stood a birthday cake, beautifully decorated, which impressed everybody.

'Good heavens, you have worked hard, Mrs Barrett,' said Eunice.

'My brother, who is a chef, helped of course,' she said. 'He made the birthday cake.'

Gemma crinkled. Her Uncle Ted, whom she loved dearly, was no chef. He was the cook at the Seaman's Mission and no doubt had done the complete buffet, but her mother loved to put on airs and graces. Gemma hated it when she did so, talking in a fake posh voice as she was doing now.

'Pour the girls a drink, Gemma,' Eve ordered. 'There's a bottle of sherry over there, the glasses are beside it.'

Gemma did as she was told and noticed that the bottle had already been opened. She handed round the glasses and urged the girls to help themselves to the food. Then she watched her mother perform.

Eve was in her element. She was the centre of attention and Gemma had to admit that when she was on form, she was good company. She had a quick acerbic wit and the others were soon laughing at her comments. Gemma sighed. If only . . . Her thoughts were disturbed by a knock on the door.

'Get that, will you.' Eve in full flow didn't want any interruption.

Outside the door stood a florist. 'Miss Gemma Barrett?'

'Yes.'

'These are for you.' She handed over an enormous bouquet. 'Happy Birthday.'

Gemma's guests gathered around, leaving Eve in mid-sentence.

'They cost a few bob,' one of the girls remarked. 'Who sent them?'

Gemma ripped open the small envelope pinned to the extravagant bow, took out the card and read it. *Happy Birthday, darling. Have a lovely day. Dad.* Her blue eyes shining, Gemma beamed at them all. 'They're from my father.' She turned towards her mother. 'Aren't they lovely?'

Eve just glared at her.

Gemma went into the scullery where she filled the sink with water and immersed the stems of the bouquet, to be unwrapped later. With her father being away so much, Ted, her mother's brother, had taken her under his wing. Without his kindness and understanding, she often wondered just how she would have coped. Eve was becoming impossible. At first Gemma had made excuses for her drinking, telling herself that it was just a phase, but Eve had continued to drown her sorrows and Gemma was getting desperate, because now she realised that her mother was fast becoming an alcoholic. She had tried everything, but her efforts always ended in confrontation.

Only two nights ago, Gemma had tried to be firm with Eve. 'Look, Mother, I've had just about enough of this!' she had declared when she had returned home, to find Eve half cut and no supper ready. 'I'm working hard all day, paying most of the bills when you get into debt, trying to keep it from Dad. But I'm not going to work my feet off to pay for your gin!'

Eve had gone berserk. 'How dare you speak to me like that! You don't know what it's like, being alone for weeks on end.'

'I certainly do. You forget, I miss my father too.'

Eve gave her a vitriolic look. 'He always spoiled you rotten. "My little angel" he called you, but he wasn't there when you played me up or when you were sick, was he? Oh no. I had all that.'

Gemma let out a deep sigh. The arguments were always the same. 'We can't go on like this,' she said. 'You have got to pull yourself together. We are only just keeping our head above water financially.' She pleaded with Eve. 'Why don't you try and get a job, then with the allotment Dad leaves you out of his money, and my contribution, you would be better off, and . . . it would be good for you to get out and meet people.'

'You think I like being like this?' declared her mother. 'What sort of life have I got? I'm still young, in my forties, although these days I feel like an old woman.'

Gemma's patience wore out. 'Then damn well *do* something about it! I won't go on saving your skin any more. I'll tell Dad what's happening and then I'll move out and get a place of my own if you don't make some effort to help!' As she stormed out and took refuge in her bedroom, she knew she was making idle threats. How could she leave Eve to cope alone? Still, the burden she carried was a heavy one.

Her uncle's arrival interrupted her thoughts. She ran to

meet him and gave him a big hug. 'Thank you so much for the spread, it's lovely.'

'It's no more than you deserve, my dear.' He helped Gemma to cut the cake and teased her friends as he handed round the portions.

Gemma noticed how Eve had quietened down at the arrival of her brother; no doubt because Ted couldn't abide her snobbish ways, as he often complained to his niece.

'My bloody sister! I rue the day someone told her she looked like the Duchess of Windsor. She thinks she's some sort of royalty now instead of a woman from a working-class background.' It became a private joke between them and sometimes he would ask, 'How's the Duchess?' but not very often.

Gemma was getting edgy as time passed and she saw Eve pour herself yet another glass of sherry. Her speech was becoming slightly slurred and there was a malevolent tone to her voice.

Eunice, sensing her friend's disquiet, nudged her friends and stood up. 'We'd best be off,' she said. 'Thanks for a lovely party, Mrs Barrett.' Turning to Gemma she added, 'See you later at the Guildhall.' They had all planned to round off the celebrations at the local dance.

There were goodbyes and thanks all round, then the girls from the shop trooped off home to get ready for the evening's frolics.

As Gemma started to clear the table she saw the familiar look of petulance on her mother's face. She ignored it and carried the plates into the kitchen.

'So now you're going out for the evening and leaving me alone,' bemoaned Eve.

Before Gemma could reply, Ted looked up and said, 'Of course she is. Today's her twenty-first birthday. You don't expect her to stay at home with *you* surely?'

She glared at him.

'You go and get ready, love,' he insisted. 'I'll wash up and clear away.'

Gemma gratefully left him to it. She didn't want a row with her mother today of all days. But as she ran a bath, she couldn't help but hear the raised voices from below.

'You're a selfish bitch, Eve. You couldn't even move yourself to put on a spread for the girl. If it hadn't been for me, she wouldn't have had a party at all.'

Trying to hide her disappointment, Gemma took her bath. How stupid of me to think Mother was behind the celebration, she thought. But later, as she laid out her sugar-starched petticoat and full skirt, she tried to push these thoughts to the back of her mind.

When at last she was ready, and ventured downstairs, Ted took her arm. 'Come on, love, I'll walk you part of the way.'

Once outside in the street, Gemma tucked her arm through her uncle's. 'Why doesn't Mum love me?' she asked. 'I can't remember her ever cuddling me when I was small. Only Dad ever showed me any affection.'

'That was half of the trouble,' he said. 'Eve always wanted to be the centre of attention. She resented the love that Jack had for you. He worships the ground you walk on, and she's jealous.'

'But she's my mother!'

He squeezed her arm. 'I know, but she was the same as a child. If she couldn't get her own way, she'd throw a tantrum. She's still doing it now. You get on with your life, my girl, do what you want. Your mother always did. Thank goodness you take after your father, you have his sunny personality. Be grateful for that.'

At the next corner, they went their separate ways.

'Anything you need, love, you come and see me.'

As she waited at the bus stop, she took comfort that there was always Uncle Ted, and for that she was eternally grateful, but there was so much she wanted to do with her life. She wanted to see something of the world. She'd been brought up with tales of foreign shores from her father, making her realise there was so much more to see out there. In one way she felt sorry for Eve, stuck here in Southampton, waiting dutifully for the return of a husband who would arrive like Father Christmas at regular intervals, bringing gifts, then sail off to exciting places, leaving his family behind.

She climbed on to the bus and offered her fare, looking around at the shop windows displaying their wares, wondering what the shops in New York would be like. She'd seen pictures of the skyscrapers, the Statue of Liberty, and was determined that one day she would see all these wondrous things for herself. Somehow she absolutely *had* to do it.

Chapter Two

Nick Weston, First Officer of the *RMS Queen Mary*, took his suitcases from the taxi driver and handed them to the porter of the Court Royal Hotel. He walked to the reception desk and signed the register, then made his way to the bar. He wasn't due to join the ship until tomorrow when it docked, but he always arrived a day early when he'd been on leave. It gave him time to get into the right frame of mind to once again take on the responsibilities of the bridge. As the First Officer, he was in total charge of the ship when on duty. It was his job to plot the course the ship would take, reporting his findings directly to the Captain. These duties sat easily with him. The sea was his life as it had been his father's and grandfather's before him.

He ordered a scotch and soda and sat looking out over Watt's Park. He preferred this establishment to the grandeur of the Polygon Hotel. The Court Royal was smaller, more intimate and comfortable. He would have a leisurely lunch, stroll to the shops and pick up one or two items he needed for the next voyage, bathe, have dinner, then he'd walk across the park to the local dance this evening. It would be just the kind of light entertainment he was seeking.

Gemma and her friends were in the ladies' cloakroom of the Guildhall, primping their hair, getting ready for the fray. When they eventually went upstairs to the ballroom, they discovered it wasn't as crowded as it usually was, but then this was a Wednesday, not a Saturday, the night they normally attended.

'I hope we won't be wallflowers.' Eunice spoke for them all.

The girls stood together, watching those who were dancing. It was a rule with them all that they never sat down on the available chairs. As Gemma once said, 'Some bloke asks you to dance, then when you stand up, he turns out to be some little short-arse, peering into your chest!'

One by one, as the evening progressed, each girl was approached by a variety of young men to traverse the well-sprung floor to the music of Bert Osborne and his band.

At the end of one number, when they were back in their group again, Gemma muttered, 'There's an absolutely beautiful chap making his way over here.' They all turned and looked. The man was six foot tall, with dark hair and broad shoulders. In his well-cut dark grey suit, he was sophistication personified. To the amusement of her friends, Gemma said quietly, 'Dear God, I have been a really good girl. Give him to me, please!'

The stranger stopped in front of them. 'Good evening, ladies.'

They all smiled at him. 'Good evening,' they replied in unison, like a chorus.

He gazed at Gemma and asked, 'Would you like to dance?'

She held out her hand to him and said, 'Thank you, I'd love to.'

As they walked towards the dance floor, she cast a glance over her shoulder at her friends and grinned. Then she looked up to the ceiling and mouthed, Thank You.

The band was playing a tango. As the stranger took her into his arms, he held her firmly, and she felt he could lead her just about anywhere. The scent of his cologne wafted beneath her nostrils. It had a tangy masculine aroma – and he *was* all man. She could feel the strength of his physique as he guided her around the dance floor. Their steps matched perfectly as Gemma relaxed in his arms and lost herself to the rhythm of the music. She loved to dance and so often the men who asked her had little idea of what they were doing, but this stranger was a dream to dance with.

The last note of the music died but he didn't release her and she stood still within his arms waiting for the next number to begin. He looked down at her as the band struck up again and she noticed that his eyes were green, flecked with hazel.

'You dance very well,' he said with a soft smile.

'Thank you.'

The corners of his eyes crinkled. 'You haven't stepped on my feet once.'

'If I do, I promise not to linger,' she said with a cheeky grin. She was curious about her partner. Who was he? Was he from around these parts? She didn't think so. What sort

of work did he do for a living? Whatever it was, it paid very
well; his suit was of the finest cloth and tailormade for
him, she was sure. But she wouldn't spoil the moment
asking any of these questions: it added to the mystery. She
smiled to herself.

'What is so amusing?'

She looked up at him, startled for a moment. Then she
gave a throaty chuckle. 'I was just wondering about you.
I've decided you are a man of mystery.'

He threw back his head and laughed. Then looking at
her with twinkling eyes he said, 'Hardly that, but I'm glad
you think I'm that interesting.' As the music stopped he
asked, 'Would you like to come to the bar for a drink?'

She nodded her agreement. Once there he settled her in a
seat beside a table. She watched him. He wore an air of
authority and she observed how the barman moved
quickly to fulfil his order, treating him with deference. As
he walked back towards her, her curiosity grew.

He held out his hand. 'Nick Weston,' he said.

'Gemma Barrett,' she replied. 'So who are you?' she
asked.

He sat back in his chair, an enigmatic smile on his
countenance. 'I'm not at all sure I'm going to tell you,' he
said.

'That's hardly fair!'

'Whatever I say is bound to be a disappointment. A man
of mystery should surely stay that way, don't you think?'

She loved the sound of his voice. It had a deep resonance
and he was obviously well-educated.

She sipped her shandy. 'Are you a teacher?'

He shook his head.

18

She studied him closely. He had strong, well-defined features, a full mouth and just for a moment she wondered what it would be like to be kissed by him. She felt the flush rise to her cheeks.

He raised an eyebrow. 'What sort of thoughts are running through your mind to make you blush, young lady?'

Now she was really embarrassed. 'I wasn't thinking anything in particular,' she protested.

'Now Gemma, I don't think you are being strictly truthful. Perhaps we'd better get back on the dance floor. Maybe that would be safer.'

But as he once again took her into his arms, to the music of a waltz, she wasn't at all sure that it *was* safer, especially as he held her even closer. She looked up at him and saw the grin on his face and knew he had done it on purpose. Well, two could play at that game. She moved her arm until her fingers were just touching the hairs in the nape of his neck.

He placed his face against hers and whispered, 'You, Gemma Barrett, are a minx.'

'My word . . . a minx and a mystery. What a combination!'

They spent the rest of the evening together and despite her efforts and wild guesses, she learned no more about him. He teased her unmercifully, but she enjoyed every moment. The band began to play Glen Miller's 'American Patrol' and as the dancers around them started to jive, she gave him a questioning look.

He grinned broadly at her. 'What's the matter, don't you think this is in my vast repertoire?'

'I'm really not sure if this is your style . . . is it?'

'Let's find out!' As he spun her around to the music,

she was even more impressed by his natural rhythm, his hips shaking to the music with complete abandon. 'Come on, Gemma, loosen up,' he urged. 'Let your inhibitions go.'

And she did. They collapsed at the end, completely exhausted.

'Well, you do surprise me,' she gasped.

'Really, why?'

'You look so, so . . .'

'Yes?'

'Sophisticated.'

'Are you sure you don't mean staid?'

'Oh, good gracious no. Not at all.'

The band began to play another tango this time and he held out his hand. 'Come along,' he invited.

Never had she danced with a man who seemed so able to interpret the mood of this Latin dance. Gemma felt the passion of the music and under his guidance she, too, danced like an expert. He gazed deeply into her eyes as he turned her this way, then the other. He made her feel sensual in his arms and she wondered just how he would act if his passion was really unleashed.

As the evening drew to a close, she asked, 'Will you be here next week?'

'I'm afraid not. I have to go away tomorrow.'

She was bitterly disappointed. 'Well, thank you for a lovely evening,' she said in a small voice.

'It was my pleasure. Come along, we may as well enjoy the last waltz.'

As the final notes died away, he placed a finger beneath her chin, tipped her face upwards and kissed her softly but thoroughly. 'Thank you for your company. You are a delightful young lady.'

'And you are still a mystery!'

He laughed. 'And you are still a minx.' He walked her to the staircase that led to the ladies' cloakroom. 'Take care, young Gemma,' he said, and walked away.

Downstairs, her friends gathered around. 'Who was he? What does he do? Has he asked to see you again? Has he any friends?' A million questions, none of which she could answer.

'I only know his name is Nick Weston and he's going away tomorrow,' she told them, sighing a little.

Eunice pulled a face. 'How could you let a man like that get away?' she demanded.

'Believe me, if there had been any way to stop him, I would have,' Gemma said wistfully, 'but it was a great way to finish my birthday.' She could still feel the impression of his mouth upon hers, recall the sensation of his arms around her, and she wished fervently that their time together had been longer.

Nick walked back to the hotel in good spirits. The young blonde girl Gemma had been amusing company and a good dancer. He had really enjoyed himself, had almost been tempted to ask her out to dinner when next the ship docked, but he thought better of it. After all, at thirty-three, he must be at least ten years her senior. Not that she'd seemed that much younger. She'd been a good conversationalist, had a sharp sense of humour, but he didn't want to get involved. A life at sea wasn't the easiest on personal relationships. Not that he didn't like women. He did. He'd had one or two affairs in the past, but marriage wasn't on his agenda yet, not for a few years anyway. But as he climbed into bed that night, the smiling face of Gemma Barrett invaded his thoughts. He recalled how she'd run her fingers through his hair as he held her close. She was indeed a little minx.

For her part, Gemma was on top of the world. As she and Eunice walked home together, she was dancing around in front of her friend, pretending she was still in the arms of the stranger. However, she was secretly relieved he hadn't asked to walk her to her door. She would have been embarrassed for him to see where she lived. Shabby council houses would not have figured in the life of Nick Weston, of that she was certain. But she would have liked to have known more about him. Being a great believer in fate, she told herself that if they were meant to meet again, they would, and she would have to be content with that. Looking up at the clear night sky, she made a wish on the first star she saw. 'Star light, star bright, first star I've seen tonight, I wish I may, I wish I might, I wish I get my wish tonight . . . I wish I get to meet that man again,' she whispered.

At last she was home and, taking a deep breath, she inserted her key in the front door and opened it. To her great relief, all the lights were out, so she assumed that her mother was in bed. Sniffing an empty glass on the draining board, the familiar smell of gin made her feel sick. She shook her head sadly. Where was it all going to end? Her father was due home in a few weeks' time; if Eve didn't improve, she would have to confide in him. She hadn't wanted to burden him with the facts. Being so far from home, she'd wanted to spare him any worries, but the situation was getting out of hand.

Gemma sat drinking a cup of Ovaltine, dreaming of the places she'd like to visit in the future. New York was first on her list. If she could work for the Cunard Company, that would be great. Unfortunately you had to be twenty-five before you could apply. How could she bear to wait that long, she wondered, before downing the rest of her hot drink and going up to bed.

Jack Barrett handed over the helm to his counterpart on the bridge of the *Edinburgh Castle* as he finished his watch, then made his way down various iron stairways through several decks of the ship, until he was able to step outside into the fresh air.

He leaned against a large bollard on the afterdeck, took a packet of Capstan Full Strength cigarettes from his pocket and lit one, inhaling deeply, enjoying the surge of nicotine to his lungs. He looked out at the far horizon, stretching his arms, bending double from the waist, turning his body first one way then the other in an effort to lessen the stiffness that had overtaken him after standing in one position for so long.

He turned his back to the hot sun and felt the warmth from its rays. Today was his daughter's twenty-first birthday and he wondered if Gemma had enjoyed it. At least he knew she'd receive the flowers he'd cabled to her, but doubted there would be much else to enliven her special day with Eve hanging around, bleating about money, making demands on Gemma's time. He hoped that the girl had gone out with her mates for a few drinks or perhaps to a dance.

He was not without a feeling of guilt as he thought of her; with him sailing away for weeks at a time, she was left to cope with the arguments and Eve's temper. It had all really started when Gemma was born. Eve resented being tied down, yet from the moment Jack picked up the small bundle that was the fruit of his loins, he was besotted with his child. As his love for her grew, the relationship between him and Eve had started to suffer, due to her jealousy.

He lowered his body, sitting on the deck, propped up against the bollard. This was his world. All his life he'd been a seaman, rising to the position of coxswain, proud to stand at the helm of his ship, his love of travel fulfilled. When he was on leave he was restless and anxious to return to sea, which hadn't helped his failing marriage.

Eve would rail at him. 'Why can't you be like other men, happy to be home with your family?'

But even when things had been good between them, the sea beckoned constantly and he was really only content when he could feel the motion of it beneath him as the ship ploughed through one ocean or another. Had it not been for Gemma, he would have regretted getting married at all. If only she too could break the chains of Eve's possessive nature and get a job as a stewardess, then she would have some chance at life, but at home, she would be stifled – as he had been.

Getting to his feet, he walked over to the side of the ship and threw away his cigarette end, watching it fly in the wind, until it was swept away in the wash. Meandering over to the stern, he looked down at the sea being churned by the ship's propellers, leaving its watery path behind it as the vessel continued on its journey. There was no other ship on the horizon, not even the sound of a gull this far out, just the noise of the screws and the swish of the ship's wake. As he walked away, he glanced up far above him at the bridge he had so recently vacated, and smiled contentedly. This surely was the life for him. He would talk to Gemma when they docked in Southampton. Try to instil in her the notion that she must get away and travel, like him. It would broaden her personal horizons and stand her in good stead for the future. In addition, looking after the passengers would teach her a great deal about etiquette and gracious living. With such knowledge at her fingertips, she could go anywhere and hold her own. After all, she already had the looks and personality . . .

Whistling merrily, Jack Barrett made his way below to the mess hall and a meal.

Chapter Three

The weather was foul. Hurricane-strength winds swept the country, bringing disaster in their wake, in particular to the East Coast, with many lives lost at Canvey Island. At least Southampton had escaped such disasters, but the high winds seemed to affect the tempers of everyone and so, when Gemma arrived home from work this evening she was feeling decidedly ruffled. Her mother was seated at the table, wearing a dressing gown, drinking a glass of milk. Gemma glared at her. 'You look like death!' she snapped.

'Thanks, that makes me feel much better.'

Since Jack had sailed, Eve had days of sobriety, then would go on a bender, but Gemma was adamant that she would no longer help her financially, except to pay for her own keep. She kept praying that Eve would come to her senses, but every time she walked into the house, she was tense, not knowing what she was going to find. When her mother was sober, the relief was almost painful, as was the despair when she would find Eve the worse for wear. It was like living on the edge of a volcano, waiting for it to erupt. Her nerves were slowly being torn to shreds.

It was all taking its toll on Eve herself. The following morning when she was alone, she took a mirror and looked at her reflection. She didn't like what she saw. Around her eyes were a few wrinkles, along her top lip also. Her skin was sallow and she had bags under her eyes. She ran her hand under her chin and was thankful that the skin had not started to sag but she knew it was just a matter of time. Her waist was beginning to thicken, her breasts were no longer pert. She was losing the thing she valued most . . . her looks. It was this, rather than the mounting bills, that fired her determination. She needed to make a life for herself instead of rotting away whilst Jack was sailing the high seas. She decided to look for a job. It would get her out of these four walls, and she would meet people, begin to enjoy her existence. She was still a good-looking woman and a bit of make-up worked wonders. It wasn't too late. She began to scour the Situations Vacant column of the *Southern Daily Echo*.

A week later when Gemma arrived home, she was surprised to see Eve all dolled up in a smart black dress, neatly styled hair, grinning broadly.

'You're looking pleased with yourself,' Gemma said, somewhat suspiciously.

'I've got a job,' Eve declared triumphantly. 'I went for an interview late this afternoon.'

'Oh, Mum. That's great. Where?'

'At the Grapes, in Oxford Street.'

Gemma looked horrified. 'Doing what?'

'Barmaid. Fulltime.'

Gemma's heart sank. It couldn't have been a worse

occupation for her mother with her addiction. She didn't say a word.

Eve's expression was like thunder. 'You ought to be pleased! You're always nagging me to go out to work, you and your father. Well, now I will be, so you can take that sour look off your face.'

'But, Mum – a pub. Why couldn't you get a job in a shop?'

'I want something with a bit of life, for Christ's sake! I don't want to spend all day serving boring housewives. I get on better with men, I always have. No, this will suit me down to the ground.'

And it seemed to do so, for a couple of weeks. True, Eve would come home slightly tipsy at night, but in fairly good spirits having been chatted up by various men, thus feeding her ego. She loved all the attention.

It also took the pressure off Gemma. Her mother wasn't buying her own gin any more and was therefore able to meet her bills, enabling her daughter to keep most of her wages without a feeling of guilt.

'You should drop in one night,' said Eve before she left for the evening shift. 'Bring that Eunice with you.'

'Mum!' What was her mother thinking of? Two women alone in a pub was hardly the done thing, especially one in Southampton's docklands. Not the most desirable of areas for young ladies, unless they were on the game, touting for business.

'I don't think so,' she said. 'Besides, you know I don't drink much.'

Eve's eyes narrowed. 'Not like your mother, is that what you mean?'

'No, of course not. I didn't mean that at all.'

Patting her hair into place, Eve said, 'I wonder what your father will say? It was his idea, after all. I'd better go, my public awaits!' She swept out of the house like a prima donna.

You'd think she was about to appear on the stage, thought Gemma as she made a pot of tea. I bet she does give a performance, too – and the girl thanked God she wasn't there to see it.

She popped in to see her uncle on the way home the following day and told him about Eve's new job.

'Working at the Grapes as a barmaid? Bloody hell!' Ted Maynard looked at his niece, perched on a stool in the kitchen of the Seaman's Mission. 'She'll just love that, being surrounded by men, listening to her every word.' He picked up a dirty glass from the draining board and pretended to pull a pint of beer, smiling and primping his hair, prancing about, fluttering his eyelashes. As Gemma dissolved into laughter at his antics he simpered and said, 'Now, who's next? Half a pint in a straight glass? Certainly, sir. Don't you think I look like the Duchess of Windsor?' He tutted. 'She'll ram her airs and graces down their throats at every opportunity. I wonder what Jack will have to say when he comes home?'

'Well, I'm not going to be the one to tell him,' she retorted.

He shrugged. 'He's away so long anyway, maybe he won't mind.'

Gemma looked dreamily into the distance. 'I'm going away to sea when I'm old enough,' she confided.

'What a great idea.'

'Dad suggested I should try for a job as a stewardess as I'm not trained to do anything else.'

'Well, darling, you're used to dealing with the public, which is a start. You really ought to work in a hotel for a bit, get some experience as a waitress perhaps or a chamber-maid – see how it's done professionally. Then you wouldn't be a stranger to the job, you'd have had some kind of training.'

Gemma looked a trifle downcast. 'You have to be twenty-five before they'll take you,' she said. 'Another four years as far as I'm concerned.'

'You could always lie a little,' her uncle suggested with a sly smile. 'Who's to know?'

The idea appealed to Gemma. She didn't generally like deceit of any kind, but in this case it would mean she wouldn't have to wait so long to apply to the company. Now her mother was working and seemed to be coping better, leaving her alone didn't seem such an impossibility and Gemma no longer felt quite so guilty about harbour-ing her secret dreams. Imagine going to New York, seeing the Empire State Building and all the other amazing sights. It made her stomach turn turtle with nervous anticipation. The desperate need to get away – to see something of the world – grew stronger by the day. And yet the very idea of working on an ocean liner filled her with trepidation. What if she were seasick? What would happen then? She asked Ted for his opinion.

'Don't you worry about that,' he assured her. 'There are all sorts of remedies on the market for seasickness, but as soon as you get your sea legs, you'll be just fine.'

'What do you mean, my sea legs?'

'It's when you get used to the motion of the ship beneath you. As it leans one way, you lean the other, to counter-balance, and that keeps you upright. You'll soon get used to it.'

Knowing that in his youth her uncle had been to sea himself, and that during the war he'd served in the Royal Navy, she asked, 'Why did you decide to work ashore?'

He sipped his coffee and said, 'A life at sea wasn't for me, love. I like my home too much. I miss my garden. Yes, it was nice seeing a bit of the world, but I don't have itchy feet like you and your dad.'

At that moment they were interrupted by a large man who came marching down the hall to the kitchen door.

One of the lodgers, Gemma assumed. His frame seemed to fill the opening.

'I want a pot of tea,' he demanded in a Scottish accent.

The reek of stale beer from his breath caught in Gemma's throat and she turned away. The man glared at her.

'I'll bring it into the lounge shortly,' Ted said.

'Well, don't take too long about it,' the man snapped before ambling away.

'Who the devil was that?' asked Gemma.

'Jock MacTaggart. He's a ship's electrician, a really bad bugger when he's riled. He stays here between ships or when he's on leave.'

'I bet his poor wife has a hellish life,' Gemma remarked.

'Not any more – she divorced him on grounds of cruelty, I heard. That's why he stays here.'

Gemma slipped off the stool. 'Best be off and let you get on with the evening meal,' she said.

He gave her a peck on the cheek. 'You take care, young lady. Come and see me again.'

As she walked back along the docks a sudden blast from the funnel of a liner filled the air, followed by another. The deep throaty roar always sent shivers down her back. Each ship had a voice of its own and she knew, listening to this one, that the *Queen Mary* was about to sail, and was being helped out of her berth by several small tugs.

Gemma had once been taken out on one such tug as it went down the river to bring in a liner. She'd been amazed how these small vessels had nudged and pushed at the side of the mighty ship, pulling on the ropes, getting the position just right so the pilot on board who had joined the crew down the river at Southampton Water could manoeuvre it safely home.

The baggage would now have been loaded, the stevedores would be untying the hawsers, and the passengers standing by the rails on deck, watching the last-minute preparations for the voyage. The docks would be a bustle of activity and one day . . . she'd be a part of it.

On the bridge of the *Queen Mary*, Nick Weston, smart in his navy-blue uniform with its gold braid, was outside on the starboard wing, watching as the hawsers were hauled in and wound around the huge bollards on the deck way below. The Captain was standing by inside the wheelhouse looking out towards the horizon as the pilot gave his orders to the coxswain.

Nick gazed down along the boat deck at all the passengers, waving to the crowds on the dockside and the balcony of the Ocean Terminal, and thought, Another trip safely under way. He hoped the guests in the dining room seated at his table would be a tad more interesting than the last lot. It was the one thing he didn't enjoy about his position – entertaining the passengers at dinner.

The most important ones – members of the aristocracy, film stars – were naturally seated at the Captain's table. Then Nick had his allocation, as did the doctor and other senior officers. Sometimes his companions were a pleasure to share a table with, but there was always someone who was a complete bore or pompous. Then, of course, some evenings he had to do his stint on the dance floor. Trundling around wealthy female passengers, being polite, exchanging conversation, making them feel special. And, sometimes, fending off unwanted advances.

The ones who were from 'old money' were usually perfectly amicable and, being well-bred, knew how to behave, but others, who had made their millions in trade or business and who had no class or manners, could make his job unbearable. Not that he ever decried anyone who was successful by their own business acumen, but crassness was never easy to handle.

Those who were used to money, never talked about it, whereas the others couldn't stop. Especially the Americans. The women wore more jewellery than you would see in a Bond Street jeweller's display window, and flashed their wealth at everyone.

He cringed when he thought of one man who had sat at his table last trip. The fellow had taken out a wad of money and waved it at the waiter as he served him, saying, 'You look after me good, boy, and some of this will come your way. Understand?'

The waiter had smiled, and quietly said, 'Yes, sir, I understand, but I would like you to know that I always take care of my passengers, whoever they are. It's part of the Cunard service.'

The American hadn't known what to say. Nick had just about managed to hide a smile. Of course, the young waiter had been quite right. The menus were not as extensive, as they would have been before rationing, but nevertheless, the food was of the highest quality, cooked to perfection, the finest of wines were on offer and the staff were hand-picked and trained to satisfy every whim of their wealthy passengers.

Nick was eternally grateful that it was only at dinner that he was forced to play mine host. Other meals were eaten in the officers' mess, or in his cabin, where his own personal steward took care of his needs, saw that his uniforms were cleaned and pressed, his shirts carefully ironed and that he had everything he wanted when he wasn't on the bridge.

As the ship left the quay he looked back at the town, and, quite unexpectedly, young Gemma whom he'd met at the Guildhall came into his thoughts. He wondered how she was and what she would be doing at this precise moment. When they next docked, maybe he'd pay another visit to the Guildhall and see if she was there. The little minx, with the twinkling eyes, who had made him laugh.

At work a few days later, Hazel sidled up to Gemma as she tidied the counter. 'Imagine your mother being a common barmaid.'

'I beg your pardon?'

'My dad went into the Grapes and got talking to the

woman behind the bar. He happened to say his daughter worked here and she said, so did hers. The Grapes isn't the most salubrious of places, is it?'

Gemma looked at her coldly. 'Good enough for your father, it would seem.'

Hazel flushed. 'It's not his local. He happened to be passing, that's all.'

'What's the matter, Hazel? Can't he walk past any pub without he has to go in – is that what you're saying?'

The other girl became flustered. 'No, that's not what I'm saying at all.'

'The trouble with you is, you don't think before you open that trap of yours. It's just a pity your brain is not as big as your mouth.'

'What's going on here? Why aren't you two working?' Mr Granger stood before them.

'I was trying to,' said Hazel, 'but Miss Barrett wouldn't let me pass. She's mucking about.'

Gemma was flabbergasted. 'That's a downright lie! I did no such thing.'

But Granger didn't believe her. 'You watch yourself, young lady,' he warned. 'There's plenty of people happy to step into your shoes.'

She watched him walk away, her cheeks flushed with anger. She turned to reproach Hazel, but the girl had made good her escape.

In the staffroom at lunch-time, Gemma confided in Eunice. 'That little bitch would get me the sack if she could.'

'She's jealous of your popularity with the customers. You must have noticed how the regulars avoid her when they can and come to you.'

'Well, who can blame them? She hasn't an ounce of patience or charm in the whole of her body.'

'You just watch your back, that's all,' warned her friend.

Gemma knew this was good advice. Hazel was always creeping around old Granger, paying him compliments, crawling to him, telling tales. To him she appeared to be a good worker, but Gemma knew her to be a dangerous conniving liar, definitely somebody on whom to keep a wary eye.

Chapter Four

The following weeks passed with life's usual ups and downs. Eve, sober some of the time, Hazel being a pest, and old man Granger as miserable and demanding as ever. Gemma couldn't wait for the return of her father. She needed someone to lean on, to share her troubles, advise her on how to cope with her wayward mother and a sneaky work associate who seemed hell bent on causing trouble for her.

Only the previous evening at the closing of the store, one of the more expensive pieces of costume jewellery had gone missing, causing both Eunice and Gemma to panic and search for it frantically, before Mr Granger discovered the loss . . . which he did, of course, having been immediately informed by Hazel.

He stormed over to the counter and Gemma was grateful for the absence of any customers. 'What's this I hear?' he thundered. 'One of our pendants is missing?'

'I'm sure it's only been mislaid,' murmured Gemma as she moved the display around in the case, searching beneath the satin cushions.

Hazel pushed her aside. 'Here, let me have a look.' She fussed around whilst Granger fumed, then with a cry of surprise, she said, 'I've found it!'

'How very convenient,' said Gemma suspiciously, certain it was all a plot to discredit her once again.

'Where was it?' the floor manager demanded.

'It had slipped down the back of the case – obviously it hadn't been properly secured to the cushion.'

'And who laid out the display?'

'Why, Miss Barrett.'

He pressed his lips into a firm line and glared at Gemma. 'Is that correct?'

'Yes it is, but—'

But he didn't let her finish. 'I really don't know what's got into you lately, young lady, but your work has been less than satisfactory.'

She blazed at the unfair comment. 'How can you say that! My sales figures are higher than anyone else's.'

A fact he couldn't deny. 'Hrumph.' He cleared his throat. 'True, but at what cost, I ask myself. I'll be keeping a close eye on you in future, Barrett.'

She swallowed her outrage. 'Will you be watching Miss Hazel Grimes too?'

He looked confused.

Unrepentant, Gemma pressed on. 'After all, if you are going to be monitoring my performance, your findings won't amount to much without someone to compare it with, will they?'

His eyes narrowed as he looked at her, then at Hazel, before stomping away.

Hazel said, 'What are you trying to do, get me into trouble?'

Raising an eyebrow, Gemma answered, 'As if I would.'

Then she gripped Hazel's arm, making her wince. 'Now you listen to me, you rotten little bitch. I know damn well that pendant was in the showcase, because I dusted it a couple of hours before we closed.'

'What are you suggesting?' blustered the other girl.

'You removed it at some time and then replaced it later, pretending it had slipped down the back when you were looking, hoping to get me in Granger's black books.'

With a sly grin, Hazel said, 'You seem to have managed that all by yourself.'

Gemma leaned towards her and said, 'Granger may not be watching you closely, but I bloody well will be because you are a scheming little hussy, so you'd better not make any mistakes or he'll know about it almost before it happens. Understand?'

As she walked home with Eunice, Gemma was still enraged. 'Why is she doing this to me? I know she's jealous, but just lately it's been like an onslaught. She never stops.'

Eunice tucked her arm through her friend's. 'Well, I did hear a rumour that there may be a department supervisor's job up for grabs.'

Gemma roared with laughter. 'And she thinks she might get it? That's highly unlikely.'

'No, but you might,' Eunice said quietly.

The laughter died. 'I see. It would be nice, I must admit. A bit more responsibility, less of old Granger, a bob or two more in my pay-packet . . . but there are so many on the staff who would fit the job.'

Eunice shrugged. 'That's not how Hazel sees it.'

Gemma longed to talk to her father about this and everything else that was going on in her life.

★ ★ ★

When Jack Barrett docked the following week, he was surprised to find the house in Duke Street empty. He knew that Gemma would still be at work, but where on earth was Eve? Normally she'd be waiting for him. He pottered around the scullery making himself a sandwich and a pot of tea, waiting for his wife to appear, thinking she must have slipped out to the shop along the road. However, when Gemma arrived home an hour later, he was beginning to get very anxious and voiced his concern.

'Mum's gone to the hairdresser's and then on to work,' Gemma told him, after giving her dad an enormous hug.

His surprise was obvious. 'Work? Eve?'

'Why are you so surprised, Dad? After all, it was your suggestion.'

He gave a smile of satisfaction. 'Yes, I suppose it was – not that I thought she'd ever do it . . . but surely the shops are closed by now?'

'She's not working in a shop. She's got a job as a barmaid at the Grapes.'

Jack's smile immediately disappeared. 'Working behind a bar, eh? With a row of optics behind her, she'll be like a pig in clover,' he said bitterly.

'She does seem to like it,' Gemma admitted.

'And what about her drinking?'

With a shrug Gemma said, 'There's no denying the fact that she still drinks, but when she comes home, she seems mostly to be in a good mood. She doesn't go off on a bender any more because she's got a job to worry about.'

Jack didn't look a happy man; a frown furrowed his

brow. 'The Grapes gets a lot of seafarers in. With a few drinks under their belt, they can be a tough bunch – ask any landlord.'

'It doesn't seem to bother Mum.'

Jack looked thoughtful. 'Perhaps we should go along and take a look? Make sure she's all right.'

'Oh, Dad. I really don't want to go.'

'Come on, love. We'll just pop in quickly, have one drink, then I'll take you somewhere else and we can sit and chat. You forget I've been cooped up on a ship. I need to let my hair down.'

She reluctantly agreed.

Although it was reasonably early in the evening, the public bar of the Grapes was already busy, mostly with Merchant Navy seamen, some of whom had docked that day on the *Edinburgh Castle*. One or two greeted Jack as he made his way to the counter.

Gemma stood behind him and watched her mother, who was busy at the other end of the bar and hadn't seen them. Another barmaid served them and whilst they waited, Gemma listened to the banter between Eve and her customers.

With her sharp tongue and witty repartee, Eve had an answer for everyone. She flirted with every customer who approached the counter, whatever his age. The cross patter was very ribald at times and Gemma, glancing at her father, saw the set of his jaw tighten at some of the remarks. Suddenly glancing down the length of the bar, Eve saw them and a look of displeasure wiped the smile from her face.

'Well, bugger me if it isn't my old man back from the

deep and my *dear* little daughter with him.' She sashayed along the bar towards them.

With years of experience behind her, Gemma could tell that already Eve had quite a few drinks under her belt, and this was when she was at her worst.

'Hello, Jack. I'd almost forgotten what you looked like.'

He gazed at her coldly and at the low-cut blouse she was wearing. 'Not afraid of catching a chill, I see.'

She ran her finger down the vee of the neck and smiled slowly. 'The customers like it,' she said, a look of defiance in her eyes.

At this, one of the punters called out, 'If she was my wife, I wouldn't leave her for too long!'

Jack coolly sipped his beer and, looking back at the man, said quietly but firmly, 'You would if you were married to her.'

The laughter that filled the bar – at her expense – made Eve's cheeks flush with anger. Gemma cringed and wished she was at home. She drank her shandy and tried to look inconspicuous.

Eve glared at her husband and was about to respond when a customer called loudly to be served and she had no choice but to go. During the next ten minutes, the time it took Jack to drink his pint, Eve put on a performance that was worthy of a cheap end-of-pier show. She pranced behind the counter, leaned forward to serve everyone, showing off her cleavage, flirted outrageously and looked across at Jack, her eyes shining brightly. She did everything but break out into a song and dance routine.

Jack swallowed the contents of his glass and said to Gemma, 'Come on, I've had enough of this. Let's go.'

She followed him quickly, grateful to be away from it all. They walked home together in silence, buying fish and chips along the way for their supper, neither one of them wanting to go elsewhere, as had been originally planned.

After they had eaten, Gemma offered to make her dad a cup of tea, which he declined. He didn't even bother to unpack his case as was his usual habit, but sat by the fire, gazing into the embers, puffing on his pipe.

'Dad, we have to talk.'

He looked up at the sound of his daughter's voice. 'Not tonight, love. I'm weary. I'll meet you outside your shop tomorrow in your lunch-hour. We'll talk then. Why don't you go on up to bed, love? You look tired too.'

Gemma kissed him goodnight and left him alone, wondering what would happen when Eve came home. What would he have to say about her exhibition? She knew in her heart it wouldn't be a friendly exchange. Tired as she was, her nerves were on edge and she couldn't sleep. She tensed when she heard her mother return.

Eve shut the front door behind her and threw her coat over the chair, then walked carefully to the kitchen, trying hard not to stagger. She made a cup of tea and carried it to the table with both hands, spilling it as she walked, aware that her husband was watching her every step. Sitting down she took a cigarette from her handbag and lit it, then glared across at Jack.

'Well go on, say it! I saw the sour look on your face when you were in the bar. Didn't like to see me having a good time, did you?'

He looked at her with distaste. 'Is that your idea of having a good time? You behaved like a cheap tart. I was embarrassed for you. I was only sorry our Gemma had to see you behave like that, although poor kid, she's probably used to it.'

Eve was enraged. 'Who are you calling a tart, you bastard! They're the kind of women you see every time you reach port. Don't tell me that you don't.'

His voice was steady and cold as he answered her. 'And who could blame me if I did? I certainly don't have much of a wife to come home to. If ever I saw you sober it would be a change – look at you now. Call yourself a wife . . . you're just a slut, and you are no example for our daughter.'

'Your bloody angel of a daughter! She can't think too badly of me – she's still here, isn't she?'

He shook his head in despair. 'Sadly, she is. She'd be much better off in a place of her own – away from you.'

Eve's mouth tightened. 'I know what you'd really like. You'd like to see me sitting in a chair waiting for your return, pipe and slippers at the ready, prepared to lick your boots, carry out your every wish, wait on you hand and foot then be ready on the bed, legs open, grateful for your attention.' She sneered at him. 'Well, I deserve better than that. I have a life too, you know, and I'm only just beginning to enjoy it . . . and you can't stand it, can you?'

'You forget, you're my wife. I keep you. It's my money that pays the bills, although you don't even seem able to do that on time. You're behind with the rates and the electricity.' At the look of surprise on her face, he explained. 'I went to the drawer to look for a box of matches and found the bills stuffed at the back.'

'How dare you come back here and start poking around!'

'This is my home, or had you forgotten? I pay the rent.'

'And you pay for me, so I'd better lie back and enjoy it – is that what you're saying?'

'You must be joking! Look at you. You stink of spirits. No, Eve. I don't want you at all.'

Her face flushed with rage. 'Then why don't you bugger off back to your bloody ship? It means more to you than I ever did.'

'That's the only sensible thing you've said.' He rose from his chair, picked up his case and made for the door.

She screamed at him, 'If you leave now, Jack Barrett, don't expect me to let you back in!'

He walked out without a backward glance, closing the door behind him.

Eve picked up her cup and hurled it with all her force at the door. It smashed into small pieces.

Gemma came rushing down the stairs. 'Whatever was that?' Looking around she asked, 'Where's Dad?'

'Gone back to his bloody ship, that's where.'

'Oh, Mum. What did you say to him?'

'Me! It wasn't my fault. He didn't want to stay here.'

'Why ever not? This is his home.'

Eve's bottom lip started to tremble. 'He said he didn't want me.'

Gemma put an arm around her mother's shoulders. 'I'm sure that's not true.' She tried to comfort Eve as her mother sobbed in her arms.

Grabbing the sleeve of Gemma's dressing gown, she looked up at her daughter, eyes smudged with mascara and pleaded, 'You won't ever leave me, will you? I can't be on my own. Please don't leave me.'

Gemma didn't know which was the more difficult to handle, her mother drunk and in a temper or drunk and maudlin. 'No, of course not,' she murmured reluctantly, thinking that when eventually the time came for her to join a ship, Eve would create a dreadful scene, and she wasn't looking forward to that at all.

Gemma slipped home during her lunch-hour the following day as Jack had popped into the shop and asked her to do so. She opened the front door and stepped into an empty front room. 'Dad?' she called.

'Up here, love,' came the call from one of the bedrooms.

She climbed the stairs to find her father packing. 'What on earth are you doing?' she asked.

Walking across the room towards her, he took her by the shoulders. 'I'm sorry, Gemma, but I'm leaving.'

She sank down on the bed as her legs seemed no longer able to hold her. 'You're leaving . . . for good?'

With an expression full of sadness he said softly, 'Yes, I'm afraid so.'

She was outraged. She stood up, eyes blazing and accused him. 'How very selfish of you!'

'What do you mean, selfish?'

'I'm surprised you even have to ask. I was under the impression we were going to talk about Mum and her problem. I was expecting you to help me sort her out.' She pursed her lips. 'Well, you've certainly done that . . . to suit yourself, anyway. But what about me?'

His expression hardened. 'Look, love, your mother and

me have been washed up for years. I don't look forward to
coming home any more – except, of course, to see you,' he
added quickly as he saw the hurt expression in her eyes. 'I
love you, Gemma, and whatever you may think, I worry
about you, and that's why it's time you stepped out into the
world and started living your own life.'

'What about Mum? Have you any idea what this will do
to her?'

'Your mother is a lush. She'll not get any better, she'll
steadily get worse. I've seen it with others – it isn't very
pretty. Surely you can see that for yourself? She'll ruin your
life, given time . . . don't you understand that? She'll drag
you down with her, if you let her.'

She appealed to him. 'But she's your wife.'

'Yes, I know that and I've given her twenty odd years of
my life.' He looked anxiously at Gemma. 'This is hard for
you to understand, but after your mother's little display at
the Grapes, I really can't take it any more. Nothing is going
to change. You and I need to move forward.' He caught
hold of her by the shoulders and stared hard at her. 'It's
time for you to go out into the world, get away from this
place . . . away from *her*. You're no longer a child, you are a
young, attractive woman. Don't let her destroy you.'

Gemma felt as if all the stuffing had been knocked out
of her and she leaned against the wall for support as her
father released his hold. 'I can't believe you are so willing
to abandon her now, when she needs you most of all,' she
said tearfully. 'How could you do that, Dad?'

He met her gaze unflinchingly. 'The only person who can
help your mother is Eve herself. She must want to . . . and
she doesn't. She's happy as she is.'

'You could stay at home with her, help her to get back on her feet, to stop the drinking.'

He shook his head slowly. 'Gemma, love, I have spent my entire adult life at sea. You know what I'm like when I'm on leave, I get restless after three days. I couldn't bear to stay ashore. What sort of job could I get? I'm a seaman, I'm not trained to do anything else. I'd be like a bear with a sore head. I know this sounds selfish, but that wouldn't help your mother. We'd be at each other's throat in no time.'

Gemma felt helpless. What could she do to make him change his mind? She knew that Eve would be devastated when she discovered that Jack was leaving, and she was frightened of the consequences.

'I have other plans,' Jack told her gently.

'Such as?'

'I'll explain when I come round later before your mother goes to work.'

'I suppose I must be grateful that you are at least going to tell Mum the news to her face,' Gemma said hotly. 'For one moment I thought you were just going, leaving me to do your dirty work for you.'

He looked askance at the idea. 'As if I would!'

She sighed. 'Maybe not, but who will have to pick up the pieces when you've gone?' Her father didn't reply.

Gemma turned towards the door. 'I must get back. I'll see you later.'

She walked back to the store in a daze. Shocked by her father's decision. Disappointed that the one person she relied upon had let her down. That really hurt, and her mood sank even lower.

Chapter Five

Back at work, Gemma was unable to concentrate. She kept making mistakes until Mr Granger, informed of this by Hazel, sent her off to the stockroom to unpack several boxes that had arrived that day.

'At least there you won't upset any of our customers with your errors,' he said angrily. 'Really, I don't know what's the matter with you this afternoon.'

It was in the stockroom that Eunice found her, sitting on an upturned box, in tears. She rushed over to her and putting an arm around her shoulders, asked, 'Whatever is it?'

Between sobs, Gemma told her friend what had transpired.

'Oh Gemma, love, I'm so sorry, I don't know what to say.'

'There's nothing anyone can say,' wept Gemma.

Eunice hugged her, then, taking a clean handkerchief from her pocket, she handed it to her friend. 'Here, wipe your eyes,' she whispered. 'Try and pull yourself together before anyone sees you. They'll only start asking questions and that's the last thing you need. I'll wait for you after work and we'll walk home together. All right?'

Gemma nodded and wiped her tears, then proceeded to unpack one of the boxes. I'll keep busy, she thought, then I won't think, but it didn't dispel her fears about the forthcoming meeting between her parents.

'Look, Gemma,' said Eunice as the girls made their way home together, 'if things get too bad, shove your nightdress and a toothbrush in a bag and come over to my place. Mum will put you up somewhere, even if we both have to double up in my bed.'

It was such a tempting thought, Gemma wished she could go there now, but it was never her way to shirk unpleasant things. One of her strengths was her ability to look life in the face and try to deal with it, but this one time, she wished she was a million miles away.

'Thanks, Eunice. You're a real sport.'

The girls parted at the top of Duke Street and Gemma walked towards her front door and put the key into the lock. To her surprise her father wasn't there, but she saw his two large suitcases pushed almost out of sight, under the stairs.

Eve, for once, was sober. She put her head around the scullery door. 'Do you want a cup of tea?'

'Yes, thanks, Mum.'

'You'll have to get some fish and chips for you and your father later,' she called, 'only I'm all behind.'

At that moment, Jack let himself into the house.

'Tea?' asked Eve.

'No thanks,' he said as he retrieved his suitcases, 'I'm not stopping.'

Eve looked at him, then at the bags. 'What's going on?'

He took out a packet of cigarettes and lit one. 'I've packed the rest of my stuff, I'm taking it over to Freda's.'

At the mention of her sister-in-law, Eve's mouth tightened in a spiteful line. 'And why would you want to do that?'

Gemma could feel her heart pounding; she scarcely dared breathe.

Jack looked straight at his wife without flinching. 'This is the end of the line, Eve. I've had enough. I'm moving out and I won't be coming back.'

The colour drained from her face. She stepped towards him. 'You won't be coming back . . . ever?'

'That's right.'

'You can't just push off after twenty-three years of marriage, just like that!' she cried.

He didn't raise his voice, but spoke clearly. 'Oh yes, I can. I'll keep your allotment going as usual and increase it, so you can look on that as your maintenance. It'll mean you can pay the rent and the bills, if you look after it, that is.'

'Maintenance? What do you mean, maintenance? Are you asking for a divorce?'

'Not at the moment,' Jack said quietly. 'There is no one else – that's not what this is about.'

Eve's temper exploded. 'You sanctimonious sod! You stand there and calmly tell me that my marriage is over. Who do you think you are?'

'Mum—' began Gemma.

Eve spun round. 'And you can shut up! You've always been your father's daughter. What do you think of your hero now?'

Before she could answer, Jack intervened. 'This is nothing to do with Gemma. This is between us.' He drew deeply on his cigarette. 'Let's face it, Eve, we haven't had any sort of real marriage for years.'

'That didn't keep you out of my bed when you came home on leave, I noticed. It was a good enough marriage for that.'

He shrugged. 'I'd been away a long time.'

'Ha! You expect me to believe you didn't have another woman in between?'

He looked angrily at her. 'That's not my style and you can believe that or not!' He paused for a moment and sighed heavily. 'I'm sorry it's come to this, Eve, I really am, but neither of us can go on as we are. As it happens, I've had an offer of another job. I had intended to turn it down because I felt my place was with my family, but after last night, I can't go on any longer . . . so now I've decided to take it. It's not easy to walk away from the past, but it seems the time has come to do so.'

Eve gave him a puzzled look. 'What do you mean, another job?'

'I've been asked to become the skipper of a private yacht, anchored at Cape Town, so I intend to sign off the ship when we get there.'

'Dad! What do you mean, you're signing off?' Gemma was startled. What on earth was he saying?

'The contract is for two years, and then if all goes well, I may be able to renew it.'

Gemma sat down, her face white, her voice strained. 'Does that mean you won't be coming home, ever again?'

'Of course not! But I won't get back for two years.' He

saw the expression on her face and tried to explain. 'The money is very good, I'll be able to save for the time that I retire. At the end of the first contract I'll come back and see you. Of course I will.'

'Two years, Dad!' To the young woman it seemed a lifetime.

He tried to make her feel better. 'If you go to sea, maybe you'll come to Cape Town and I could see you then.'

'And if I don't?' Tears filled her eyes and Jack Barrett's face became a blur. 'Dad, how could you do this to us?' she asked passionately. 'Don't we mean anything to you at all?'

He came over to her and knelt beside her. 'Of course you do, you know how much I love you, but I have this chance and for a man of my age, it's a great opportunity, one that will never come again. And you know how I hate the climate in this country.'

She looked at him accusingly. 'How easy it is for you to walk away from your responsibilities.'

'That's not fair, Gemma. I'm providing financial support for your mother and now you are of age. At twenty-one, you can find your own way. I know how much you want to travel . . . so do it. You will discover a very different world from all this.'

She couldn't believe her ears. By making this decision, her father had just destroyed any chance of her fulfilling *her* dream, and he couldn't even see it!

Gemma rose from her chair and walked over to the window. The street was full of children playing. Some were skipping; two girls had tucked their skirts into their knickers and were doing handstands against the wall. This view was to be her future now as well as her past.

No longer could she dream of sailing the ocean, of seeing New York. Once her father walked out of the house, he had made it her prison. Once *he* had gone, *she* couldn't do the same to her mother, it wouldn't be fair. She turned and looked at Eve, who had been stunned into silence. The expression in her eyes made Gemma's heart reach out to her. Inside she knew that Eve was in great pain.

Walking over to her mother, Gemma put an arm around her shoulders. 'Don't you worry, Mum. Let him go if that's what he wants. We can manage without him.' Her words seemed to give Eve a sudden strength, for she straightened her shoulders.

'You'd best be off then, Jack. You've made your decision. Fine. Let's face it, we didn't see that much of you anyway. I shouldn't hang about, I'm sure your Freda will welcome you with open arms.' She slipped her arm around Gemma's waist and hung on tightly.

It was Jack now who was uncertain. His wife and daughter stood before him, united, and he didn't know what to do. 'Right then.' He looked at Gemma, but the coldness in her eyes stopped him from kissing her goodbye. 'I'll send you my address when I get settled,' he said to her.

'If you like,' she said carelessly.

It was his turn to be hurt. 'Don't be like this, love. Try to understand. After all, I am still your father.'

'I suppose on paper you are. It just doesn't feel like it any more. But don't you worry, Uncle Ted has always been there when I've needed him. He's never let me down – I'll be just fine.'

She knew how much she was hurting him, but she

wanted to get back at him. Had she not been a woman, she would have punched the daylights out of him, this man whom she had adored from the moment of her birth. Right now, all she felt for him was a raging anger. He had betrayed her. Cast his love for her aside, easily, or so it seemed. She would have walked through fire for him if she'd been asked to, without reservation. But not now. Not any more.

Jack picked up his cases and opened the front door. He turned to look at the two of them for a second, then he walked out, closing the door behind him.

As soon as he'd gone, both Eve and Gemma clung to one another, and wept. Gemma patted her mother's back as if she was a child and between her own sobs tried to comfort her.

'It'll be all right, you'll see,' she assured her. 'After all, we have each other.'

'Oh Gemma, how could he do such a thing?' cried Eve.

Gemma led her mother to a seat at the table. 'I'll put the kettle on and we'll have a cuppa, while we plan for the future.'

'What future?' The despair in Eve's voice was pitiful.

Gemma made a pot of tea and took it into the other room on a tray. She poured a cup for Eve, who took it and gazing at her daughter said, 'If I was really honest, I could see why your father would want to leave me, but you . . . that I don't understand. He idolised you, I used to be jealous of the attention he gave you when he was home, yet you see it didn't make any difference in the end. Men are such selfish buggers!'

'We'll be all right, Mum. Dad said he would increase

your allowance, you're working, I'm working. We'll get by, you'll see.'

Eve put a hand to her forehead. 'I have such a head-ache, and I don't seem able to get my head round what's happened. I don't feel a bit like work. Perhaps I'll take the night off.'

'Now that won't do at all,' said Gemma sharply. 'I'll get you some aspirin, then I'll make a sandwich for you while you get ready for work. We have to go on. Look, Mum, nobody died. Dad just left home and as you told him, we didn't see that much of him. So put on a bit of slap, doll yourself up and go to the Grapes. You'll be a damn sight better there, surrounded by people, than here at home with your thoughts.'

Eve looked at her, knowing that Gemma must be as devastated as she was, and couldn't help but admire her spirit. 'What will you do?'

'I'll wash my face and pop round to see Eunice for a while. What do you say? Stiff upper lip and all that.'

'You're absolutely right,' said Eve defiantly. 'Why should we let that bastard ruin our lives. When he came home it wasn't that special anyway. I'm not going to be missing much. There are plenty of men who want me, even if he doesn't. No, I won't miss Jack Barrett at all.'

'Now look, Mum. Don't go and do anything stupid.'

Her jaw tight with suppressed anger, Eve said, 'But I'm a free woman now, Gemma. I can do as I please, your father has no say any more. Right, I'd better go and get ready for action.'

Gemma sat at the table and wondered just what her mother had in mind. Eve could be so unpredictable; she was capable of anything. She wouldn't take this rejection lightly, but why should she? Yet Gemma was scared of what she might do to soothe her injured pride.

In the scullery, as she made her mother a sandwich, Gemma thought how, unlike Eve, she *would* miss her father because after every voyage, his company was the one thing she really looked forward to; however angry she was, there would be a great void in her life from now on. She wondered if she would ever be able to forgive him for what he'd done.

When Eve came downstairs, she was carefully made up, with her hair dressed like the Duchess of Windsor's and wearing a smart black dress with a full skirt. Around her neck was a string of pearls she'd bought at Woolworths the week before. Below the mid-calf hem of the dress, she was wearing black court shoes, and Gemma couldn't help but think that by the end of the night, her mother's feet would be killing her.

'How do I look?' asked Eve as she did a twirl.

'Lovely, Mum. You look lovely.'

'Good,' smiled Eve as she put on her coat. 'I'll see you later,' and she let herself out of the door.

Yes – but in what state, Gemma wondered. Tonight she could understand it if Eve came home plastered!

Gemma tidied away the dishes and then, instead of visiting Eunice, she made her way to the Seaman's Mission. There she sat on a high stool in the kitchen and told her uncle just what had transpired. He was flabbergasted.

'I honestly find this hard to believe,' he said. He cocked his head on one side. 'Leave Eve – well, who could blame him? Even though she's my sister, I know she's a pain, and Jack's done well to put up with her all these years. But you, darling, his pride and joy . . . are you sure there isn't another woman involved?'

'He said not.'

'Well, at least he's done the decent thing by your mother financially. How's she taking it?'

'Pretty hard, despite all she says to the contrary.'

He nodded sympathetically. 'Her pride will have been dented. Poor old Eve – nobody likes rejection. Never mind, love, life has to go on and soon you too will be spreading your wings.'

'How can I go to sea now?' Gemma said despairingly. 'I can't leave Mum alone, can I?'

'That's enough of that nonsense, my girl,' Ted said firmly. 'When the time is right, you apply for a job with Cunard. Bloody hell, you would only be away for twelve days at a time. Eve could certainly survive that. Besides, you have your own life to lead. What happens if you fall in love and some man proposes to you? What are you going to say? "Sorry but no, I can't leave my mother"?'

She couldn't help but smile. 'When you put it like that it sounds pretty ridiculous.'

'Listen, sweetheart, you've had a shock, but after a few days, you'll be able to put all this into perspective. The end of the world, it isn't.'

She hugged him. 'I told Dad you never let me down and you don't. Thanks, Uncle Ted.'

He looked slightly abashed. 'On your way now, I've got lots of paperwork to do.'

As she walked home, Gemma thought over her uncle's words. In theory of course he was right, but in reality it would all depend on Eve. If she could hold herself together . . . Gemma unconsciously crossed her fingers and hoped.

Chapter Six

That night in the Grapes, Eve put on an act of cheerfulness that was worthy of an oscar performance. She was bright, witty and flirtatious. Several of her customers asked to take her out on her night off, but she declined all their offers, making some excuse each time. It didn't seem to matter how much drink she consumed, she was stone cold sober as she made her way home.

Gemma was waiting up for her with a bowl of hot soup at the ready. Eve saw the anxious look she gave her as she walked through the door, and said wearily, 'I'm not drunk, if that's what you're wondering. I could have drunk the bar dry tonight, but it would have had no effect. Funnily enough, I had several offers of a date from blokes, so you see, I'm still attractive to some men ... just not my husband, it would seem.'

The bitterness in her mother's voice was painful to hear. 'You're a good-looking woman, Mum,' Gemma told her gently. 'It's Dad's loss. In time perhaps he'll come to realise that.'

'I doubt it. Swanning around at the helm of some swanky yacht, he'll be having the life of Riley.'

'Don't you think he'll miss us at all?'

Eve looked at the sadness reflected in Gemma's eyes and said, 'I don't honestly know. Men don't think like us at all, and the sooner you realise that, the better it will stand you in life. Don't expect too much from men, Gemma, then you won't be disappointed. That's my advice to you.' Eve finished her soup and said, 'Come on, let's go to bed. You'll be tired in the morning, otherwise.'

The shop was busy the following day, for which Gemma was grateful. She had no time to chat with Eunice, and was secretly relieved, since it was all still much too painful to dwell on.

During mid-afternoon, she was attending to one of the showcases when a man's voice caught her unawares. 'Gemma? Is that you?'

She looked up and saw Nick Weston standing there. 'Good heavens, the man of mystery!'

He chuckled softly. 'And how is the minx today?'

'Very *un*minx-like. What are you doing here?'

'It's my mother's birthday and I'm searching for a present. She likes brooches so I stopped to look at the display . . . and there you were.'

Seeing Mr Granger in the distance observing her, Gemma said very professionally, 'Perhaps I can help you?'

Between them they looked over her selection. 'This is a lovely brooch,' she said, removing a large pearl one from the display case. It was indeed a handsome piece. The large centre pearl was shaped like a tear drop, surrounded by a double row of smaller ones, with a drop pearl at the base.

'Do you think this would appeal to her?' She held it against her blouse.

Nick looked at it admiringly. 'You have very good taste, Gemma. I'm sure my mother would love it.'

'Would you like me to gift-wrap the box for you?' she asked.

He said he would.

Whilst she was tying the bow, Nick said, 'Look, I'm free this evening. How about coming out for a meal with me?'

She looked up into his smiling eyes and knew she would accept. 'Only if you tell me about yourself. Being a man of mystery is only interesting for so long, you know.'

He burst out laughing. 'Very well, it's a deal. I'm staying at the Court Royal Hotel. Meet me in Reception at eight o'clock. We can have a drink at the bar, then find a decent restaurant. Does that suit you?'

She smiled at him. 'That sounds fine. I'll see you there.'

He settled his bill and took the package from her, holding on to her hand as he said, 'Until later then.'

She was aware of the warmth of his flesh against hers and felt the colour rise in her cheeks. She pulled her hand away and looked up into his twinkling eyes. 'Thank you, sir. I hope your mother likes her gift.'

He just grinned at her and walked away.

Eunice came racing over. 'Wasn't that the bloke from the dance?' she asked excitedly.

'Yes,' Gemma answered, 'and I'm having dinner with him tonight. I'm meeting him at his hotel.'

'Oh, yes?' said Eunice. 'If he invites you to his room, don't you dare go!'

Chance would be a fine thing, Gemma thought. Then she remembered Eve's words. *Don't expect too much . . .* but she wasn't expecting anything, except to find out exactly who he was and what he did for a living. She thought he might be a solicitor or something professional. And again she was intrigued by the man.

Wearing a smart emerald-green dress beneath her coat, Gemma arrived at the hotel ten minutes late, not wanting to appear too eager. She walked up the steps, and saw that Nick was already waiting. As she went through the swing doors, he stepped forward to greet her.

'Come through to the bar,' he said. There he took her coat from her and settled her in a comfortable chair. 'What can I order for you?' he asked.

'A gin and tonic would be nice,' she said thinking that her usual shandy would be out of place in these sophisticated surroundings, and sat back as the waiter came over. Nick still had the air of authority about him she'd first noticed at the Guildhall bar and she got the feeling he was used to giving orders.

Once they had been served, he raised his whisky and soda. 'Cheers. It was a bit of luck, running into you like that this afternoon. May I say how lovely you look. That shade of green really suits you.'

She sipped her drink. 'Thank you. So, what have you been doing since last we met? Then I seem to recall you were going away somewhere.'

He wasn't giving too much away too soon. 'Yes, I've been travelling quite a bit since then. How about you?'

She gazed at him and said, 'You are being evasive.'

He raised his eyebrows in mock surprise. 'Evasive – me? Why would I do that?'

'Are you some sort of commercial traveller?' she asked.

He seemed to find this highly amusing. 'Is that what you think I am?'

'Frankly, no. I see you more as a professional man.'

'Yes, you could certainly say that.'

'You now know what I do for a living,' she persisted. 'It's only fair that you tell me what you do.'

He grinned broadly. 'There's no secret, I promise. I'm the First Officer on the *Queen Mary*.'

Gemma was completely taken aback. Never for one moment had she thought of him as being in the Merchant Navy. She was speechless. 'Good heavens,' was all she could think to say.

Nick looked bemused. 'What's that supposed to mean?'

'Absolutely nothing. I just hadn't imagined you being a seafarer, that's all. What does a First Officer do?'

'I have my Master's ticket and I work on the bridge, navigating, plotting the course the ship takes. Sometimes when the Captain isn't on duty, I'm in charge of the vessel.'

'Vessel doesn't sound grand enough,' said Gemma. 'I've seen the ship sail out of the dock. She's huge.'

'The liner, then.'

Remembering when her father took her on the bridge of the *Edinburgh Castle*, she asked, 'Isn't it scary in rough weather?'

'It certainly has its moments, but the ship isn't going to sink every time she gets into a rough sea.'

'They said the *Titanic* was unsinkable.'

'O ye of little faith,' he chided. 'In rough weather, you

change the ship's course to ride the waves.'

'And you love every minute of it, don't you?'

He looked surprised. 'Yes, I do. I'm from a long line of seafarers.'

'I know, don't tell me . . . it gets in your blood.'

'You sound as if this life is familiar to you, Gemma.'

'Oh yes, I know all about it. My father is a coxswain with the Union Castle line.'

'That explains it then. I expect he's told you what a great life it is.'

'Many times.' She paused. 'It's a lonely life for wives though,' she said quietly, thinking of her mother and how she herself used to miss her father when he was away.

Nick looked at her thoughtfully. 'I agree, but if you marry a seafarer, you should be prepared for the separations. If not, your marriage is in trouble from the beginning. But think of years ago when men went exploring. They could be away for years on end; and what about war? Families were parted for ages then, and of course, many merchant ships were torpedoed.' Nick knew that from his own experiences as a young Able Seaman during the war. 'Compared with that, present-day voyaging isn't nearly so bad.'

'No, I suppose not.'

He looked at his watch. 'I've booked a taxi to take us to a club I know. I hope you like it.'

The club was small and exclusive, situated in The Avenue. The dining room was attractive and a three-piece band was playing as they sat down at their table. Nick handed Gemma a menu and said, 'Knowing how you enjoy dancing, I thought you might like it here. Besides, the food is excellent.'

And it was. Gemma found her hors d'oeuvre of white-bait crispy and fresh; her navarin of lamb was succulent, served with new potatoes and fresh vegetables. Nick chose the wine for them and she was impressed with his considerable knowledge. She herself had only ever drunk one glass of wine, and she resolved to take it slowly. How sophisticated he was, she thought, and how delightful it was to be in such company.

The two of them decided to wait a little before ordering a dessert, and Nick suggested they should dance. 'Come along, Gemma, it's a slow waltz. It'll help the food to go down.'

He took her hand and led her on to the dance floor. His strong arms enfolded her and she felt as if she belonged there, as they moved as one around the floor, neither speaking, until the music stopped and they returned to their table.

'That felt so good,' he said quietly and Gemma was pleased that he seemed so happy. After their dessert and coffee, they danced together for the rest of the evening, enjoying each other's company.

'Why do you stay in a hotel when the ship is in port?' asked Gemma.

'I need to get off the ship each trip, otherwise I'd go stir crazy as the Yanks say,' he explained. 'I'm cooped up on board so much, I need the break. It's good to get back to reality, the real world . . . so that I can spend my time in pleasant company,' he said with a cheeky grin. 'Why don't we have one more dance, then go back to my hotel for a nightcap?'

She looked at him warily, thinking of Eunice's warning.

She saw he was struggling to keep a straight face. 'We can have a drink in the residents' lounge, or you can have coffee if you prefer.' He leaned forward. 'I'm not abducting you to my room to have my wicked way with you, Gemma, if that's what you're thinking.'

She chuckled softly. 'Of course not. Would I think of such a thing?'

'No, but I might.' He rose to his feet as he said it and looked at her with a mischievous grin. 'Come on, you'll be quite safe with me. After all, I am an officer and a gentleman. Well, most of the time!'

They sat on a comfortable settee in the residents' lounge, with a tray of coffee and a liqueur, talking. For Gemma, it was bliss. This was the type of conversation she used to enjoy so much with her father. Nick was well-travelled and he told her about the West Indies cruise he'd recently done, about the various islands in the Caribbean, and of the different European countries he'd visited when cruising the Mediterranean. It only increased her desire to see them for herself.

'What do you do when you're in New York?' she asked, eager for information.

'I certainly don't spend my time shopping, like the female members of the crew,' he said with a laugh. 'There are museums to visit, I sometimes see a show on Broadway, go to a concert at Carnegie Hall, and I have a distant cousin who is a lieutenant in the New York Police Department. We go for a meal and a drink together sometimes. He's an interesting chap to talk to.'

'What a fascinating life you do lead,' Gemma said

enviously. 'How lucky you are. I would love to travel, to see all these places.'

'Maybe one day you will,' he said. 'The world is getting smaller all the time. Now the war is over, more people are travelling every year.'

She didn't tell him of her dream. She couldn't see him being impressed with her wanting to be a stewardess, somehow. Suddenly she realised how late it was. 'I must get home,' she said.

'I'll get you a taxi,' he volunteered and she was relieved that he hadn't planned to take her home himself.

Nick walked her out of the hotel when the car arrived, gave some money to the driver, then taking her firmly in his arms, he drew her towards him and kissed her soundly. 'Thank you for a delightful evening,' he said as he stared into her eyes. 'We must do it again some time.'

'Yes, I'd like that,' she said, and climbed into the car, giving the driver her address. She waved to Nick as they drove away, disappointed that he hadn't made a date for a further meeting and wondering if he really meant it when he said they should get together again. He had certainly meant it when he kissed her. She could still feel the imprint of his mouth on hers, the warmth of his arms around her. It had been an experience she certainly would like to enjoy again.

When Gemma arrived home, she was relieved that Eve was already in bed. She didn't think her mother would be very impressed by the fact she'd been out with a seafarer. At the moment any man who went to sea was a bastard, without morals, in Eve's eyes. In fact no man was worth his salt, but

Gemma hoped that as time passed, Eve would feel less bitter and get on with her life, although Gemma realised that the break-up of her marriage was a huge hurdle for any woman to overcome. She could only cope herself by putting the incident of her father's departure to the back of her mind, but it kept surfacing at different times, unexpectedly, and the pain of her loss was intense.

She found he invaded her thoughts a lot this particular evening when she was talking to Nick. He had been to so many places that Jack had told her about, in glowing terms. Nick reminded her of her father, through his obvious love of the sea. Nick hadn't talked at all about his home-life. She didn't think he was married – had she suspected that he was, she would never have gone out with him, of course. Perhaps like Jack, he was married to whatever ocean he was travelling. Seafarers were certainly a breed apart. And the worrying thing was, she could totally empathise with their way of thinking.

But this didn't help her when, a few weeks later, her mother received a letter from Jack giving them his new address, somewhere in Durban, in South Africa. He made the mistake of telling Eve how hot the weather was, and Eve went berserk.

'The rotten bastard! He's just ramming it down our throats, showing us how little we mean to him. Well, that's fine by me. He can sail his bloody yacht to hell and back for all I care.' There was a look of triumph in her eyes. 'There are plenty of men in the pub who want me. Before, I turned them down.' She looked at Gemma. 'Stupid, isn't it, but you see I still felt like a married woman. What an idiot

I was.' She tossed her head defiantly. 'I won't miss Jack Barrett at all. You just watch me . . . I'll show him!'

'Now look, Mum, you take care.'

Eve gave her a look filled with malice. 'Don't you tell me how to run my life, my girl. It's none of your business what I do from now on.'

Gemma stood her ground. 'It *is* my business. This is my home and you are my mother.'

Eve was suddenly beside herself with rage. 'A lot you care! Now get out of my way, I've got to get dressed for the evening. And I'm *really* going to enjoy myself!' She stormed upstairs and slammed her bedroom door shut.

To calm her own nerves, Gemma set about cleaning the kitchen. She turned out the cupboards and scrubbed the floor, aware of Eve running a bath, slamming each door as she went from room to room. The house reverberated with anger.

Eventually Eve stalked downstairs, ready for work. She was carefully made-up, her hair done in a chignon, and she was wearing a smart red dress with matching beads and earrings. Ignoring her daughter, she put on her coat and swept out of the house, leaving a waft of scent in her wake.

Unable to stay in the house any longer, Gemma decided to visit Eunice.

Her friend welcomed her and took her straight to her room. 'What's up?' she asked.

Gemma told her about her father's letter and Eve's bad mood.

'You can understand your mum being furious,' said Eunice fairly. 'I would be too. She'll get over it by the time she comes home.'

73

'It's when she comes home I'm worried about.' At the look of puzzlement on Eunice's face Gemma explained. 'You see, my mother is an alcoholic.'

'Oh, my God!' The other girl put an arm around Gemma. 'I had no idea.'

'It isn't something you brag about. But you see, now that Dad's left, I have to take care of her.'

'What a situation, but listen to me. I know you feel responsible for your mother, but you have a life of your own, and knowing your mum, she'll lead you a dog's life if you let her. You have to stand up to her.'

She knew that Eunice spoke the truth. After an hour chatting about incidental things as girls do, Gemma said, 'I'd better get back. Thanks for listening.'

Not wanting to go back to an empty house and dreading Eve's return, Gemma wandered along Canute Road, past the Cunard Company offices, looking with envy at the large colourful posters with pictures of the *Queen Elizabeth* and the *Queen Mary*. Behind the ships, the background was of the New York skyline with its towering skyscrapers. She read the exciting itinerary of the *Caronia*'s cruise around the North Cape and all about a trip to the West Indies at the end of the year on the *Mauretania*.

Travel the world with Cunard, it said. Barbados, Jamaica, Nassau, St Thomas in the Virgin Islands. A different world was out there. Gemma felt excitement growing inside her as she thought of palm trees, golden sands, a large expanse of ocean, moonlit nights at sea. How romantic. She closed her eyes, trying to visualise it all. She took a deep breath and could smell the tang of the sea.

'You all right, miss?'

The voice made her start. Beside her stood a policeman.

She gave a throaty chuckle. 'I'm fine.' She pointed to the posters. 'I was just trying to picture these places in my mind.'

He smiled benignly. 'Can't help you there, miss. A caravan at Highcliffe is all me and the wife can afford. But we all should have a dream.'

'One day I'm going to visit those places,' she vowed. 'If you close your eyes, you can smell the sea. Try it,' she invited. He looked bemused. 'Go on,' she urged, and closed her eyes.

They stood side by side with their eyes shut. After a few seconds she said, 'You can, can't you?'

He nodded. 'Yes, miss. You certainly can. Right – I'd best get back on me beat and you best be off, otherwise I'll have you up for loitering with intent to travel!'

She laughed. 'All right, officer.' As she walked away she felt much better. If only she could get Eve settled after this recent shock, she would then be free to get right away from Southampton, to travel, to discover this other world that seafarers kept talking about. She wouldn't be satisfied until she did.

Chapter Seven

It was almost eleven o'clock that night before Gemma heard her mother return. There was the sound of Eve giggling outside on the pavement and then a man's voice speaking softly. Gemma pulled back the corner of the front-room curtain to see Eve clasped in the arms of a stranger. Feeling like a voyeur, she watched her mother kiss the man, and then let go the curtain.

Eve eventually let herself into the house. Seeing Gemma, she said belligerently, 'What are you doing up at this hour? Spying on me, were you?'

'No, of course not,' Gemma replied guiltily. 'I was worried about you, that's all.' She saw the glazed look in Eve's eyes, which was a fair indication of the amount of alcohol she had consumed, and noticed that her lipstick was badly smudged.

Taking off her coat and flinging it on the settee, her mother declared, 'I told you earlier – the way I lead my life from now on is my business.'

'Who brought you home?'

There was a defiant gleam in Eve's eyes as she said, 'One of the customers. He's asked me out on my night off.'

'Are you going?'

'Bloody right I am. I intend to enjoy my life from now on.' She walked into the scullery to make a cup of tea.

As Gemma made her way upstairs to bed, she sighed. She could well understand Eve's need to prove to herself that she was still attractive to the opposite sex, but she was concerned about the type of man she was meeting. Customers in a bar was one thing, but as an escort or a potential husband, that was something different. She realised she was in for a difficult time during the weeks ahead.

The situation at work only added to her problems. It was now common knowledge that a place for a supervisor was up for grabs and everyone was on their toes, knowing they were being watched by their departmental heads. For once, Gemma was in Granger's good books, having made a few really good sales, which didn't suit Hazel when she heard her being praised. She wanted that job and if she had anything to do with it, that stuck-up madam wouldn't stand an earthly. But what could she do? The opportunity she craved to discredit Gemma happened by chance.

Hazel had been invited to a cousin's birthday party. She'd bought a new frock but it needed dressing up a little. On display in the jewellery department was the very thing – a long, 1920s-style necklace made of amethyst and small pearls. It was exactly the right colour to match her dress.

Just before closing time on the Saturday, Hazel took the necklace out of the case and slipped it into her skirt pocket, rearranging the other pieces of jewellery to fill the empty space. She would return it early on Monday morning, she told herself, before anyone noticed. However, on that morning, Hazel's bus was late again, and by the time she arrived at the store, Gemma had already discovered the necklace was missing.

Remembering the débâcle before, when Hazel had set her up, Gemma searched diligently for the necklace, but it was nowhere to be seen. She felt her heart sink at the thought of Mr Granger's displeasure when she reported the loss. As she turned to tell Eunice of her fears, Hazel arrived. When she saw the open lid of the display case, she became very furtive, which Gemma picked up on immediately.

'Have you seen the amethyst and pearl necklace from here?' she asked.

'How could I?' Hazel said sulkily, cursing her late bus. 'I've only just arrived.'

'Well, it's missing – and this time it isn't tucked down at the back of the case.' As she spoke she saw Hazel's hand go instinctively to the pocket of her skirt. The guilty flush to her cheeks gave her away.

'You've got it, haven't you?' she rapped out.

Hazel was emphatic in her denial. 'Of course not. You're mad. How could you think such a thing?'

Gemma made to grab hold of Hazel's hand. 'What have you got in your pocket? Show me.'

From the corner of her eye, Hazel could see Mr Granger approaching. She panicked and pushed Gemma away, saying, 'I've got to go to the locker room.'

She took off at speed, followed by Gemma, calling loudly, 'You come back here!'

Mr Granger followed them angrily, wondering just what

was making two of his staff behave in such an unseemly manner.

Seconds behind Hazel, Gemma pushed open the door to the locker room, just in time to see Hazel remove the missing necklace from her pocket. 'I knew it!' she said triumphantly. 'You rotten little sneak. You took this home at the weekend, didn't you?' She took it off the girl and held it aloft, out of Hazel's reach.

At that moment there was a rap on the door and Mr Granger strode in.

'Just *what* is going on here? I could hear your voices halfway down the corridor.'

Hazel stepped forward. 'Thank goodness you're here, sir,' she said quickly. 'Miss Barrett has stolen a piece of our jewellery. I came here to get it back. She had hidden it in her locker and I found it.'

Gemma was shocked. 'That's a bloody lie.'

Mr Granger glared at Gemma and the offending article in her hand. 'Then perhaps you can explain why you have possession of the piece of jewellery?' he asked coldly, taking it from her.

'It was her, not me!' Gemma exclaimed, pointing to the other girl. 'When I dusted the display case this morning, I saw it was missing and from the way *she* was behaving I knew she had it in her pocket. I came after her to get it back.'

Hazel looked at her boss and said, 'She's lying, of course.'

'Did you inform anyone else that this was missing?' he asked Gemma, and she cursed silently. Hazel had arrived before she'd spoken to Eunice.

'I didn't have time.'

'You will both return to your places. I'll send for you later . . . and in the meantime, you'd better behave with decorum. Understand?'

They both nodded.

As they walked back together, Gemma said quietly, 'You won't get away with this, Grimes.'

'I don't know what you're talking about,' Hazel smirked. 'I saw you take it out of the case. It's your word against mine.'

An hour later, Hazel was summoned to Mr Granger's office. She returned to the department later with a self-satisfied look on her face and told Gemma that Mr Granger wished to see her.

With a sense of foreboding, Gemma made her way to the inner sanctum. Granger faced her from a chair behind his desk. He didn't invite her to take a seat and Gemma stood in front of him feeling like the accused in the dock.

'It pains me greatly to have to say this, Miss Barrett, especially as you have been doing so well of late, but I'm afraid I'm going to have to let you go.'

She gave him a startled look. 'Let me go? I don't understand.'

'Then let me be more clear. You no longer work for this store.'

'You're giving me the sack?'

'Exactly. I couldn't have put it more plainly myself.'

'But on what grounds?'

His face reddened with anger. 'I can't believe you even have to ask, when you have been caught red-handed with stolen goods.'

Gemma's outrage was boundless. 'You have absolutely no proof at all that that was the case. I had, in fact, just removed the necklace from Hazel. She'd taken it home over the weekend, but I found out before she had time to replace it. She was trying to hide it, and that's the truth!'

It was obvious he didn't believe her. 'We have decided not to call the police in to deal with this matter. The necklace is back and we don't need adverse publicity over a piece of costume jewellery. For that at least you should be grateful.'

'Call them!' Gemma demanded. 'At least then I would get some kind of justice. I'm getting none from you. You are taking Miss Grimes's word against mine.'

Granger rose from his chair. 'There is nothing more to be said. Your wages and cards are being made up. Wait in the locker room, Barrett. They'll be brought to you there. That'll be all.'

'Not quite,' said Gemma firmly. 'You have made a serious mistake today, because I'm the innocent party here, so your judgement is called into question. I was always loyal to this firm and honest, and you are letting me go for a girl who couldn't care less about you or the customers, who lies and steals. I only hope it doesn't all come tumbling down around your head in the future, Mr Granger, and that you end up paying dearly for the decision you made here today.' She turned and walked out of the office, her head held high.

Still stunned by the turn of events, Gemma was empty-ing her locker when Eunice popped her head around the door. 'What happened?'

'He fired me! That little bitch fed him a pack of lies and

he believed her. You'd best get back or you'll be in trouble. I'll keep in touch, I promise.'

It was with a heavy heart that Gemma made her way home. Now she was without a job – and what would she say at the Labour Exchange if she went to sign on? They would ask why she had left her last position. 'I was accused of theft and fired!' didn't exactly have a good ring about it. Thank goodness that Eve was working.

Her mother was surprised to see her when she returned home from her morning shift and more than a little perplexed to learn that she was now the only breadwinner. Gemma's wages would be missed. When her daughter eventually explained the painful events that had led to her dismissal, Eve was all for storming into the store and facing Granger. But Gemma begged her not to.

'It won't do any good, Mum. It won't get me my job back, so there's no point.'

'It's our good name that's at stake here. I don't want the neighbours pointing the finger!'

For Gemma this was the final straw. 'For one minute there, Mother, I thought you had my wellbeing at heart. I have been called a thief when I'm innocent but all you're concerned about is what the neighbours will say.' She put on her coat and opened the door. 'You don't seem so concerned about the gossip when you come home legless!' She slammed the door behind her. She knew it was a cruel taunt, but even so it was true. She felt the rage building up inside. My father should be here to sort this out! she thought. I've been unjustly accused and there is no one around who gives a damn!

That wasn't quite true, she discovered, when Eunice called round to see her that evening after work. 'The staff have all sent Hazel to Coventry,' her friend informed her. 'She can't stand it. If she comes along, we all turn our backs on her.' She giggled. 'Actually, Gem, I'm really enjoying myself.' Then realising what she'd said, she apologised. 'I didn't mean that entirely. I'm sick that you got the push through her lies, but I am enjoying getting back at her. We all make a great show of locking up our belongings when she's around. We're really getting to the little cow.'

'It serves her right,' said Gemma gloomily, 'but she's the one who still has the job, despite all that. She told a barefaced lie about me and what's worse, Granger believed her. She got away with it and there's nothing I can do about it. I'd like to throttle her.'

'You'll get something else soon, you'll see. What you need to cheer you up is another evening out with that gorgeous bloke. Have you heard from him?'

Gemma shook her head. 'He doesn't know where I live and if he comes into the shop again, I won't be there.' She looked quite stricken. 'Oh Eunice, wouldn't it be awful if I was to miss him?'

'Don't you worry, love. I'll keep an eye open for him, never you fear. I'll even be a real friend and offer to keep him warm for you.'

'Over my dead body. You lay off.' Gemma sighed. 'Anyway, he's probably a ship that passed in the night.'

'Yes, but he's passed twice,' quipped Eunice. 'And the last time, he kissed you!'

'Yes, he did,' said Gemma dreamily, 'and it was lovely.

Why can't he arrive out of the blue and take me away from all this?'

'On a white horse, you mean?'

'Why would he need a white horse, Eunice, when he has a whole liner to ride? He rides the waves, you see.'

'I can see you've lost your marbles. Rides the waves? Whatever next!'

Gemma spread her arms wide. 'Anything! God, I need something to happen. Dad has left home, Mum has hit the bottle and I've got the sack.' She turned quickly to Eunice. 'We could rob a bank. That's it, it would solve all our problems. What do you say?'

Eunice was now beginning to worry about her friend. 'You aren't serious, are you?'

Gemma sank into an armchair. 'Of course not, stupid. I don't want to end up behind bars. It's just that life is so rotten at the moment I want to scream with frustration. I'll have to go to the Labour Exchange tomorrow. I'll tell them the store was cutting back on staff, or I'll never get offered anything.'

But when she went to the office the following day, there were no jobs on offer. She had to report weekly, draw her meagre National Assistance money and be prepared to go for an interview if anything came along. That evening she bought a copy of the *Southern Daily Echo* and searched the Situations Vacant column, but could find nothing. They would have to tighten their belts at home meantime to make the money go further. She would have to impress this on Eve, make her understand how difficult their situation would be for a while until she was once again employed.

But Gemma had such a headache that evening, she took two aspirins and went to bed early. It was around midnight that sounds from below woke her. She sat up in bed, rubbing her eyes, trying to gather her senses, when she realised she could hear male voices. She rose from her bed and putting on her dressing gown, hurried downstairs.

Her mother was leaning against the table, hanging on to a chair, swaying on her feet. With her were two seamen, dressed in Merchant Navy rig – navy trousers, matching polo-necked sweaters and thick short coats. They both looked at Gemma with a smile of anticipation. One turned to the other.

'It's all right, mate. We've got one each now.' He staggered towards Gemma, arms outstretched. 'I thought we were going to have to share,' he said. 'Come here, my little darlin'. We're going to have a great time.'

She stepped away from him, looking anxiously at Eve for help, but her mother had slumped on to the settee. Picking up a dining chair, Gemma held it in front of her, using the legs as a means of defence. 'Get out of this house, now!'

The man just grinned at her. 'I like a woman with spirit. Come here, you little wildcat.' He lunged at her. As he did so, she swung the chair with all of her might, catching him a sturdy blow across his chest, sending him reeling. She turned to the other man. 'Take your mate and get out before I smash the window and call the police!'

He saw the look of determination on her face, and tugging at his friend's jacket, dragged him towards the door. 'We was invited,' he grumbled.

'Yes, by a drunken woman! You scum, taking advantage of her like that. Now bugger off and don't come back again!' Gemma slammed the door behind them and drew the bolt across, then slid to the floor, every part of her body trembling with fright.

Eve hauled herself to her feet, looking dazed. 'Where's Jim?' she asked.

Gemma was consumed with rage. She got up off the floor and taking her mother by the shoulders, shook her hard. 'How dare you bring strange men into the house at this time of night?' she demanded.

Pushing Gemma away, Eve said sulkily, 'I'll bring who I like when I like.'

'But one of them thought I was here for his benefit. We could have both been raped . . . don't you realise what you have done? The danger you put us in?'

But Eve was too far gone. 'They only wanted a good time, that's all.'

'For God's sake, Mother! When am I going to get through to you?'

Eve pushed her aside and made for the stairs. 'I'm going to bed.'

Gemma let her go, knowing there was nothing to be gained by talking to her in this state, but in the morning it would be a different matter.

And it certainly was. Eve, nursing a hangover, listened as Gemma raged about the previous night. The girl lost her temper when Eve refused to believe what she told her about the men's expectations. It wasn't until Gemma threatened to leave if it ever happened again, that Eve took any real notice.

'What do you mean, leave?'

Realising that at last she had her mother's full attention, Gemma glared at her. 'How can I rest in my bed at night knowing you are bringing men home. Strangers! They could be anybody. I could be murdered in my bed – and so could you. If you don't give a damn about me, at least have some pride in yourself. Some bloody Duchess of Windsor you are, Mother! Take a good look in the mirror and see what you're doing to yourself. As it is we are short of money, now I'm out of work. It's time you pulled yourself together.' She grabbed her coat and stormed out of the house.

Eve was stunned. She already knew her looks were suffering, but to have this pointed out by Gemma of all people, was more than she could bear. She was coming up to her forty-third birthday and was scared of getting old, without a man to care for her. She knew she would have to do something about her drinking. Only last night her boss had warned her about it after she'd upset someone with her acid tongue, whilst being half cut, and without her wages now, they would really be in financial trouble.

It was all right for others to criticise; for her, a drink was a panacea to all her troubles. It made her forget, for a while anyway. She picked up a hairbrush, but winced as she used it. Her head was so tender. In truth she couldn't remember very much about last night, but Gemma's anger was such that she now believed her account of what had happened. She realised at last that it had indeed been a mistake, and had it not been for Gemma's presence . . . and then she began to cry.

Chapter Eight

After the *Queen Mary* had docked in New York, Nick Weston was sitting in the comfort of his cabin on board, entertaining his distant cousin, Lieutenant Gus Carter of the NYPD. He liked Gus. Here was a man, just turned forty, portly and balding, but as dedicated to his chosen profession as Nick was to his. Gus didn't have the smooth sophistication of his cousin; he was a tough New Yorker, and he'd earned the rank he held the hard way. At the bottom of a drawer in the bedroom of his apartment were several citations for bravery. Gus didn't put much store by awards. He just wanted to stay alive to do his job, and in this dangerous city, that wasn't always easy. Although very different, in many ways the two men were similar.

Gus leaned back in his plush chair, enjoying a cooling glass of beer and tucking into the club sandwiches served by the steward. He wiped his brow with a handkerchief. 'Thank God for air conditioning!' he exclaimed. 'New York in the summer is a real bitch, and in a couple of months' time, we'll all be sweating like pigs. The humidity really gets to me.' He sipped his beer. 'I came looking for you last trip,' he said.

'I was in London taking another exam,' explained Nick. 'I needed it to help towards my own captaincy in the future.'

'How did you make out?'

'I have to wait for the results,' said Nick, 'but I think I did all right.'

Gus gazed around the splendid cabin with its comfortable bed, writing bureau, table and easy chairs, and remarked, 'Not a bad life, Nick. Not bad at all.' His eyes twinkled as he joked. 'I can't believe you actually get paid to enjoy this life of luxury. After all, for a few hours on the bridge, all you have to do is point the ship in the right direction, and the rest of the time you're dining with all these rich people, eating the finest food, drinking the best wines, dancing the night away with beautiful women. There's no hardship to your job as far as I can see! You don't even have to dock this brute; the pilot does it for you *and* takes it down the river when you sail!'

Nick was highly amused. 'In comparison, you have a hard life, is that it?'

'Damned right I do. Whilst you are mixing with the high and mighty, the movie stars, I have to make do with the dregs of New York. Gangsters, pimps, hookers and murderers. There's no comparison.'

'It certainly sounds more interesting. You wouldn't believe how boring some of our passengers can be. Even the pretty ones.'

'Oh, come on! On board here, it's like a world all of its own. You are so protected with the crew on hand to fulfil your every whim. It would do you good to see a little of my world, get a taste of real life.'

Nick gazed at his cousin. 'Now that really would be fascinating. I would enjoy such an experience.'

Gus took a long swig of his drink. 'If you mean that, maybe I can do something about it.'

Nick was intrigued. 'How?'

'Do you have anything planned for tonight?' Gus asked.

'Not really. A movie and a meal, perhaps. I hadn't given it much thought as yet.'

Looking at his watch, Gus said, 'Why don't you come along with me and my partner in our patrol car? You can see what life on the streets here is really like.'

'You're not going to get me shot, are you?' Nick joked. 'Only I don't think the Captain would appreciate sailing without his First Officer.'

'Jesus, I hope not. Mainly we're on a stake-out, but you might find the scenario behind the job interesting. I'll tell you more about that later – but anything I say is strictly confidential, you realise?'

'Of course. Now you've made me very curious . . . how could I refuse?'

Gus rose from his seat. 'Wear something comfortable, Nick. Savile Row will not be suitable.'

'You're confusing me with the skipper. Savile Row is beyond my salary, old boy.'

Gus raised an eyebrow. 'Don't tell me you buy your suits off the peg, 'cause I don't believe it for one minute.'

'No,' Nick conceded. 'I have a very clever Jewish tailor in Southampton.'

With a grin, Gus said, 'I knew it. I'll pick you up at the dock gates at seven-thirty, OK? You'd better eat first. Stake-outs can be long and tedious. Sure you want to come?'

'Of course! I wouldn't miss such an opportunity for anything.'

At the allotted time, Gus pulled up at the dock gates in an unmarked car but as Nick walked towards it, Gus and another man stepped out. He introduced Lou Masters, his partner.

'Hi, how you doing?' asked Lou.

'Fine, thanks. Where are we going?'

'We'll be cruising downtown for a while, but first we're going across the road for a beer.'

Along the dockside opposite pier 90 was a market diner, a one-storey building with a bar at one end and a diner at the other which served short-order food to eat in or take out. Nearby was a newsagent and tobacconist where the British crews could buy papers from home. Another bar on the opposite corner was a very seedy-looking place, used mainly by the longshoremen – American stevedores – and by a few locals and transients. Nick had never been inside the place before and as he stepped into the scruffy bar, he hoped never to enter it again.

Lou went up to the counter and ordered the beers as Gus gestured at a table, covered in spilled beer and cigarette ash, near the open door.

'Sit and watch,' said Gus with a grin. 'All manner of life walks in through these doors.'

And so it seemed. As Nick observed the customers come and go, he turned to Gus and said, 'These men all look like gangsters out of a James Cagney movie.'

Returning to the table, Lou overheard his remark. 'Many

of them are – and have a long crime-sheet to prove it, ain't that right, boss?'

Gus nodded. 'That little guy over there with the scar on his cheek served time for armed robbery. The big Negro by the bar served ten years in Leavenworth after a stabbing. Lucky for him his victim survived.' Nick grew increasingly uneasy. Sensing this, Gus quietly remarked, 'You're quite safe. Both Lou and I are armed and that dirty-looking guy at the end of the bar is an undercover cop, so relax.'

It was obvious that one or two of the regular customers recognised Gus, as they greeted him warily. 'Hi, Lieutenant. Slumming, are you?' He answered them good-naturedly, but there was an air of hostility in the room and soon, Gus said, 'Come on, let's go.' It was with a feeling of great relief that Nick followed them across the street to the car.

They drove away, eventually making for Broadway and Times Square. Nick looked out at the garish neon signs towering over the well-lit stores. This was familiar territory, and it felt more comfortable. As always the city gave him a buzz of excitement. At Times Square, there was a huge hoarding advertising a make of cigarette with the face of a man, blowing out real, large smoke-rings into the air.

They drove through Greenwich Village with its bars and restaurants until Gus made for the Lower East Side. Here the affluence faded fast; the real poverty was now unhidden and it felt menacing.

Gus drove slowly, cruising the streets, casting glances either side as he went. Nick felt himself tense. He sat up in the back seat and peered out of the window into the now dimly lit street. Prostitutes stood around, touting for trade.

Men gathered in small groups outside rundown stores, talking, smoking, drinking from beer cans, which they tossed onto the sidewalk when they were empty. Further along, two drunks were arguing.

In front of them a car pulled into the side and a prostitute walked to the window of the vehicle and spoke to the driver. Gus stopped his car and looked at Lou. 'Come on,' he said, 'let's spoil his night. You stay put,' he told Nick.

He and Lou got out of the car and walked one either side of the other vehicle. Gus made for the driver's side. The man looked up at him, startled by his arrival. When Gus flashed his police badge at him, the man cursed loudly.

'Kerb crawling is a federal offence, buddy,' Gus said.

'I was just asking the way,' the driver said nervously.

'Of course you were. Show me your driver's licence.' The man did so, reluctantly. Gus started to write down the details.

On the other side of the car, the prostitute was struggling as Lou held her. 'Let me go, will you! Damned cops!'

'Shut your mouth, honey,' he said, 'or I'll take you down to the station and book you for obstruction.'

'I'm only trying to earn an honest buck.' When he ignored her she changed her tune. 'Please don't book me,' she pleaded. 'I'm having enough trouble paying my last fine. My pimp will kill me if I get another.'

Nick was observing the scene in front of him with interest when suddenly a tap on the window alongside the back seat startled him. A woman grinned through the glass at him. Her clothes were dishevelled and her blouse was open, showing her full breasts. 'Hi darlin'. There's room back there for us both.' She poked the tip of her tongue out and ran it along her top lip before wiggling it at him, in what was supposed to be a provocative fashion. It just made Nick feel sick. He wound the window down a little and said, 'This is an unmarked police car.' He then indicated the two men in front of the vehicle. 'And they are cops.'

'Oh, shit!' she said, and walked away.

Gus meantime handed back the driving licence to the man behind the wheel, who asked, 'Does my wife have to know about this?'

The policeman looked at him with distaste. 'You should have thought of that before you came round here.'

'I've got three kids,' he said dully.

'You piece of garbage!' exclaimed Gus. 'You come here for sex, then go home to your wife. Don't you ever think you could give her some kind of disease?'

The man turned pale.

Gus gave him back his licence. 'Go home,' he said, with disgust. 'If I see you around any of these streets again, I'll book you. Understand?'

'Yes, sir. Thanks.' The man put his car into gear and took off at speed.

Lou let the girl go. 'You're lucky this time,' he said. 'My boss is in a forgiving mood.'

She glared at him and walked quickly away.

The two men returned to their car. As Gus drove away, he said angrily, 'These kerb crawlers make me sick. Most of them are family men with nice homes, loving wives, but they come here to get their kicks. Sick bastards!'

They drove on to Little Italy, an area inhabited mainly

by Italian immigrants from years back, and drew up opposite a restaurant. To Lou Gus said, 'I wonder if our boy is on time tonight.' Shortly after, a red Dodge sports car drew up and the driver got out of the car with a leggy blonde and went inside. 'There he goes,' said Gus. And lit a cigarette.

'Who is he?' asked Nick.

'This young blade works in the docks. The longshoremen work in gangs and he's a boss of one of them. That's fine as it goes, but he's employed by Tony Anastasio, a mobster. His brother, Albert, is head of one of the Mafia families. Tony runs the docks, here and in New Jersey.'

'The Mafia!' exclaimed Nick.

'Now don't tell me you haven't heard they run the docks – you're not that naïve,' Gus challenged him.

'Of course there are rumours, but as long as it doesn't interfere with the movement of the Cunard shipping, I really don't want to know,' Nick confessed. 'So why are you watching this chap?'

'Call it a gut feeling. Recently he's had a couple of meetings with Tough Tony himself, which means that he's into something else and I want to know what.' He turned round in his seat and faced Nick. 'You see, my assignment is to try and break the stranglehold the Mafia have on the docks.'

Nick cursed. 'Christ, Gus . . . isn't that dangerous?'

The two Americans laughed. 'This is New York, not cosy Olde Englande, my friend. Jeez! Your limey cops walk the streets unarmed. Here, without my gun, I'd have been dead meat years ago.'

'I need a piss,' Lou said suddenly.

'So do I,' said Nick.

'Then go to the alley back there, but don't make a noise closing the car doors.'

As Nick stood next to Lou Masters, peeing up against a wall in a narrow alleyway strewn with rotting vegetables and papers, he thought, This can't be real. And he realised just what a cosseted life he really did lead. Gus was right, he had no idea how the other half lived in the city of New York and fascinating though it was, he was grateful for his own way of life.

Two hours later, the couple emerged from the restaurant. Under the streetlight Nick saw the young man clearly. He was tall and good-looking, with dark hair. He was wearing a lightweight suit, but he carried the jacket over his shoulder, tossing it into the back of the car. The girl was attractive in a coarse way, with flowing bleached blonde hair.

The police car followed the red Dodge at a discreet distance, parking way back when the driver of the other car pulled up outside an apartment block off Broadway. The young couple entered the building.

'We can all go home,' said Gus. 'He'll be there all night. There is obviously nothing else on his agenda but sex.' He glanced at Nick. 'Do you want to stop off somewhere for a drink or a meal?'

Shaking his head Nick said, 'No, I'll go back to the ship if you don't mind. I'm on duty early in the morning. I'll have a bath and go to bed, but thanks for the offer.'

'I'm pretty tired myself,' said Gus, 'and Lou here will want to go home to his wife, won't you?'

The other man smiled. 'Yeah. Betty will have something hot for me to eat, then I'll hit the sack.'

Nick was driven back to pier 90 without further delay. As he got out of the car he said, 'Thanks, fellows. That was quite an eye-opener and I'm sure it was nothing to some of the stuff you have to deal with. Gus, my friend . . . you're absolutely right. I *do* have an easy life, thank the Lord!'

'Hey, one day, Nick, I'll take a trip to the old country. You can give me the VIP treatment. Share some of those pretty English dames with me.'

'Gladly,' he laughed and made his way along the dock, towards the gangway and the safety of his cabin.

As Gus drove home, he grinned to himself. Tonight would have been quite an experience for Nick. It gave the American a kick to show his British cousin the seedy side of New York, even though he'd only skimmed the top this evening. He wondered what his cousin's reaction would be if he knew that Albert Anastasia – he'd changed the spelling of his surname – was not only a crime boss, but the head of Murder Incorporated, an organisation that would kill or maim anyone for the right price. He was also deeply involved with the union of the International Longshoremen's Association.

Through his grip on the union, millions of dollars each year were funnelled into syndicate coffers from kickbacks on dues; in addition cargoes were purloined, and there were payoffs from shipping companies to maintain the smooth running of the docks and protect their ships.

With a sigh, Gus thought how Nick had no idea what his American cousin was up against. Frankly, he himself wasn't at all sure how much he could do about all the corruption . . . but he had to try.

Chapter Nine

Gemma was getting desperate. No matter how hard she tried, she couldn't find employment. She went for several interviews, but either the situation had been taken by the time they got to her, or she didn't hear anything further. She realised that Mr Granger might have put in a bad word for her, if anyone had asked him for a reference as her previous employer.

After the incident of the two seamen, Eve Barrett was trying to behave, but the atmosphere at home was so unnatural and strained that Gemma felt she was sitting on the edge of a volcano, waiting for it to erupt. One evening she'd had enough and made her way to the Seaman's Mission to visit her uncle. She had no one else to turn to.

Ted was in his office, going over his paperwork when Gemma arrived. He gazed at his niece with surprise as she entered.

'What's wrong?'

She related the whole sorry tale.

Ted was furious. 'That's really tough, Gemma love. Is there anything I can do to help?'

'Yes. Give me a job.'

He looked horrified. 'You wouldn't want to work here, pet. This isn't the place for you.'

'Why not?'

'Seamen can be a bit of a handful, especially when they come back here with a bellyful of beer. Their language is pretty choice, for a start.'

With a sardonic smile she said, 'I can shut my ears to the swearing, and as for dealing with drunks, I am well-trained in that department.'

'Now you stop that kind of talk,' he scolded. 'Dealing with your mother is entirely different.'

She pleaded with him. 'Look, Uncle Ted, I desperately need a job and if I worked here, you could give me a bit of training at the same time – show me what to do if ever I get a job at sea. We would kill two birds with one stone.'

He laughed heartily. 'This place isn't a bit like work on an ocean-going liner. More like a leaking rowboat!'

She ignored his humour. 'But beds still have to be made, don't they, rooms kept clean and meals served. I'll do anything.'

He was filled with admiration for her. 'You really mean it, don't you?'

'I've never been more serious in my life.'

He stroked his chin thoughtfully. 'We are short-handed, as it happens. This manager asked me only the other day if I knew of anyone. I'll have a word with him later.' He frowned as he explained. 'You do realise if there is a job, you'll be a sort of dogsbody? It's dirty work – you'll be scrubbing floors, serving meals, turning out bedrooms, and I have to warn you, cleaning up after some of these boys isn't the most pleasant job in the world. Are you still interested?'

'I certainly am.'

'All right, love, I'll ask and let you know sometime this evening. If you can stick with this for a couple of months, I'll teach you all you need to know about being a stewardess. Then I suggest you apply to one of the shipping lines for a job.'

Her eyes widened with surprise.

Ted lit a cigarette. 'Listen to me, my girl. By always being here, ready to bail your mother out whenever she gets into trouble, you aren't helping her one bit. She'll never learn to stand on her own two feet whilst you are there to pick her up every time she falls by the wayside.'

What he was saying made a lot of sense, but Gemma still had her reservations. 'But what if she hurts herself . . . if she gets drunk and falls?'

'Gemma! You can't spend the rest of your days being her crutch. If my sister is going to make any life for herself, she has to learn to do it alone. And you have to give her a chance.'

'What if she doesn't make it?'

He looked earnestly at her. 'Eve has a choice. If she goes down the pan, she probably would have done so anyway.' At her hesitation he added, 'You want to go to sea, don't you?'

'You know I do.'

'If you miss the opportunity, you'll regret it for the rest of your life.'

She was reluctant to agree with him. Then: 'You're right, of course. It's just that I feel so responsible for her.'

'That's because you are a dutiful daughter.' Ted gave a harsh laugh. 'Your mother has failed miserably in her duty to you, so there is no need for you to harbour any feelings of guilt. Those belong to your parents. In my book, they both failed you.' He caught her by the arm. 'Come along, I'll show you around, then if the boss says the job is yours, you'll be familiar with your surroundings.'

As she went from room to room, Gemma realised that this job would be a far cry from her clean and comfortable employment at the store. The furniture in the so-called residents' lounge was shabby and she was appalled by the untidiness of the inmates. Her father had been very clean and tidy in his habits due to his time served on board, living in confined quarters, but the same couldn't be said for the seamen living here. Ashtrays overflowed, news-papers were strewn everywhere, and dirty cups were still on the table. But she didn't care. She needed a job – and she desperately needed the money.

In the bar of the Grapes, Eve was not her usual exuberant self. Being the sole breadwinner in the family worried her. It was a responsibility she'd never shouldered before. Lately she'd always relied on Gemma to dig her out of any financial hole. Now she couldn't.

If only she could give up the drink, she thought, or limit herself to just a few, but as each day passed, her need for alcohol grew stronger. Without it, in the mornings her hands shook so badly she had to hold a cup of tea with two hands to prevent any spillage. She felt ill, and vulner-able. The drink made her feel good, for a while anyway. Too much and she became belligerent, she admitted. That was a worry to her now. She had to keep control, because if she got the sack, they could be in real trouble.

True she had her allowance from Jack, but apart from spending too much on booze, she liked to treat herself to something new to wear. Something that would maintain the image of the Duchess of Windsor, ignoring her unpaid bills. It was the one thing in life that gave Eve pleasure. To have to live off Jack's money alone, would mean she'd have to give up all she now enjoyed.

When she arrived home that night it was to find Gemma in despair. Ted had called round to say the job at the Mission was filled.

'I didn't know you'd asked for one there,' Eve remarked.

'I had to do something!' snapped Gemma.

Eve looked uncomfortable. 'Look, I know I drink too much and I am trying to do better.'

Gemma gazed at her in surprise. This was something new, Eve admitting she was in the wrong about anything. 'Why do you do it, Mum? You're a good-looking woman still, smart. You can be good company when you're sober.'

Eve flinched at the remark and for once there was an expression of vulnerability about her demeanour. She let out a deep sigh. 'I don't know.' She hesitated then admitted, 'I suppose I expected so much more out of life.'

There was such a note of sadness in her voice that it moved Gemma. 'So, what was missing? You were married with a home and a child. What else could you possibly want?'

The fire inside Eve flared suddenly. 'I wanted to be somebody! I wanted to be admired like I was when they let me dress up as Amy Johnson to advertise the film. I had my picture in the paper. People pointed to me in the street. I liked feeling special! But that died away and I was nothing. Nothing.'

Gemma felt anger rising within her. 'You were a wife, a mother. There was Dad, and me. We both loved you. Why wasn't that enough?'

Eve looked at her coolly. 'Yes, Jack loved me then, but it wasn't enough for me. Then I had you, and after that, what chance of a future did I have?'

The tone of her mother's voice hurt Gemma deeply. 'You could have loved me,' she managed.

'Your father loved you enough for both of us,' she retorted.

Gemma gazed at her and asked, 'How could you be so jealous? I am your child too, after all.'

Sipping her tea, Eve said, 'I wasn't ready for motherhood. I was much too young to be tied down.'

Gemma appealed to her. 'I try to help, try to please you. I always have, but whatever I do or did, you always found fault with me.' She stared hard at Eve, willing her to admit that she had some feelings for her. 'I do love you, Mum.'

But Eve remained silent, drinking her tea.

With a heavy heart, Gemma rose from the table. 'I'm going to bed,' she said, and left her mother sitting alone with her thoughts.

For the next week, there was an air of neutrality between mother and daughter. Eve was drinking very little, but as the days passed, she would jump down Gemma's throat whenever she spoke. Truth to tell, Eve was suffering from withdrawal symptoms. She was battling to stay sober, but the craving for alcohol was getting to her. Even her customers remarked on her bad temper. Her boss had words with her.

'People come in here to enjoy themselves,' he said, 'not to be treated like dirt by the barmaid. Pull yourself together, Eve, or look for another job.'

Eve pulled a face at his retreating back. That's rich, she thought. If she was drunk he told her off, and now she was in the wrong because she was sober! But at least when she was drunk she was a damn sight happier.

It was a great relief to Gemma when, a couple of weeks later, Ted called round to tell her that if she still wanted the job at his place, it was hers. It seemed the person who took it couldn't stand the pace and had left. 'You can start at seven in the morning, if you still want to. But it won't be a piece of cake,' he warned her.

Gemma couldn't have cared less. All she wanted at this moment was to be employed. When she relayed the news to her mother that night, Eve felt as if a weight had been lifted off her shoulders. She was not in the least concerned about some of the dirty, menial tasks her daughter would have to do, and when Gemma went to bed, she searched for a miniature bottle of gin she'd been keeping for emergencies and drank it. Never had anything tasted so good.

The following morning, Gemma set about cleaning the residents' lounge. She emptied the ashtrays, threw away all the papers and empty cigarette packets and hoovered the somewhat threadbare carpet. She then opened all the windows to try and rid the place of the smell of tobacco.

After that she scrubbed the tiled front entrance, polished

the brass front step, cleaned up the vomit in a hallway where a drunken seaman hadn't made it to the toilet in time, and changed the sheets in three of the bedrooms, cleaning and polishing so the rooms were ready to let.

The fourth room was in a terrible state. The previous occupant wouldn't allow anyone in to clean, consequently it was disgusting. Tea cups with mould inside crowded the bedside table; in the corner were crumpled stale newspaper wrappings from a fish and chip shop, according to the odour, and the mattress was badly stained and stank of urine. She had to get help to drag it outside in the back yard to be dumped, as it was now useless. Then she set to and scrubbed the place with disinfectant. Her hands were red raw by the time she'd finished. Ted commiserated with her in the corner of his kitchen over a warming plate of stew. 'Dirty buggers, some of them,' he complained. 'They come here to a clean room and treat it like a pigsty. God knows what their homes must be like.'

For pudding he gave her a portion of spotted dick with some thick creamy custard, saying 'Here, love, get that down you. You've earned it.'

Gemma couldn't remember when she'd tasted anything so delicious.

When she arrived home, she washed her face, cleaned her teeth, and fell into bed. She was so tired, she didn't even hear Eve come home.

During the second day, Gemma saw more of the occupants of the Mission as she helped to serve the midday meal. They were certainly a mixed bunch, arriving from all parts of the country. Some were waiting for their ship to dock, others were visiting shipping companies, looking for work. One or two just needed a bed for the night whilst they waited to be transferred from one vessel to another.

The majority were inoffensive and chatty, exchanging pleasantries with the cheery young woman serving them whilst discussing the fact that Gordon Richards, the jockey, had been knighted, arguing that riding the waves in a heavy sea was more worthy of a title than riding a horse. One or two flirted outrageously with her. A few were a bit surly, mostly due to suffering with a hangover from the previous night's drinking. And then there was big Jock MacTaggart, whom Gemma had encountered briefly once before.

The Scot had an abrupt manner and his broad Glaswegian accent made it difficult for Gemma to understand him when he addressed her. It infuriated the man when he had to repeat himself.

'What's up wi ye, woman. Are you deaf or daft?'

She stared boldly at him. 'I'm neither, thank you very much. Just speak a little slower, then perhaps I'll understand what you say.'

He glowered at the chit of a girl who dared to defy him where others made sure they kept well clear of him. 'Just get me some more toast and stop your blethering.'

Gemma went into the kitchen, complaining bitterly to Ted about Jock's rudeness.

'You just watch out for him, my girl,' her uncle warned. 'He's a troublemaker, a nasty piece of work and when he's had a few he can be lethal.'

'Then why do you have him here?'

Ted shrugged. 'I can't do anything about him. I'm only the cook.'

'Then do us all a favour and put some ruddy arsenic in his tea!' exclaimed Gemma as she returned to the dining room. I hope it chokes you, she thought as she placed the toast rack in front of MacTaggart.

Gemma had a couple of hours' break for her evening stint and, needing some cotton for mending, she went into Cussons, where she used to work. As she walked through the entrance she did feel uncomfortable for just a moment, but told herself she was the innocent party in her sacking and she had as much right to shop there as anyone.

After completing her purchase, she walked over to the jewellery counter to have a quick word with Eunice.

'Where have you been?' asked her friend. 'I've been worried sick about you.'

Gemma greeted her with a warm smile. The two girls were very close and apart from her uncle, Eunice seemed to be the only other person who really cared about her.

'I'm working at the Seaman's Mission with my uncle.'

'Doing what, for goodness sake?'

'Anything and everything. Tell me, did Hazel get the supervisor's job?'

Eunice grinned broadly. 'No. Some relative of the boss got it and very professional she is too. She used to work in a big store in London. Hazel didn't last five minutes. She told her, "Pull your socks up or you'll go!" '

'And?' asked Gemma, dying with curiosity.

'She got the push just last week. It was glorious. We stood outside waiting until she left, and cheered like mad!'

'I would have paid money to have seen that,' laughed Gemma.

'How's your mother?'

With a grimace Gemma said, 'Not too bad. When I was out of work she had to pull her socks up, but for how long it will last, now I've got a job, we'll have to wait and see.'

'Maybe she's seen the light,' suggested Eunice.

'And I'm the Virgin Mary!' Gemma retorted, then suddenly mindful of her friend's religious beliefs, quickly apologised. 'I'm sorry, Eunice. I didn't mean to be offensive.'

With a chortle Eunice replied, 'Don't apologise. Some of our parish priests have been known to like the taste of the communion wine a little too much.'

'Best be going,' said Gemma. 'I'll be in touch and perhaps we can see a film on my day off. I'll call round.'

'How about another trip to the Guildhall in search of your mystery man?'

With a grin Gemma answered, 'Why not? A bit of romance is just what I need.'

Chapter Ten

Gemma was settling into a routine at the Seaman's Mission. In the mornings she served the breakfasts, then did the rounds of the bedrooms, before she completed her general cleaning duties. In the afternoon she had four hours off, before serving dinner. When she'd cleared the tables, she was finished for the day.

In the bedrooms, her uncle showed her how to neaten the corners of the bedsheets, tucking them into what he called 'hospital corners'. He demonstrated how to turn the sheet back ready for the new occupant. 'We don't usually do that here,' he said, 'but it won't do any harm to get into the habit. On board you would usually lay out your passenger's pyjamas or night-gown, but for heaven's sake don't try that here! Half the blokes sleep in their underwear.'

She learned how to set out a tray with the correct cutlery, folding the napkins into fancy shapes. This was done within the confines of the kitchen when uncle and niece had a quiet few minutes.

'You see, love, sometimes a passenger will require their meal in their cabin, but they will expect the same professional service as they get from the steward in the dining room. And remember, no matter how demanding the passenger, you smile and say, "Yes, madam, No, madam. Three bags full, madam".' He grimaced and then warned her, 'American women in particular can be very difficult, very demanding. They can also cause a scene at the drop of a hat, so beware. But they love an English accent,' he chuckled, 'so talk softly and be charming, then at the end of the trip, if you're lucky, you'll get a hefty tip.'

'Really? I didn't know that.'

'You can make some serious money if you work hard and do a good job.' As they sat drinking tea, Ted tried to advise her on other aspects of passenger care. 'You have to be discreet sometimes.'

'What do you mean?'

'When you deliver a breakfast tray for instance, there's no way of knowing the state of dress the passenger may be in, or who may be in the bed. Just make sure you don't actually stare at them. Look past them, put the tray down with a cheery "good morning!" and off you go.' He looked at her anxious expression and laughed. 'It's all part of the game, love. And if you find a male passenger making a pass at you, send the bedroom steward in next time.'

'You *are* joking?'

He shook his head. 'No, love, I'm not. You'll see a bit of life when you work on a ship, Gemma, but you'll learn. To begin with, by the end of the day, you'll be exhausted, but you'll get used to it.'

A couple of days later, Jock MacTaggart returned to the

Mission. He'd booked in for two nights and was his usual belligerent self as Gemma discovered when she served him the following morning.

'I'll have a full cooked breakfast,' he demanded, 'with lots of toast and a pot of freshly made tea.'

She stared back at him and said firmly, '*All* our tea is freshly made,' then she walked into the kitchen to place his order, observing the smiles from a couple of the other residents at her audacity.

There was a young seaman of whom Gemma made an extra fuss. He was just seventeen, joining a ship for the first time as a commis waiter, and she knew he was feeling homesick because he had admitted as much to her as she tidied the residents' lounge the previous day. For some reason, big Jock had got it in for him.

'You are too lily-livered to be leaving home,' he remarked as the boy asked for a glass of milk with his breakfast. 'You're still tied to your mammy's apron-strings. Real men drink strong tea or whisky. Milk is for babbies!'

The boy blushed crimson and Gemma immediately rushed to his defence. 'You leave him alone and keep your opinions to yourself!'

Jock nearly choked on his toast. 'Don't you talk to me like that, young lady.'

The room became silent as everyone stopped eating.

Gemma strode over to the Scot's table and stood defiantly before him. 'You, Mr MacTaggart, are a bully,' she declared. 'Well, you don't frighten *me*.' Which wasn't true at all because Jock put the fear of God in her, but she wasn't going to let him see that. 'And I'll thank you to let my customers eat their breakfast in peace.' She turned on her heel and made for the kitchen where she leaned against the wall for support as her legs had started to shake.

'Whatever is the matter?' asked Ted.

'I've just told Jock MacTaggart that he's a bully.'

'You what?'

She glared at him. 'Well, he is and you know it.'

'You watch yourself, my girl. He wouldn't take kindly to a remark like that.'

'No, he didn't,' she said. 'He was furious.' She returned to the dining room with some trepidation, but MacTaggart had left. Gemma breathed a sigh of relief.

'Blimey, girl,' said one of the seamen. 'You'll end up with your head in your hands if you tackle that bastard again. You just look out.'

Young Ken, the lad she'd defended, came over. 'Thanks, Miss Gemma,' he said, 'but I don't want you getting in trouble on my account.'

She smiled as she reassured him. 'Don't you worry about me, I can take care of myself.' But as she left the building for her afternoon break, she found that Jock was waiting for her outside on the steps.

He gripped her by the arm. 'Now you listen to me, lassie,' he said in menacing tones. 'You cross my path again like you did this morning, making me look a fool in front of the others, you'll be very sorry.'

Although her heart was racing with fear, she looked straight back at him. 'You let me go. Touch me again and *you'll* be the one to be sorry. I'll have the Law on you.' She shook off his hold and walked quickly away. But she knew she had made an enemy and she was scared.

She said as much to her friend Eunice when they met up

to go to the pictures the following Sunday. 'He really frightens me,' she shuddered. 'He's got such a cruel face. No wonder his wife left him.'

'You look after yourself,' urged her friend. 'I know you, Gemma, you rush in where angels fear to tread. Talking of which, how are things with your mother these days?'

With a shrug Gemma stated, 'She's started drinking again, but she seems to handle it most of the time.' She sighed. 'I don't know what she'll be like if I do go away to sea.' She turned to her friend. 'If I do get a job with Cunard, I can be a greater help to her, as I'll be earning more money. I can treat her, bring her things back from New York.'

'You're too soft for your own good,' admonished Eunice.

Gemma was able to forget her troubles as the two of them sat in the cinema and enjoyed seeing Burt Lancaster and Deborah Kerr in the film *From Here To Eternity*. As they ate their ice creams in the interval before the B picture that followed, they discussed the film they had seen.

'That Burt Lancaster was a bit of hot stuff,' remarked Eunice. 'I wouldn't mind rolling around a wet beach with him.'

'Yes, you would,' Gemma chuckled. 'Sand gets in all the wrong places.' But she looked wistful. 'It must be great to be kissed with such passion. I mean, he was so masterful.'

'Yes,' agreed Eunice dreamily as she scooped out the last of her ice cream from the small tub with a wooden spoon. 'Ooh, it makes me go all unnecessary.'

Gemma nudged her. 'Imagine telling him to stop.'

'No,' whispered Eunice. 'I would rather try and imagine what came next when you didn't say anything at all . . .!'

★ ★ ★

Gemma had been working at the Mission for several weeks when during a coffee break, her uncle told her he thought it was time for her to apply for a job with the Cunard Company.

She looked at him apprehensively. 'Do you really think I'm ready for it?'

'Why not? I've taught you the basics, the rest you'll learn on the job.' He saw the uncertainty in her eyes and said, 'Life doesn't come knocking on your door, Gemma, love. If you want a slice of it, you have to go looking for it yourself.'

'I want to do it so badly,' she admitted, 'but it is a big step to take.'

'You're thinking about Eve now, aren't you?'

'Of course I am. She'll have a fit!'

He lifted his cup to his lips and sipped the contents. 'She'll get used to the idea in time.'

Gemma sat quietly ruminating about the consequences of such a step. Eve was still hanging on to her job, despite her drinking. She occasionally went out with one or other of her punters and on those nights, she usually came home the worse for wear. Gemma could always gauge how much liquor her mother had consumed by her mood. A few drinks and she could be amusing, a few more and she was vitriolic; any more and then came the tears and the self-pity. It was hard to live with and Gemma knew in her heart she badly needed to get away as soon as possible.

'I'll think about it this evening,' she said. And she did, knowing that once she wrote for an interview, there was no turning back; even if she didn't get a job with Cunard, she would write to all the other shipping lines until someone took her on.

Whilst she was reading the local paper, she saw an advertisement for Alcoholics Anonymous, and thinking it might be the answer to her problems and Eve's, she showed it to her mother.

Eve flew into a rage. 'How dare you!' she raved. 'I'm not an alcoholic, I just drink to be sociable. You really are Miss High and Mighty thinking you can talk to me like that.'

'No, Mum. But I am your daughter and I worry about you.'

'My daughter – my bloody keeper, more like! That's what you think you are. Well let me tell you, if I'd had my own way you would never have been born.'

Gemma felt the blood drain from her face. 'What do you mean?'

Eve faced her, her eyes flashing with anger. 'I never wanted you. I never wanted *any* children.' She leaned towards Gemma until her face was within inches of her daughter's. 'I tried to abort you.'

Gemma felt faint as the words were hurled at her. 'You what?' she asked, her voice trembling.

Eve stood up and placed her hands on her hips. 'Yes, that's right, don't look so shocked. I took some stuff someone gave me, but it didn't bloody well work . . . so I gave birth to you after all, and that was the end of my gallivanting days. Well, now I'm making up for it.'

Gemma gazed at the cruelty written in her mother's expression and from that moment she hated her. She wanted to hit out at her, swipe the smile from her face. Scared that she might not be able to control the rage that was boiling inside her if she stayed near this monster who was her mother, she rose quickly to her feet, sending the chair tumbling and fled to her bedroom where she collapsed on her bed in tears – thumping her pillow with her fists. Eve was wicked, selfish, vicious, heartless. All these things . . . so why did it hurt so much? But at least now Gemma felt able to please herself. There was no more guilt. Why should she care about such a woman? Tomorrow she would write to the Cunard Company. It was time to leave.

The following day, Gemma purchased some Basildon Bond writing paper and matching envelopes, and with Ted's help she wrote to the Cunard Company, asking for an interview. She bought a stamp at the Post Office and, taking a deep breath, with trembling fingers she pushed the letter into the letterbox.

Afterwards, she walked along Western Esplanade and wandered towards the water's edge, kicking pebbles into the water. It was a warm July evening, and she was comfortable in her blue pedal-pushers and sleeveless blouse. She stood still, staring out over the water towards the far horizon. There's a whole new world out there, she thought, and with a bit of luck and a following wind, I'm going to see some of it. Her stomach was in knots with excitement at the enormity of what she'd done and she was bursting to tell someone.

Eunice opened her front door and was momentarily surprised to see Gemma there. She ushered her into the kitchen. 'Come in,' she said. 'Mum's taken the younger kids to Gran's so we've got the place to ourselves.' She gave

Gemma a suspicious look. 'What's going on? What have you been up to?'

'What do you mean?'

'I know you too well. Do I have to guess or are you going to tell me?'

Gemma couldn't contain her excitement any longer. 'I've just posted a letter off to the Cunard Company, asking for a job on one of their liners.'

Eunice let out a squeal of delight and hugged her friend. 'How marvellous! I never thought you'd screw up the courage to do it, but . . . oh Gemma, I'm so pleased for you.'

'Hang on a minute, I haven't got the job yet.'

Eunice clasped her hands together. 'But just imagine if you do, all those places you'll see. New York for one.' She looked intently at Gemma. 'If you ever come across Clark Gable or Errol Flynn, would you get their autographs for me?'

Gemma dissolved with laughter. 'You're thinking about Hollywood, not New York.'

'No, I'm not!' insisted Eunice. 'I read in the *Picturegoer* that you bump into all sorts of stars on the streets of New York.' She sat down and looked at her friend in wonderment. 'Oh Gemma, wouldn't it be marvellous if you went?'

Gemma, filled now with even more enthusiasm after having shared her news with her best pal, hugged herself with delight. 'Imagine being there . . . even without Clark or Errol! Oh Eunice, wouldn't it be awful if they turned me down! I lied about my age, you know,' she confessed. 'I said I was twenty-five. I feel very guilty but otherwise I'd have had to wait another four years and I just couldn't!'

Eunice dismissed her anxiety. 'Unless they ask for your birth certificate, they'll never know. For goodness sake, work out the year of birth you should have if you really were twenty-five, so you can rattle it off if need be.'

'What a good idea,' agreed Gemma. 'I could have come unstuck there. You really are quite bright at times . . . when you try!'

'Cheeky monkey. Have you told your mother yet?'

Gemma shook her head. 'No, I haven't. What's the point? I may not even get an interview so I'm keeping quiet. If I get a job, I'll worry about it then, but at the moment all I want is a quiet life.'

A week later, Gemma was in the scullery when she heard the thud of the postal delivery on the linoleum. She hurried to the door and picked up the mail. Emblazoned on a brown official-looking envelope were the words *Cunard Company*. Hearing her mother moving about upstairs, she thrust the envelope into her coat pocket, her heart thumping wildly as she wondered at the contents of the letter. She couldn't get out of the house quickly enough to open it. As she read the typewritten page, Gemma caught her breath. She then wanted to yell out loud when she read the proposed date and time for her interview with the Lady Superintendent of the company.

Arriving at work, breathless from running, she waved the envelope under the nose of her uncle. 'I've got an interview on Friday morning. How about that?'

Ted came over and gave her a big hug. 'That's absolutely marvellous, but for now, dump your coat, love, and get stuck in. The dining room is heaving this morning. We haven't an empty bed in the place.'

Gemma flew from table to table as if on winged feet, she was so happy. Some of the regulars teased her about her cheery smile. 'Got a new boyfriend, is that it?' asked one.

'You men are all the same,' she quipped. 'There is far more to a woman's life than men.'

'You give me a chance, darling, I'll prove you wrong.'

She raised an eyebrow in the speaker's direction. 'You just behave yourself,' she cautioned him, 'or I might upset a pot of boiling coffee in your lap. That'll put an end to your shenanigans!'

The man winced at the thought, but grinned at her. 'You're a hard woman, Gemma,' he said, before stuffing his mouth with some fried egg.

One of the others came to her defence. 'Listen, this girl is all right. Anyone who can stand up to big Jock MacTaggart's all right in my book.'

The first man looked at her in admiration. 'Blimey. It's more than I'd want to do.'

'It was nothing,' she said airily, 'so you behave yourself,' and she swept out of the room and into the kitchen. What she really longed to do was question them about working on a liner, pick their brains, get first-hand advice, but she couldn't. She had to wait until Friday, until she'd had her interview. This week would seem endless.

Chapter Eleven

Friday morning eventually dawned, and after Gemma had served the breakfast at the Seaman's Mission, she changed her clothes in Ted's office, putting on her smartest light-grey suit, with a hemline just below the knee and a jacket that nipped in at the waist. Beneath this she wore a plain white blouse. When fully dressed, she went into the kitchen and asked her uncle, 'How do I look?'

'You look fine,' he assured her. Kissing her on the cheek he said, 'Good luck. Come back and tell me what happens.'

The Cunard offices were not very far from the Mission. Gemma skirted the park keeping to the path, so as not to soil her highly polished shoes, and walked along Canute Road where she entered the building she'd so often gazed at from outside, and was directed to the office of the Lady Superintendent.

'Miss Barrett, please sit down.'

The short rounded figure of Miss Webster in a neat navy suit, faced her across the desk. The woman looked at Gemma through steel-rimmed glasses. 'I have your letter here,' she began, 'but first of all, tell me about yourself and what kind of work you have been doing before you applied to us for a position as a stewardess.'

Gemma told her about working at the store, but said that she had left to gain experience from her uncle at the Seaman's Mission. She told the woman about her father working for the Union Castle Line and that she would like to follow in his footsteps.

'Why?' asked the woman. 'Why do you want this kind of work?'

'I long to travel,' Gemma told her, 'to see a bit of the world. I'm well aware that it isn't an easy job. Both my father and my uncle have told me about life at sea, the long hours and the responsibility, but I'm not afraid of hard work. I'm not qualified for any post other than a stewardess, but I am used to dealing with the public, and I'm good at it,' she added confidently.

'Even the difficult ones? Some of our passengers can be very demanding, you know.'

'Whenever you deal with the public, Miss Webster, it is never easy, but I'm quite certain that I could cope with them.'

'So you can handle the passengers – what about the members of the crew?'

Gemma looked at her with a puzzled expression. 'I don't understand, I'm afraid.'

Miss Webster sat back in her chair and folded her hands. 'Being in such close proximity as you would be on board, can lead to difficult situations,' she explained. 'Unfortunate liaisons. Many of the men who go to sea are married and we don't welcome calls from irate wives telling us their husband is having an affair with a female member of our staff.'

Gemma met the penetrating gaze of her interviewer. 'I can see where that would be difficult, but you don't have to go to sea to meet married men, do you?'

'No,' agreed Miss Webster, 'but being at sea makes such a situation that much easier.'

'I can assure you that going out with a man who's already married doesn't appeal to me at all,' Gemma said firmly.

'Good. I'm happy to hear it,' said the woman. She studied Gemma intently as if making her mind up before saying, 'As it happens, I do have an opening for a stewardess. We are having a difficult time of late as several of our girls have gone down with some summer virus. You will need to see our doctor, to make sure you are fit, and if you pass your examination, I would like you to sail on the *Queen Mary*, when she docks, next trip. That would be in twelve days' time – would you be able to sail then?'

'Oh, yes, Miss Webster, that would be no problem at all.' Gemma couldn't believe what she was hearing.

'You will need several uniforms and at least one pair of white shoes, and our stewardesses wear starched caps. I can give you the address of an outfitter in the town. Your uniforms must be pristine at all times, so kindly purchase at least three – one to wear, one to wash and a spare, in case you need to change in the middle of the day.'

'Is there anything else?' Gemma asked, her head reeling with all the details.

'You'll need a passport. Do you have one?'

Her face fell. 'No, I don't.'

'Then you need to go to London and get one. You won't have the time to do it by post. You'll need photographs. Here.' Webster handed Gemma a printed page. 'This will give you all the information you require. I'll take you to see the doctor now.'

Gemma followed her to another room. 'Come back and see me when the doctor has finished, and bring any papers he gives you.'

Her head in a whirl, Gemma was hardly aware of the examination before, having been passed as fit by the doctor, she was back with the Superintendent, listening to her instructions.

'You will be sent a boarding pass for the day you have to report on board; on doing so, you will go immediately to the leading stewardess. You will be under her jurisdiction whilst you are at sea. Go to the crew gangway on that day and they'll direct you. The ship only has a matter of 36 hours to turn round before the next voyage, so there will be a lot to do.'

In a state of stunned elation, Gemma looked at her and said, 'I understand. Thank you so much. This is far more than I expected.'

There was just a glimmer of a smile on Miss Webster's face as she said, 'You were lucky. Some girls wait as long as two years for a place. Now keep out of trouble, Miss Barrett, or you'll have me to answer to.'

Gemma thought she wouldn't like to cross this woman, pleasant as she was. There was a sense of steel running through her and Gemma didn't doubt that the lady could be tough if necessary. 'I'll do my best,' she said, as she rose from her seat.

'I certainly hope so, Miss Barrett!'

Once outside, Gemma sat on a bench in the park, trying to gather her thoughts. She looked over at the South Western Hotel, its imperious façade sweeping the corner opposite the dock gates. Passengers sometimes chose to stay here, prior to sailing. The trains from London's Waterloo station came right into the docks station beside the hotel, before trundling those people who were going on board, inside the dock gates to the Ocean Terminal, where they alighted beside the liner of their choice.

Gemma sat and closed her eyes, remembering when she'd stood outside the Cunard offices, looking at the posters, smelling the tangy salt air. Then it had been nought but a dream, now it was reality. When next she heard the mighty roar of the *Queen Mary*'s funnels on sailing day she, Gemma Barrett, would be on board as a member of the crew.

She couldn't contain herself any longer; leaping to her feet, she danced in a circle, letting out a mighty yell of delight, which made one or two passers-by stare, but she didn't care. My God! she thought, I've so much to do. Passport pictures to have taken, a trip to London to find the Passport office, uniforms to buy, white underwear, shoes . . . a myriad of things ready for the great day. She'd rush back to Ted and tell him the good news. She made to leave, then realised with a sinking heart that, at some stage, she would have to tell Eve.

When she arrived back at the Seaman's Mission, Ted took one look at her face and said, 'They've taken you on!'

When she nodded, so filled with happiness she couldn't answer, he picked her up and swung her round before setting her down again. 'Well done, Gemma. I'm proud of you.'

'I'm sailing on the *Queen Mary*, in twelve days' time,' she said breathlessly.

'Bloody hell!'

'I've got to go to London for a passport and to some place in town to buy uniforms and shoes.' She looked confused. 'It's happened so quickly, I can't think straight.'

'Sit yourself down, girl, and I'll make you a cup of tea.' Ted put the kettle on the stove and got the tea-caddy ready. 'I've a mate who's a photographer, he'll do your passport pictures for you in a hurry,' he said. 'He owes me a favour. You can go off this afternoon and buy your uniforms and shoes.'

'I need white underwear too,' said Gemma, mentally ticking things off in her mind.

'How are you fixed for money?' Ted asked.

'I've been saving my wages,' she told him.

'Well if you're short of a few pounds, give us a shout. I'll help you out.'

'Thanks, Uncle Ted.' A worried frown creased her brow.

'What's the matter?' he asked.

'There's just one thing. I'm worried that the company will discover I've lied about my age. I wish I hadn't had to tell a lie,' Gemma fretted.

Ted tried to reassure her. 'Look, love. When you sign on you'll be given a seaman's book. They won't ask to see your passport. They'll assume as you have one that you must have had the appropriate documentation. Besides, from what you say, they're up the creek at the moment as they want someone immediately. You were lucky – you applied at just the right moment. Stop worrying!'

'I can't, Uncle Ted. You see, I've now got to face telling Mum.'

He let out a deep sigh. 'Best get it over with soon as you can. Give her time to get used to the idea. If she gives you more trouble than you think you can cope with, I'll have a talk to her, all right?'

She looked at him with affection. 'You are such a dear. What would I do without you?'

He rumpled her hair. 'Nonsense. It's time you went out into the world, away from Eve. Tasted a bit of freedom. There's nothing like being your own person, but a word of warning; when you first settle on board, keep your own counsel. Watch and observe for a few trips. You'll be surprised at what you see.'

Gemma was intrigued. 'Whatever do you mean?'

'Life on board an ocean liner is a strange environment. You will make many shipboard acquaintances, but choose your friends carefully. Do your job well and keep your nose clean. Look and learn.'

She gazed at him apprehensively.

'Don't look so worried,' he chuckled. 'Once you settle in, you'll love every minute of it, I promise. Now I can manage here, so go and sort out your uniforms, but first I'll see about your photos.'

As Gemma waited for Ted to organise an appointment with his friend, she sat sipping her tea. The reality of the situation seemed beyond her comprehension. Before she had too much time to think, she'd be walking up the gangway of an ocean-going liner and into a new way of life. She suddenly wondered if she'd see Nick Weston on board, but doubted it. A First Officer wouldn't be seen around the passenger decks, she thought.

The rest of the day passed in a haze. She had her photos taken, bought her shoes and uniforms. She felt strange trying on the pristine white button-through dresses with a label above the breast pocket which stated *Stewardess* in red lettering. She grinned when she tried on the starched hat. She'd have to buy a card of Kirby grips to keep it on her head, but it did look kind of cheeky, she thought.

She looked at her reflection in the mirror. Gemma Barrett, stewardess! She smoothed down the creases. She'd have to buy one of those travelling irons she'd seen in the shops. She'd need to take washing powder too, as she'd been told that the girls washed their uniforms in their cabins. Where on earth would they hang them to dry, she wondered.

Clutching her shopping, she hurried back to the Mission to do her evening shift, before rushing home to put all her packages away before Eve saw them. She put them in her sturdy wardrobe and turned the key. She wondered why she felt the need to do this but something in her subconscious was telling her to make them secure.

She next sorted out her chest of drawers, rummaging through her underwear and stockings, preparing for the great day. She told herself that as long as she had enough to get her to New York, she could always buy more there, if need be. Then she sat on her bed amazed at her thinking. Shopping in New York! She couldn't even begin to envisage the changes she would be facing.

Gemma had to admit that she was nervous about the new environment she would be entering. It wasn't the work that bothered her. Ted had trained her well enough, she could hold her own there, she thought. It was the lack of knowledge of the workings of an ocean liner. She had voiced these fears to him earlier that day.

He explained, 'You'll be working with a bedroom steward; he'll tell you where to go and what to do.' Seeing her worried frown he added, 'He won't let you flounder, love. It will be in his best interest to help you so you can do a good job. Remember, at the end of the trip, you are tipped for your good service!'

She eventually settled for the evening in an armchair, listening to Bebe Daniels in *Life with the Lyons* on the radio with one ear and trying to read the paper as well. Anything to kill the time until her mother returned. She'd practised her speech a million times, but when eventually she heard Eve's key in the lock, she had an awful sinking feeling in the pit of her stomach.

'Why are you still up?' asked her mother irritably.

Gemma was thankful to see that this was one of the nights when Eve hadn't had a great deal to drink. 'Shall I make you a cup of tea?' she asked.

Eve flopped down in a chair and kicked off her shoes. 'Yes, I could do with one, my bloody feet are killing me.' She unpinned her hair and ran her fingers through it. 'God, I'm tired.'

In the scullery, Gemma made a pot of tea and placed it on a tray with two cups and saucers, some milk in a jug and a small plate with a few biscuits. She carried it into the other room.

Eve glanced at the tray, then at Gemma. 'What's all this about, then?'

'What do you mean?'

'This waitress service is a bit unusual, isn't it?'

'Well, I'm usually in bed when you come home, aren't I?'

With a suspicious glance in Gemma's direction, Eve said, 'You haven't lost your job again, have you?'

'No, I haven't,' said Gemma with great indignation. 'How could you say such a thing?'

With narrowing eyes, Eve studied Gemma as she sipped her tea. 'What's going on then? You've got something up your sleeve. I can read you like a book.'

Taking a deep breath, Gemma said, 'In fact, I am going to change my job. I'm leaving the Seaman's Mission.'

Eve's gaze didn't falter as she asked, 'And what might you be doing?'

Gemma was feeling uncomfortable beneath her mother's close scrutiny, especially as she was going to be dropping a bombshell in their midst. But she didn't avert her gaze as she said, 'I'm going to be a stewardess on the *Queen Mary*.'

Eve spluttered on a mouthful of tea, spraying it over both of them. 'You what!'

Gemma tried to keep her voice steady. 'I've been for an interview with the Cunard Company. I'm sailing on the *Queen Mary*, on her next voyage.'

Her mother slammed her cup down on the saucer in front of her, spilling the contents on to the table. She glared at Gemma. 'You sly little bitch! You've been planning this behind my back, haven't you? For how long, I wonder.'

'It wasn't like that at all,' Gemma protested. 'You know I've always wanted to travel. I wrote away for an interview, not thinking I'd get one, let alone a job . . . well, certainly not that soon. There was no point in telling you anything until there was something *to* tell.'

But Eve's anger was increasing with every word. 'You're just like your father. Selfish! Only thinking of yourself. Well, what about me?'

Gemma steeled herself for the ensuing battle for her rights. 'And what about you?'

This was not at all the reaction Eve was expecting. 'How can you sit there and say that? I am your mother. First your father leaves me and now you are going to bugger off too!'

'I'll only be away for twelve days at a time. That's hardly a lifetime, is it?'

Eve looked accusingly at her. 'I'll be all alone.'

'For heaven's sake, stop being so bloody dramatic!' Gemma tried to reason with her mother. 'I'll be earning good money, so I'll still be able to contribute financially. You have your job and Dad's allotment.' At the baleful look on her mother's face, Gemma became impatient. 'If I was getting married, I'd be leaving home for good.'

'But you are not getting married.'

Sitting down and pouring another cup of tea, Gemma tried to keep calm. 'I must be allowed to get on with my life, Mum. I'm a woman now.' She ignored Eve's snort of derision. 'I want to see the world and please don't think you can stop me, because no one will. This is my chance. I have a great opportunity, why can't you be happy for me?'

Eve's lips pressed into a spiteful line as she rose from her chair and crossed to the sideboard. She took out a half-bottle of gin and looked defiantly at Gemma as she poured herself a stiff measure. 'Fine. Get on with your life and I'll get on with mine. I don't need you *or* your father. In fact, it suits me just fine. I'll have the house to myself, then if I want to bring anyone home, I'm free to do so, without your disapproval.'

This is emotional blackmail, thought Gemma, and I'm not playing this game any more. She rose from her seat and walked across to the stairs. 'That's settled then,' she said to Eve. 'You go your way and I'll go mine. It should work very well. Goodnight.' As she reached her bedroom, she heard a scream of rage from below followed by the sound of breaking glass. No doubt her mother would have drunk the contents of the glass before she broke it, she thought sardonically.

Chapter Twelve

During her last days ashore, Gemma continued working at the Seaman's Mission. It gave her something to occupy her time and was a means of earning extra money. It also got her out of the house, where the atmosphere was oppressive, with Eve scarcely speaking to her and only then when it was absolutely necessary. It was as if Eve was trying to punish her for leaving, mused Gemma, whereas all she achieved by her attitude was making her daughter feel relieved that she'd finally made the move.

The men at the Mission were pleased for her and many tried to give her advice about treating seasickness, teasing her. Telling her it was inadvisable to eat greasy pork chops when the ship was rolling.

'I'm sure the chefs never serve greasy food, ever!' she retorted.

There was a chorus of, 'Ooh, listen to her,' from the men. 'Now keep off the decks at night,' advised another. 'Especially with a fellow.'

'Why?' she asked, in her innocence.

The seaman looked very serious. 'Well, young Gemma, you see the sea does funny things to a woman. Especially if the moonlight is shining on the waves – it makes her go all funny.'

'What do you mean, funny?'

'It is said, Gemma, that at sea, on an open deck at night beneath the moonlight, a woman loses her inhibitions *completely*. So keep out of the lifeboats!'

She had to laugh. 'You lot are awful,' she said. 'I don't know why I waste my time with you.'

Later, as she was tidying up before leaving for the night, her peace was disturbed by Jock MacTaggart, who stumbled into the deserted residents' lounge as she was emptying the ashtrays on her way out. His bloated face looked more ruddy than usual and it was evident that the man was in a foul mood. He glared balefully at her.

'Get me a pot of tea,' he demanded.

Gemma backed slowly away. 'I'm sorry, I can't do that. The kitchen is locked up for the night.'

He grabbed her by the arm. 'You do as I bloody well say, or you'll be in trouble.'

'I don't have the keys.'

'Then get them,' he bellowed, and gave her a shove.

She cannoned into the half-open door and caught the side of her head against it. The impact was such that for a moment she saw stars, but she managed to stagger out into the corridor and headed, somewhat unsteadily, for her uncle's room where she hammered on the door, loudly calling his name.

'Gemma! What on earth has happened?' he asked when he emerged and saw the red mark on the side of her face.

She told him about MacTaggart.

He pushed her inside his room. 'Lock the door,' he said.

'I'll sort this out once and for all.'

She sat on the side of Ted's bed, trembling but listening intently to the raised voices outside. There was a sound of broken glass, furniture being overturned and, fearful for her uncle's safety, she unlocked the door and raced along the corridor to the residents' lounge.

A couple of seamen were trying to assist Ted as he struggled with MacTaggart on the floor, but with a sudden roar, the Scot sent them flying. Ted made a grab for him, but Jock, now incensed, caught him round the throat with both hands – and squeezed.

Seeing the danger her uncle was in, Gemma sprang like a tiger on to the back of the drunken man, clawing at his eyes in an effort to stop him. Letting go of Ted, Jock threw Gemma off his back, sending her flying across the room. Then he turned back and caught hold of Ted by the front of his shirt.

There was a heavy ashtray on a nearby coffee table and in desperation, Gemma grabbed it, bringing it down with all the force she could muster on to the head of the huge Scot.

He slid to the ground. 'My head, my bloody head,' he moaned as a trickle of blood ran down his neck.

Gemma flew out of the room and out of the main entrance and on to the street where, to her relief, two policemen were strolling by on their beat.

'Thank God!' she cried. 'Come quickly, I need your help!'

The constables followed her and realised at once what had been happening. One of them looked at Jock, still in a dazed condition, holding his head, complaining that he could feel a lump.

Seeing the blood for the first time, Gemma let out a cry of alarm. 'Oh, my God! I could have killed him!'

The policeman didn't look concerned. 'In trouble again, eh Mac?' He examined the man's head and turning to Gemma said, 'I've seen worse, but we'll take him to the station and get a doctor to look at him, then we'll put him in the cells for the night.' He looked around at the broken furniture and shaking his head said, 'They never learn, do they?'

'No, I'm afraid not,' said Ted who had now recovered.

'You want to make a complaint?' asked the officer.

'No, just get him out of here. I'll bring his stuff to the station in the morning. When my boss sees this he won't want him back here and we'll all be grateful for that. He can pay for the damages.'

One of the officers called the station to send a car for their prisoner. MacTaggart staggered as the men hauled him to his feet and handcuffed him. He glared at Gemma.

'I'll get you for this, lassie,' he muttered. 'You best keep looking over your shoulder, because one day I'll be there.'

She felt her legs weaken beneath her as she looked into the menacing gaze of the man and was glad she would be far away from him in the near future, because he terrified her.

Ted took her into the kitchen and sat her down. He unlocked a cupboard and produced a half-bottle of brandy. Pouring a measure into a glass, he said, 'Drink this, darling. You deserve it. Without you, I might have been a goner!'

Her hands were shaking so much that she had to hold the glass with both hands, but the burning sensation as the liquor went down her throat was strangely comforting, as was the cigarette her uncle handed her.

'Bloody hell!' he exclaimed. 'What a turn-up for the book.' He gazed at the side of Gemma's face and getting a clean cloth from the drawer, he filled it with ice cubes and held it against her cheek. 'Can't have you going to sea with a black eye, can we?'

She looked horrified. 'Will it show?'

'If it does, you'll just have to cover it with make-up.'

'Blimey, Uncle Ted, I hope all seamen with a few drinks under their belt aren't like this!'

He laughed at her. 'There's good and bad everywhere, my dear. Seafarers are no worse or better than anyone else.'

As she finished her brandy, Gemma was relieved that she'd be in bed before Eve came home. She'd certainly kick up a fuss if she saw the marks on her daughter's face. What she didn't know wouldn't hurt her.

But as she climbed into bed that night and closed her eyes, Gemma could clearly visualise the look on Jock MacTaggart's face as he had threatened her – and she knew that he meant every word.

It was now just two days before the *Queen Mary* was due to dock and the tension in the Barrett household was intense. Gemma had now left the employ of her uncle, with his blessing and twenty pounds he'd given her on top of her wages. 'As a bit of extra security,' he'd said. 'You never know what will crop up, Gemma love.' And she was grateful, because she'd spent nearly all of her money on her uniforms, shoes, underwear and bits and pieces, all under lock and key in the wardrobe.

The stout door of the old but strong piece of bedroom furniture looked as if someone had tried to force it open recently, which was a worry, so Gemma was pleased to be around the house to keep an eye on things. If Eve tried to stop her leaving by destroying her uniforms, she'd be in a real quandary. Her boarding pass and passport she kept safely in her handbag which was with her at all times. She had enjoyed her trip to London, it made her feel very adventurous finding her way around on her own.

Sitting alone in her bedroom, Gemma went over the documents and read her instructions. She was to report to the leading stewardess, an hour after the ship docked, when she would be shown her quarters and the section where she would be working. She could feel her heart thumping away with excitement as she read the words. It wouldn't be long now.

She'd popped into the Cunard office one day and asked them for a brochure of the *Queen Mary*, and had marvelled at the pictures of the grand interiors: the First-Class Main Lounge with its wonderful Canadian maple panelling, the observation lounge where through the windows you could look out over the bow of the liner at the expanse of the ocean beyond. The shopping arcade took her breath away, it looked so very sophisticated, with Austin Reed, W.H. Smith, a bank, jewellery shops for the indulgence of the passengers, the cashmere sweaters on sale, skirt lengths of material. Then there was the library, cinema, a printer's shop – and the ship even had her own hospital! It was like a world all of its own, a floating island. Imagine having enough money to be a passenger, Gemma thought. She was delighted simply to be a member of the crew.

Gemma wondered just what her father would say if he knew about this latest development in her life. She realised then that she hadn't given a thought to him for some weeks, and felt guilty. After all, he was her own flesh and blood, but she still felt that betrayal. There was still a part of her which couldn't forgive Jack Barrett for walking out on his responsibilities.

The night before she was due to leave, Gemma was busy packing her things in a suitcase borrowed from her uncle. She had to take clothes to wear in New York, too. She had been warned about the autumn heat and the humidity, so she'd packed a couple of summer dresses, a light duster coat, a pair of both sandals and court shoes.

She was very much on edge waiting for the return of her mother. Eventually she heard Eve's key in the lock and, taking a deep breath, walked downstairs to meet her. When she entered the room it was to see Eve attempting to remove her short jacket, swaying on her feet as she did so. Gemma's heart sank.

'Here, let me help you,' she offered.

But with a hostile glance in her direction, Eve rudely declined, pushing her hand away. 'Leave me alone,' she grumbled. 'After all, I'm going to have to get used to looking after myself in the future. I might as well start now.'

'Please don't be like this, Mum,' Gemma pleaded, stepping towards her. 'You should be happy for me, thrilled that I have this chance.' But the look of intense dislike on her mother's face made her recoil.

'A chance to behave like a cheap little tart is what you

mean!' Eve spat the words at her.

Gemma paled at the venom in her tone. 'Whatever do you mean?'

'I've heard stories of what goes on at sea. Well, if you get yourself pregnant, don't come running to me, that's all. You've made your bed, now lie on it.'

Thinking of the strong terms in which she'd been interviewed by the Lady Superintendent of the Cunard Company on the subject, Gemma looked at her mother with disdain. 'You don't know what you're talking about,' she protested. 'It wouldn't be allowed, such carryings-on. You're just being spiteful, that's all, because you don't want me to leave.'

Eve turned on her like a raging bull. 'Don't want you to go? I can't wait to see the back of you! For over twenty years I've been stuck with a daughter to take care of. Now as last I'm free! Free to do *what* I like and *with* anyone I like. Your father left to lead his own life and now I can do the same. You can't go soon enough for me, dearie!'

Gemma was at a loss for words. What was the point of any further discussion? It just proved to her, once again, that she was doing the right thing. When she could afford it, she would find a flat of her own, then she could finally break the chains of this destructive relationship.

For once she'd been able to see beyond the love she had for her mother and saw Eve for the selfish, self-centred woman she really was. Eve had never shown her any love, despite giving birth to her, so why was she wasting time trying to reason with her? Gemma turned on her heel and went quietly upstairs, leaving her mother alone.

The following morning, Gemma heard the throaty roar of the funnels of the *Queen Mary* as it docked and felt the adrenaline pumping through her veins. She shut the suitcase, checked that she had her boarding pass and passport safely in her handbag and glanced at her reflection in the mirror on her dressing table. Well, this was it! Time to go. She picked up her suitcase, hesitated outside the door of Eve's room, but decided against entering. With her head held high, she walked down the stairs and out of the front door.

She took a taxi into the docks and when the policeman on the gate stopped the car, she looked at him, showed her boarding pass and said, '*Queen Mary*, crew. I'm joining the ship this morning.' As he smiled at her and waved her through, she sat back and grinned broadly. That had sounded so good.

She looked around her. It was the first time she'd been inside the dock gates. The taxi trundled unevenly over the railway lines leading in different directions. A goods train passed behind them, laden with coal. Ahead she saw the tall cranes, already busy unloading the cargo from various vessels, the contents swinging over the quay, enclosed in large nets, then unloaded by waiting stevedores. She was amazed at the traffic coming and going. Trucks, full of packing cases, dockers on bicycles, weaving in and out, and a steady stream of taxis, making their way to the various destinations.

At the Ocean Terminal, the driver stopped the car, took her suitcase from the boot and handed it to her. Gemma paid him and gave him a tip.

'Thanks, miss. Have a good trip,' he said as he got back into the driving seat.

Inside, the terminal was a bustle of activity. Through an open gap in the side of the building, she could see stewards in white coats, rushing around with luggage that was being unloaded from a moving belt from within the liner. Customs officials were already dealing with passengers who had disembarked, standing under large signs, each depicting a letter of the alphabet, waiting for their bags. Gemma rightly assumed that if your surname began with the letter B, then under that initial was where you waited.

She walked through the terminal and out onto the dockside, where she looked up in awe at the liner. She hadn't realised just how huge it was. How majestic it looked with its smooth lines. She felt very insignificant standing beside it, the ship's hull towering over her. She looked towards the bow and read the words – *Queen Mary*.

There were several gangways, which confused her. She made her way to one with a man in uniform standing at the bottom.

'Can I help you, miss?' he asked. 'You look a bit lost.'

She was grateful to him. 'I'm joining the ship for the first time,' she confessed nervously, 'and I don't know where to go. I have to report to the leading stewardess.'

'I'm the master-at-arms,' he told her. 'You come with me.' He took her suitcase and led her up the gangway and on to the ship. She could scarcely hide her excitement.

Chapter Thirteen

As Gemma followed the master-at-arms up the gangway, she couldn't help but remember doing the same as a five-year-old, following her father to board the *Edinburgh Castle*. Now at long last she was fulfilling her dream. Although inside her nerves were taut with excitement and expectation, she was also deeply thrilled. This was the start to her new life, and she wondered just what the future held.

As they stepped off the gangway into a large foyer, the master-at-arms stopped a stewardess who was passing and said, 'This young lady is one of your lot, come to sign on. Show her the way to the leading stewardess's cabin, will you?' He smiled at Gemma and said, 'You'll be all right now, miss.'

'Welcome aboard,' said the girl. 'Follow me.'

Gemma gazed at everything in wonder as they walked up several decks on wide grand staircases. She saw window displays full of goods for sale, a barber's shop and beauty parlour, and what looked like a long reception desk with men and women smartly dressed in navy uniforms with gold braid on their sleeves. 'The purser's office,' her companion explained. Stewards and stewardesses scurried about, arms full of bed linen, disappearing into various cabins. Gemma was both nervous and elated by such unfamiliar sights.

Eventually she was led along a corridor to a cabin with the door open. Inside was a woman in a smart white uniform and cap, sitting at a desk, talking to another stewardess.

'I'll wait with you,' said the girl. 'My name is Gwen, by the way.'

'Mine's Gemma, and I'm finding all this a bit overwhelming,' she confided.

'Never mind. It is a bit daunting to begin with, but you'll soon get used to it.'

Gemma was ushered into the cabin as the other girl left.

'New stewardess,' announced Gwen. 'Do you want me to wait?'

'Please. Come and sit down,' Gemma was told. 'Do you have your boarding card?'

She handed it over and the woman read it. Looking up she said, 'Ah, yes, Miss Barrett, your first trip. Right, I'll get Gwen to show you where to sign on after she's taken you to your cabin. Here's the key, make sure you don't lose it. I'm Mrs Reader. When you've signed on, go back to your cabin and unpack, change into your uniform and report back to me, then I'll take you to your section. All right?'

Gemma's head was spinning by now but she managed a smile. 'Fine, thank you.'

The next hour passed in a haze. Gemma was taken to her cabin through twisting alleyways, like a rabbit warren lined with doors, all closed. 'These cabins belong to the female members of the crew,' Gwen explained. 'We call it Virgin's Creek,' she said with a grin, 'although I'm not at all sure how many girls who sleep here deserve the title.'

Gemma's cabin was small with two bunk beds along one side, a hand basin, and two built-in cupboards which served as wardrobes. Beneath the bottom bunk were two deep drawers and along the other side, a sofa-like seat that Gwen called a day bed.

'I'm not sure who you'll be sharing with as I live at the other end of the ship,' said Gwen. She opened one of the wardrobes which was empty and said, 'This one is yours, and one of the drawers. But put your case down now and I'll get you signed on.'

They made their way out of the cabin, down several interior iron stairways through various decks and then along what Gwen told her was 'the working alleyway'. Here kitchen porters were pulling trolleys piled high with vegetables and fruit. She saw a butchery with sides of beef, lamb and pork, hanging in refrigerated rooms. At last she was led into a room where she queued to sign on and join the Seaman's Union. As she rifled in her handbag to find the money to pay her dues, she was relieved that her uncle had given her extra cash, because goodness knows what else she'd be required to pay out for now she was at last on board.

When she finally returned to her cabin, she looked at Gwen and said, 'I'll never be able to find my way around. I had no idea the ship was so big.'

Gwen laughed at her concern. 'It'll take a couple of trips, but after that you'll be fine. I'll give you an hour to get settled and changed, then I'll come and collect you.'

Gemma sat on the day bed and looked around. This was to be her home for a while. She wondered who she'd be sharing this confined space with and which bunk would be hers. If it was the top one, how the dickens was she going to climb into it?

An hour later, Gemma was unpacked, dressed in her new, slightly creased uniform, her cap securely pinned to her head with kirby grips, and freshly applied make-up as she wanted to make a good impression. She now had a Seaman's book to add to her collection. She put this with her papers and handbag into her wardrobe, locked it and waited, somewhat apprehensively.

Gwen arrived at the allotted time and took her back to Mrs Reader. She was told about her working hours and that she would be teamed up with a bedroom steward who would show her the ropes. 'Any problems, you come and see me,' she was told. She then took Gemma along to B deck and introduced her to Charlie Black. Mrs Reader had a brief word with him before leaving the pair together.

Charlie was a dapper man in his forties. His sleek black hair was greased back neatly. His white shirt was a little crumpled where he'd obviously been working, but nevertheless, he looked very smart in his black tie and matching trousers. On his nose was a pair of dark-rimmed glasses, but behind them his grey eyes twinkled as he said, 'Well, Gemma, this is your baptism of fire. These fourteen staterooms are our responsibility.' He led her into a small pantry, stacked with china and glasses, condiment sets, a toaster, tea, coffee, with pots to serve and a large boiler for heating water.

'This is our little haven,' he said with a broad grin. 'Here, we care for the needs of the passengers. Any food we need, we get from the galley, but I'll show you that later.' He handed her a key. 'This is for the segregation gates.' At her puzzled expression he led her outside the pantry and pointed to a white slatted half-gate in the distance. 'It divides the different classes,' he explained. 'We are in Cabin Class, then there is First Class and beyond the gate after that is Tourist. It stops them from wandering about the ship. Now we have to prepare for the next lot of passengers. I've collected the fresh linen from the linen room so . . . let's get started.'

It was hard work, changing the sheets, hoovering the carpets, polishing the furniture, removing every speck of dust until each cabin was pristine. At lunchtime, Charlie took her down to the working alleyway and showed her where the cold pantry was. The man on duty grinned at Gemma when Charlie introduced her.

'Always nice to see a good-looking girl,' he said. 'You need any cold cuts of meat or sandwiches, you come and see me.'

She was shown the confectioner's shop and marvelled at the host of cakes and pastries being made. The decorations and artistic icing took her breath away, especially the delicate spun sugar which topped one such offering.

'Are you hungry?' asked Charlie.

'More peckish than hungry,' she said. 'I'm so hot from working, I couldn't eat anything heavy.'

He took her to another area where one of the chefs, resplendent in his white uniform, tall hat and blue and white chequered trousers, made them a delicious-looking salad with cold fresh salmon. 'It'll be a pleasure to look after you, darling,' he said with a wink.

As they made their way back to the pantry with their food, Charlie explained. 'That chef will supply all our meals and at the end of the trip we bung him some money. It's a way for them to make extra bunce and for us to get some decent grub.' They settled on a couple of high stools and ate.

'During the day when we're at sea, we sometimes have to eat on the run, maybe make do with a sandwich,' he told her, 'or you can eat in your two-hour break. If it's calm, the passengers will all be in the dining room, which gives us a rest, but in rough weather, that's a different matter. Some of them feel queasy before we've even left the dock!'

Gemma's face fell. 'I hope I'll be all right,' she said anxiously.

He laughed at her. 'If you feel a bit dicky, love, I've got a certain cure. A drop of brandy and port will put you on your feet.'

'It will more likely put me flat on my back!' she exclaimed.

He looked at her thoughtfully. 'I can see by the way you worked today that we'll get along just fine. I'll teach you all I know. You need to be quick and efficient . . . and polite. Then you'll make money.'

Her eyes shone. 'That sounds good to me, and I'm more than willing to learn.'

'That's half the battle,' he said, 'now let's get on. We've got a full complement of passengers so make sure you get to bed early tonight. No staying up late with your boyfriend.'

'That's no problem,' she assured him. 'I don't have one at the moment.'

With a broad grin Charlie said, 'That won't last long. A good-looking girl like you, the men will soon start to wander along this section, trying to get to know you.'

She looked perturbed, remembering her lecture at her interview and the caustic comments from her mother.

Seeing her troubled look, Charlie said, 'Be friendly with everybody, but not too much. Some of the female staff are very snobbish, it doesn't get them anywhere. A friendly smile and a word doesn't do any harm. Anyone steps out of line, I'll deal with them, all right?'

And suddenly she knew she had an ally in Charlie Black. 'Thanks, I'll remember, but I can handle most people. A spell working for my uncle at the Seaman's Mission in Southampton taught me a thing or two, I can tell you.'

He raised his eyebrows. 'Blimey. Now that really *is* a baptism of fire.'

Thinking of Jock MacTaggart she nodded. 'It had its moments.'

At the end of her first day, Gemma was exhausted, but happy. She decided to sleep on board, rather than go back to Duke Street as she could have done. It was pointless to return home for the night, she decided, only to have yet another confrontation with Eve.

Fortunately, her cabin was on the same deck as she was working, so Gemma didn't have too much trouble finding it. She opened the door and was surprised to see a slender dark-haired girl sitting on the bottom bunk. Although she was attractive, there was a hardness about her that immediately made Gemma wary.

'Hello,' she said. 'I'm Sally James, your cabin-mate.' She cleared some clothes off the top bunk and said, 'This is yours, I sleep on the bottom.'

'How on earth do I get into it?' asked Gemma.

'It's not that difficult,' said Sally. 'You stand on the ridge of wood at the end of mine and haul yourself in. You'll soon get used to it. There's a bathroom along the corridor, but we have to share it with the others. It's a case of first come first served . . . and make sure you leave it clean after you. There is cleaning stuff in there for you to use.'

'Where do we wash our uniforms?'

'In the wash basin, last thing at night.' She pointed to a large hook in the bulkhead above the basin. 'Put your uniform on a hanger and it will drip dry.'

'And ironing?'

Sally showed her a unique device – a piece of wood shaped like an ironing board without legs which went over the basin, held by the two taps.

Gemma shook her head in disbelief. 'Ingenious,' she said.

'I hope you're tidy,' declared Sally abruptly. 'The last girl I shared with was just a slut. She never put anything away. It drove me mad.'

Gemma stared straight at her. 'I am. How can you be anything else in this small space?'

Sally took a towel and wash-bag and made for the door. 'I'm off to have a bath before I go ashore. I won't be back tonight. What are you doing?'

'I'll get changed and go ashore, have something to eat, then I'm for an early night.'

'I'll see you in the morning then.' With that her cabin-mate left the cabin.

Gemma felt as if her feathers had been ruffled. There was something about Sally that irritated her and she felt that sharing this small space with her wasn't going to be easy.

After a quick snack and a cup of coffee at the local café, Gemma returned to the ship, washed out the uniform she'd worn that day and ironed the one for the morning. The board worked very well, she found. Eventually she hauled herself into the top bunk with some difficulty and was pleased that Sally wasn't there to watch her. No doubt she'd soon become adept at it. Then she tried to settle down for the night, but the ship seemed to make strange noises, and people went in and out of their cabins and the bathroom, chatting to each other, keeping her awake. Eventually she slept from pure exhaustion until her alarm clock woke her with a start, the following morning.

When she arrived at her section, somewhat bleary-eyed, Charlie took one look at her and made her a cup of coffee. 'Didn't sleep too well?' he asked.

She shook her head as she drank the coffee.

'Too much excitement and strange surroundings, I expect. We sail at noon,' he said. 'When our passengers embark, show them to their cabins if they can't find them. Most will want to be on deck when we sail, but if any have visitors and want drinks, then we'll have to go to the service bar for them.'

'How do the visitors know when to leave the ship?' she asked.

'A man goes around banging a gong. If any get stuck, they can go off down the river when the pilot leaves the ship. But that doesn't happen very often.'

Already there was an air of excitement on board. Florists were arriving with bouquets for the passengers. These were steeped in water before being arranged and placed in the corresponding cabins. Charlie disappeared to the baggage room to sort out the luggage for their section, disgorging bag after bag from the elevator, puffing with the effort, grumbling away to himself as he did so. Gemma heard him muttering, 'Why these bloody people have to take so much with them I'll never know. Haven't they ever heard of travelling light!'

Gemma was busy dispensing vase after vase of flowers to various cabins, complete with the cards that came with them, praying she wouldn't get them muddled. She gave a glass of water to one of the young bellboys who stopped at the pantry and asked for one. He looked hot and tired, but she thought he was very smart in his uniform with the brass buttons down the front of his maroon jacket and she liked his cheeky pillbox hat.

'Thanks, miss,' he said as he gulped the water before rushing off. He seemed so young to be away from home, she thought. He couldn't have been more than fifteen.

The next few hours flew by and Gemma learned that she worked well under pressure. Charlie had shown her where the service bar was and she'd rushed along with orders for champagne for one or two of the cabins, but as Charlie had said, most of the passengers, once settled, made their way on deck. At last she heard the steward banging the gong calling, 'All visitors ashore!' She was surprised the time had gone so quickly.

Then she heard the familiar roar of the ship's funnels. The sound always touched something deep inside her, but never more than today, because at last she was on board.

Charlie popped his head around the pantry door. 'Go up on deck, girl. It's your first trip – go and see us sail out of port. It's quite a sight.'

'But the passengers . . .' she began.

He grinned at her. 'They're all up top. I can manage, away you go.' He told her how to get there, and she flew until she found herself outside on the boat deck. The sun was shining and there were few clouds in the sky. The deafening roar from the funnels above her made her jump. She looked over the ship's rails and saw the stevedores let loose the ropes. There were tugs alongside, ready to move the mighty liner away from her berth. Gemma's heart was thumping with excitement as the last hawser was hauled inboard . . . then she felt the ship move.

There was a mass of people on the veranda of the Ocean Terminal, all waving madly and calling out to various passengers, who were waving back, and she found herself waving madly too. She didn't care that there was no one on the dockside she knew, she was filled with a euphoria that carried her away.

As the ship made its way down the river, the passengers started to disperse and Gemma reluctantly made her way back to B deck. She walked into the pantry, bursting with happiness. 'It was wonderful,' she told Charlie. 'Now I know I'm really here, and it isn't a dream.'

'Listen, sweetheart, by the end of the day you'll be in no doubt you're on board, as you'll be completely knackered! I've got to see a passenger now,' he said, 'but I want you to do a little job. The bulb has blown in one of the lights in the alleyway outside – look, it's that bulb there. I've sent for the electrician. When he comes, show him, will you?'

Five minutes later there was a tap on the pantry door. Gemma turned round with a smile which quickly died as she looked straight into the eyes of Jock MacTaggart.

Chapter Fourteen

MacTaggart was the first to recover from the surprise of this unexpected meeting. He glared at Gemma. 'What the hell are *you* doing here?'

'I would have thought that was fairly obvious,' she retorted, determined not to show the Scot how much she'd been thrown by the encounter. 'Are you the electrician we're waiting for?'

He didn't answer. 'I haven't forgotten it was through you that I spent a night in the cells,' he growled.

'That wasn't my fault. You nearly throttled my poor uncle,' she said.

'That was my first mistake. It was you I should have throttled,' he snapped.

'You're lucky he didn't have you up for assault,' she said and made to walk out of the pantry, but he barred the way.

'I owe you one, lassie, and I won't forget it.'

At that moment Charlie arrived. 'Ah, the electrician,' he said. 'I'll show you the blown bulb.' Turning to Gemma he told her, 'You'd better pop back to your cabin and get your lifejacket ready for boat drill.'

With great relief, Gemma left to do as she was bid. She

was stunned and a little edgy to discover that Jock was on the same ship, and she wondered just how much opportunity he would have to harass her if that was his intention. She didn't want to always be looking over her shoulder as she worked – that would be unnerving to say the least. Nor did she want to tell Charlie of her concerns, not at this stage.

When she returned to the section, MacTaggart had gone. 'Do we have much work for the electricians?' she asked Charlie when she had an opportunity.

'God, I hope not, love. If we do, it means something's wrong with our equipment and that's the last thing we need. You know where your lifeboat station is, don't you?'

Gemma had read the card in her cabin which told her that, if necessary, she was to stand by the elevator on B deck. 'What happens?' she asked.

'When the bells sound, put your jacket on and direct the passengers to their gathering point.' He showed her where it was. 'It only takes a little time, then it's over. Some don't bother, which is very foolish.'

'You're not expecting any disaster, are you, Charlie?'

He chuckled. 'Of course not. It's Board of Trade rules that we go through the drill, that's all.'

Earlier that morning, Gemma had experienced her first difficult passenger. Mrs Myers was constantly ringing the bell for service. She wanted more towels, a bucket of ice, she needed some dresses pressed and she wanted an appointment booked with the hairdresser.

Taking the garments, Gemma asked when she wanted her hair attended to. Armed with the information, she made her way first to the room where all the valeting was done, then on to the beauty parlour. The first of many trips, before Mrs Myers was satisfied.

Charlie advised her to try and persuade the passengers to go along themselves to the hairdresser's. 'It saves time and you have others to look after. Mind you, that old bat will run you ragged, I know the type.'

And he was right. When the bells sounded for lifeboat drill Gemma was summoned to help the woman into her lifejacket and direct her and her husband to their station. Then before dinner, Mrs Myers wanted the back of her dress fastened. 'I don't trust Mr Myers,' the woman snapped. 'He's so damned clumsy. He caught my flesh in the zipper last time.' I'm not surprised, thought Gemma as she tried to tuck the extra flesh inside the tight-fitting garment.

Fortunately her other passengers were less demanding, but by the end of the day, Gemma was smiling at Mrs Myers through gritted teeth. However, she maintained her politeness, albeit with some difficulty.

'That woman doesn't have the words please or thank you in her vocabulary,' Gemma complained to Charlie as they went round all their cabins turning the beds down for the night. 'It's I want this, get me that. She has no manners at all.'

With a grin Charlie said, 'She's like one of those spiders who eats their mates after having sex.'

Gemma started to laugh. 'Mr Myers is still alive, so it doesn't say a great deal about their sex-life.'

'He probably married her for her money,' was Charlie's response. 'Let's face it, it wasn't for her good looks and charm.'

Eventually the night steward appeared and took over.

'I'm off to have a pint on the pig deck,' said Charlie.

'The what?'

'The Pig and Whistle. It's a crew bar for the men only, otherwise I'd buy you a drink,' he said. 'See you bright and early in the morning.'

'I'm going up on deck,' said Gemma. 'I desperately need some air.'

'We should be docking at Cherbourg soon,' Charlie informed her, 'but we won't have any new passengers to worry about. All of ours are already on board. Now don't go falling overboard,' he teased. 'Mrs Myers wouldn't like it!'

Gemma went to her cabin for a cardigan, then made her way to the crew deck, aft of the ship. She wandered over to the ship's rail and peered at the sea below, being churned up by the propellers, leaving a foaming path in its wake.

'Some say if you look at the wake of a ship long enough, you are tempted to jump.' Jock MacTaggart leered at her as Gemma turned to see who had spoken. 'It would be so very easy to tip someone over the side, wouldn't it?' he said menacingly. 'A body would soon be pulled beneath the water . . . and who would know, eh?'

She stepped away, fearful of his close proximity. 'What are you doing here?' she asked.

'Same as you, lassie. Getting some air.'

'I'll leave you to it, then,' she said and started to walk quickly away. She could hear him chuckling to himself. He knew he'd unnerved her, which was exactly what he'd intended to do, of that she was sure and she was angry with herself for allowing him to do so.

Once back in the safety of her cabin, she chided herself for her foolishness. MacTaggart was a violent man, she'd seen that for herself at the Seaman's Mission, but not for one moment did she think he was capable of murder, so why had she been so scared? It was his unexpected appearance, taking her by surprise – that was it. Well, should they meet again, she would stand up to him. He mustn't think he had the power to frighten her. Men like him thrived on such things and she wouldn't give him that satisfaction.

When she returned to her cabin, Sally was there. Her cabin-mate had changed into a black dress, sheer stockings and high-heeled shoes. She put on a coat and said casually, 'Bye. I'll be back late.'

Sitting alone on the day bed, Gemma wondered where Sally was going. Surely not to one of the public rooms. That would mean instant dismissal if she was discovered. To a passenger's cabin? She'd lose her job . . . so where? She remembered Ted's advice to take care with whom she mixed. She decided that Sally James was trouble.

The following morning was frantically busy on Gemma's section as several passengers decided to take breakfast in their cabins. Charlie and Gemma rushed around with trays laden with different orders. 'Bloody hell, Charlie,' she gasped as they took trays into yet another cabin, 'I'll certainly lose some weight rushing up and down the stairways like this.'

'It'll keep you fit, love,' he said.

'Especially bloody Myers. I've made three trips to the galley to get her boiled eggs just right. I swear I'll shove them down her throat before the trip is over!'

They tidied the pantry, washing all the dirty dishes after everyone had eaten. Charlie looked around. 'The Captain's inspection is due about now, so keep everything as neat as possible.'

'What inspection?'

'Every morning there's a Captain's inspection,' he explained. 'They go around different sections, some they just walk through but every now and then they pick on a section and give it a thorough going-over. You know, a finger along a ledge to make sure it's clean.'

'Really?' Gemma said with surprise.

'Oh yes, and some of them are absolute buggers. They forget just how many people we have to look after.' He looked out of the door as he heard voices. 'Talk of the devil,' he said quietly, 'here they come.'

Gemma stood with her back to the sink inside the pantry, not quite sure what was to happen next as the voices came nearer. A well-built man stopped outside and stared at Gemma. He had a lot of gold braid on his hat and uniform and she was in no doubt from his stature that he was someone of importance.

'Everything all right, Mr Black?' he asked Charlie.

'Yes, sir, everything's fine.'

The officer glanced behind him and said, 'Take a look, Mr Weston, will you.'

Nick Weston stepped inside the pantry.

Gemma just stared at him. He looked so different in uniform. He gazed at her and said, 'Good morning.' There was no hint of recognition as he looked around before saying, 'Everything is as it should be, sir.'

Gemma watched the inspection party move away. 'Who was that?' she breathed.

'That, my dear, was Captain Matthews, the Staff Captain, and with him, the First Officer and a master-at-arms.'

'Oh, I know the First Officer, Charlie. We've met before,' she said casually.

The look of surprise on his face made her chuckle. 'Not that you'd think so. He blanked me. We could have been strangers.' She gave a sardonic grin. 'A lowly stewardess is probably beneath him.'

'It depends on how well you know him,' Charlie told her. 'Maybe he couldn't say anything with the Staff Captain breathing down his neck. He could hardly sweep you into his arms, now could he?'

She saw the twinkle in his eye and said, 'I don't know him that well . . . but he is a good kisser!'

Laughing, he said, 'Oh my, I can see I'm going to have to keep an eye on you.'

At the end of the day, Gemma was again feeling the need to get out into the open, but fearful of meeting MacTaggart, she decided to walk along the boat deck. As she emerged into the fresh air she saw Nick walking towards her. He was dressed in a white short jacket trimmed with gold braid and she thought he looked devastatingly handsome. To her surprise he stopped and greeted her.

'Hello, Gemma. We meet again, although I must admit to being surprised at seeing you this morning – and as a member of the crew.'

'You did recognise me then,' she said tartly. 'I would never have known.'

The corners of his mouth twitched as he tried to suppress his amusement. 'It was hardly the time to renew our acquaintance, was it?'

'A polite "hello, Gemma" wouldn't have gone amiss.'

'Oh dear, I've made you angry. I am sorry, but you must be aware of the rules, that there is to be no fraternising between members of the crew.'

' "Hello, Gemma" is fraternising?' She stared up at him. 'But of course, I forgot, you have your position to think of.'

'Yes I do,' he said. 'And you have your reputation to consider too.'

She hadn't thought of that, and looked at him, trying to decide whether he was teasing her or not. 'Should we be seen talking to each other now, or would that be against company rules, also?'

'It wouldn't be very discreet, I must admit, but how about letting me take you out to dinner in New York?'

Cheekily she asked, 'Would we have to get permission?'

He started laughing. 'Still the minx. No, we wouldn't and it would give me great pleasure to share your company once again. Don't be cross, say yes.'

She considered his offer for a moment, then said, 'Yes, that would be nice.'

'I'll let you know the time when we dock. I have to see which watch I'm on first.'

'Will you send the message secretly, by pigeon?'

He shook his head. 'No, Gemma, by bellboy!'

When they parted company, Nick Weston smiled broadly to himself as he walked along the deck. Seeing Gemma this morning had been a real surprise. He wondered just what had made her make this change in her life. He loved her impish sense of humour, but she would have to be made aware that they could not be seen to be friends on board ship. It was something he usually steered well clear of; anything in that line was fraught with difficulties. Any women he'd ever had a relationship with had always been as far removed from sea life as possible. Which made the fact that he'd invited her out in New York most unusual, but there was something about this young woman that appealed to him.

Gemma returned to her cabin, mentally reliving her conversation with Nick. He was such an attractive man, but besides his obvious good looks, she liked his personality. She'd been very surprised when he'd asked her for a date . . . and delighted. She wondered if they would go to a place where they could dance because she so enjoyed being held by him. She wondered also if he would kiss her again. She must write to Eunice and tell her what had transpired. She'd post the letter in New York. She ought to write to Eve too, but it was difficult knowing what to say. If she was too enthusiastic about her life on board, Eve would be furious. She'd have to think carefully before putting pen to paper.

Had Gemma known what was going on in Southampton with her mother, she would have been more than concerned. Eve was having a tough time, trying to come to terms with Gemma leaving. She felt totally abandoned and to her chagrin, realised just how much her daughter's presence had meant to her. The house felt so empty now when she came home. And despite all her boasting about still being attractive to the opposite sex, no one who was halfway decent had asked her out recently. This was indeed a blow to her self-esteem, but she knew she'd let herself go a bit. The polish on her nails was chipped, for example, her hair needed washing. This wouldn't do at all. Her appearance was the one thing in which she usually took a pride. It was time to pull herself together . . . to start again, to prove to herself that she was still desirable. That she could have a life.

Filled with a sudden burst of determination, she ran a bath, washed her hair, pressed a dress for the evening then repolished her nails. When she was ready to leave for her stint at the pub, she did a little twirl and looked at her reflection in the mirror. She knew she was a good-looking woman when she was well turned out. She figured she looked quite classy. Perhaps she should look for a job in a bar at a decent hotel, meet a better class of person. Commercial travellers as opposed to seamen and the usual locals. Yes, she liked that idea. She'd show Jack and Gemma she could do without either of them!

For the first two hours behind the bar at the Grapes, she was really on form, exchanging witty banter with the customers, flirting with every man who came to order drinks, until one of the wives took exception as she watched Eve stroke the cheek of her husband. The woman stormed up to the counter.

'You keep your thieving hands off my old man, you cow! Just 'cause you don't have a bloke of your own, don't you come sniffing round mine!'

Eve looked at her with disdain. 'You think I'd fancy anything you've touched, dearie?'

The husband, who'd enjoyed Eve's attentions, took this slight personally. 'Don't give me that,' he said to Eve. 'If I'd taken you up on your flirting, you'd have broken your neck to accommodate me.'

Eve laughed in his face. 'I flirt with everybody. It's part of the service. Any fool knows that.'

'Who are you calling a fool?' The man's face was flushed with anger.

His wife flew to his defence. 'My Ernie ain't no fool.'

'He must have been to marry you,' Eve retorted.

'Anything in trousers would do for you,' the woman accused Eve. 'You're just a common tart!'

She couldn't have said anything more insulting. Eve picked up a glass half-full of beer and threw the contents in the woman's face. 'You wouldn't know a bit of class if you fell over it.'

There was a dreadful commotion. The woman, hair dripping, was livid. She picked up her husband's glass and emptied the contents over Eve's head. 'You rotten bitch! I'll show you.' She leaned across the counter and grabbed a handful of Eve's hair and pulled with all of her might. Eve retaliated by grabbing a fistful of her adversary's.

It took four men to part them.

The landlord hauled Eve from behind the counter. 'You're sacked!' he said. 'Come back in the morning and collect your money and cards.' He led her to the side door, opened it, handed Eve her coat and pushed her out into the street, slamming the door in her face.

She stood outside, dishevelled and shocked. This wasn't how it was meant to be at all. Tonight was supposed to be the start of her new life. She pulled her coat around her, pushed back the sodden remnants of her hairstyle and, leaning against the wall, started to cry.

Now what was to become of her? Apart from the money she earned at the pub, she'd enjoyed being with people. Her customers had filled what would have been many a lonely hour. She was used to Jack being away, and her anger that he might have found someone else to take her place filled any void left by his permanent departure; however, she had begun to realise just how much Gemma had contributed to her life, and that didn't sit easy with her after so many years filled with resentment against the girl.

What would Gemma say when she came home and found out she'd been sacked? She couldn't bear the humiliation. Eve decided she wouldn't tell her. It would be easy to hide the fact during the short time she was home and that would leave her at least with a little dignity.

Eve wiped her tears away. She couldn't face going home to an empty house this early. She opened her handbag and checked the contents of her purse. She had enough for a few bevies. Christ! She needed something to cheer her up. She walked along the street and headed for the nearest bar.

Chapter Fifteen

Whilst Nick was on duty on the bridge of the *Queen Mary*, his cousin, Lieutenant Gus Carter, was sitting in his office of the 52nd Precinct in New York, talking to two of his detectives.

'They fished a body out of the Hudson River last night,' one of them said. 'Shot through the back of the head.'

'Any identification?' asked Gus.

'No, but it made no difference, he was soon identified by one of the Department. He'd just been let out of Leavenworth Prison. It was Bobby Santano, one of Anastasio's men.'

'Albert, or his brother Tony?'

'Albert.'

'I wonder why he was disposed of,' said Gus.

The detective said, 'His tongue had been slit down the middle. Obviously they thought he'd been talking too much.'

'And had he?'

Unwrapping a stick of gum, his colleague said, 'Well, let's say he'd been a little careless. The guy was crazy. After all, when the man you work for runs an organisation like

Murder Incorporated, you should become tongue-tied, but not Santano. Like all smalltime hoodlums, he had to brag, show what a big man he was in organised crime.'

'Mm,' mused Gus. 'No idea who did the hit, I suppose?'

The man shook his head. 'No, and you can be sure everyone will have a watertight alibi, but I'll go around the usual haunts. We may get lucky.'

When he was alone, Gus rifled through his papers, then sat back in his chair, sipping his strong black coffee, thinking of the task ahead of him. Of Albert Anastasia, originally Anastasio, until he'd changed the spelling, although his brother Tony hadn't followed suit. Albert Anastasia was a crime boss, head of Murder Incorporated and deeply involved with the union of the International Longshoremen's Association. Through his grip on the unions, millions of dollars each year were funnelled into his coffers from kickbacks on dues, cargoes that were purloined, and payoffs from shipping companies to keep the docks running smoothly and their ships in particular.

The mob had so many people on their pay-roll that finding hard evidence that would hold up in court was almost impossible, but he would keep digging. Someone had to make a mistake somewhere along the line. Gus was still interested in the young blade who had appeared on the scene and, understanding human nature the way he did after so many years on the Force, was hopeful that this flash young man might just be the one to put a foot wrong. If he did, then Gus could use him to enforce the law and break the stranglehold of these gangsters.

He smiled to himself as he thought of his last meeting with young Nick. He knew his cousin had been shaken by his first insight into the seedy side of the city. In Merrie Olde Englande, thought Gus with some amusement, things were so docile in comparison. The gun laws were different, for a start. He couldn't envisage doing his job, unarmed as the British bobby did. To him that was plain crazy.

Later that evening, whilst Gus was having a lonely meal in a small restaurant, Vincente Morelli climbed out of his Dodge convertible, having first fitted the silencer to the muzzle of his Smith & Weston, which he tucked into the belt of his trousers. He could feel the adrenaline pumping through his body and his eyes glittered under the streetlights as he made his way silently towards a small warehouse, situated near the New York docks.

In the distance he could see a light shining through the window of the haulage company. He sidled up to it and peered inside. There, sitting alone at a desk in his shirtsleeves, was the man he'd come to see. An evil smile spread across Morelli's features as he shifted the gun to his jacket pocket.

The man looked up as the door opened. 'Hi, Vince. You're out late, ain't you?'

Vince closed the door behind him and leaned nonchalantly against it. 'Herb. How you doing?'

The man shrugged. 'You know how it is. Struggling to make an honest buck.' A slight frown creased his forehead. 'What can I do for you?'

'My boss, Mr Anastasio, isn't too happy with you, Herb. He asked me to call and have a chat.' He watched the other man's face turn pale as he stared at him.

'What do you mean? Why ain't he happy? I've been

171

sending my money every week.'

'Sure you have, after you've creamed more than your share off the top. Now Mr Anastasio isn't a mean guy. He expects every businessman to have his own scam going – in fact, he allows a small percentage off the top of the take. An honest man makes him nervous but you, my friend, have been greedy and my boss, he don't like that.'

Herb started to bluster, making excuses. 'Business ain't been so good lately. I ain't making the usual turnover. I wouldn't try and pull a fast one on Tony Anastasio. You think I'm crazy or something?'

Vince casually raised one eyebrow. 'That's exactly what I'm thinking, and I'm here to put things right.'

There was an expression of terror on the man's face as he rose to his feet. 'What do you mean?'

Morelli took his gun from his pocket and pointed it at Herb.

'No! No, please! I've got a wife and kids, for Christ's sake!'

'You should have thought of them before,' said Vince as he pulled the trigger.

There was a look of surprise on Herb's face as he sank to his knees, blood spreading on his shirt, just where his heart used to beat.

Walking over to the body, his killer looked coldly at him, then he carefully searched through all the desk drawers, spilling their contents on the floor, breaking the lock on one. Eventually he came across a large brown envelope, stuffed with dollar bills. 'Well, what do you know,' Vince muttered as he leafed through the money, looking at the large denominations. With a smile of satisfaction, he placed the envelope and its contents in an inside pocket of his jacket and walked out of the office, carefully closing the door behind him.

He drove to Lower Manhattan and Greenwich Village, parking his car outside a delicatessen on Clancy Street, then went inside and ordered coffee and a sandwich – pastrami on rye. Killing always made him feel hungry. He sat at a small table and bit into the sandwich and the large dill pickle that came with it.

He thought of the envelope, snug inside his jacket. There must be at least five grand in there. Jesus! What a break. The juices of the pickle ran down his chin and he fastidiously wiped it away with a paper napkin. He didn't want anything marking his new suit.

Although he could well afford to dine at the top restaurants, he enjoyed the simplicity of the deli. Good food sold without any frills. Basic. A bit like him, really.

He knew he was doing well, working for Tough Tony as an enforcer for Murder Incorporated, the same boss he worked for in the docks during the day. His employer was pleased with him; one of Tony's men had taken him aside and told him so.

'The boss is happy,' he was told, 'because you don't mess up. You do the job quietly and efficiently.' But there was a warning also. 'Watch out for the broads. When you're screwing around, we don't want no pillow-talk. It only leads to trouble – understand?'

Vince nodded. 'Sure, you got nothing to worry about.'

'Good,' said the man. 'Only we've got the NYPD breathing down our necks and we don't want no trouble.'

Getting into his car, Vince remembered these words and

the words of his father when he told him he'd got Vince a job working for the mob.

'Listen to me, son. I've done good all these years doing what I was told and not asking questions. You do the same. Tony Anastasio don't take no prisoners. I'm related to him, but if I was to mess up, that would make no difference. Just keep your head down. Don't get smart!'

And he had followed this sound advice. Now he had a small apartment off Broadway and money in the bank. One day he'd move to the Upper East Side to one of those plush apartment blocks, but he was content to wait. He was still young, only twenty-five. He would work his way up the organisation. After all, he was a smart cookie . . . but above all, he was patient.

He patted his jacket. There was no way his boss would get this money. After all, who was to know it was there? Only Herb and him, and Herb was dead.

The following morning, Gus Carter was staring at a body slumped on the floor of a small haulage company. He looked at his sidekick, Lou Masters, and said, 'One clean shot through the heart. A professional hit. Who was he?'

'Herb Kranz,' Lou informed him. 'Owner of the company. Not one of Anastasio's.'

'Not on paper, but in his pocket, I'll bet. Make sure Forensics do a good job. I want every fingerprint checked, all right?'

'Yes, sir.'

'The mob is behind this, I'll bet my pension on it.'

The officer handed Gus a photograph. 'This was found in his wallet.'

Gus looked at the snapshot of a family gathering. 'A wife and two kids. Tough.' He handed it back and walked out of the room.

Sitting in his car, he took out a packet of Camel cigarettes and lit one. This killing had all the hallmarks of a professional hit and he was sure it had been a contract carried out by the mob. There had been a spate of these killings lately, all tied up with the docks in some way or another. All done with the same precision. He puffed on his cigarette. There had to be something or someone who tied them all together. But no fingerprints found at any of the crime scenes matched those of any known criminals. He desperately needed a lead.

He wasn't worried that this was the start of a gang war. It was more likely that the victims were being taught a lesson for some misdemeanour, being used as an example to others.

Gus removed his straw fedora and mopped his sweating brow. He wished he was out of the city, fishing beside a nice lake somewhere. He could do with a change of scene. Never mind, in a couple of days' time, Nick was due to dock. He'd look him up, pick up the latest gossip about the family. He liked to keep in touch. Although he had been born in New York in the Bronx, his grandfather was always talking about the 'old country' and their way of life in the UK. He promised himself that when he retired, he'd take a trip and see the place for himself.

Gus put the key in the ignition and started the engine. Ever since his wife divorced him because she couldn't stand the stresses of his job any longer, he'd been lonely . . . and he was getting older. In his mid-forties now, he felt it was too late to marry again and put another woman through all the worry of being married to a cop. Besides, he was becoming used to living alone. There had been no children from the marriage, which was why he was so interested in Nick.

As he drove home, he couldn't help but compare his young relative to the lowlifes he had to deal with on a daily basis. There was no doubt about it, mixing with criminal types coloured your view on life altogether. But he tried to keep a level head. There were decent people around, but being in the Force made you cynical, no matter how hard you tried not to be.

Chapter Sixteen

By the third day of her first voyage, Gemma was beginning to settle into her new routine. She and Charlie worked well together, both being speedy and efficient and sharing the same sense of humour. She was now finding her way around the working alleyway and the Cabin-Class galley, ready with a witty quip when some of the young chefs teased her whilst she waited for service, either for herself and her colleague or for the passengers.

'Here you are, love,' said one of the chefs, handing her a tray of croissants for the breakfast serving. 'Where are we going when we get to New York then?' he asked with a broad grin.

'We, you cheeky devil? And what would your wife have to say about that?'

With a look of surprise he said, 'How did you know I was married? I never told you.'

'You didn't need to, you have that look about you.'

'What look?'

She gazed at him with twinkling eyes. 'Henpecked!'

The others standing waiting all started to laugh. 'There

you are, Lennie,' said one. 'She's a bright girl, she's got your number.'

'How about me, darling? I'm not married,' called another.

'Sorry boys, I've got plans,' she retorted as she picked up the tray.

'You've got a great pair of legs, I know that, Gemma,' said one as she walked away.

She turned and pointing at him said, 'Watch it, you!'

On her return to her section, she laid a breakfast tray, adding a compote of fruit and a fresh pot of coffee and carried it along to a nearby cabin and knocked on the door.

'Come in,' called a voice.

Gemma entered the cabin, placing the tray on a nearby table, wishing the lady in the bed a cheery, 'Good morning, madam.' As she did so, the husband of the couple emerged from the bathroom. Gemma looked up to greet him too. The man was completely naked, except for a towel which he was using to rub his wet hair. He made no effort to cover himself and Gemma quickly averted her gaze and made a hasty retreat.

When she returned to the pantry, Charlie was there. 'What on earth's the matter?' he asked. 'Your cheeks are bright red.'

She told him what had happened and was not impressed when he doubled up laughing. 'It's all right for you,' she exclaimed, 'but it was very embarrassing for me.'

'So, was he well hung?' Charlie asked coarsely between loud guffaws.

'Hung! There was nothing *hanging* there,' Gemma said

indignantly. 'His wife won't be having any breakfast yet, from what I saw. Food is the last thing on his mind.'

'We'd best not be in too much of a hurry to tidy the cabin then,' he said, still grinning.

'You can be the first to go in when we do,' she shuddered. 'And if they want breakfast tomorrow, you can take it.'

'He might make me feel inferior,' Charlie said, trying to keep a straight face.

'That man would make a bloody Hereford bull feel inferior!'

The leading stewardess called on Gemma during the morning. 'How are you getting on?' she asked.

'Fine, thank you, Mrs Reader.'

'Any difficult passengers?'

With a grimace, Gemma said, 'Only one, but she's not a real problem. How do you handle rude people?' she asked.

The leading stewardess gave a sardonic smile. 'The ruder they are, the more polite I become. They don't know how to cope with that.'

Gemma thought she'd have to remember that when she next saw Mrs Myers. This morning, she'd already tried a different tactic. When she put the breakfast tray before the woman, Mrs Myers had looked at it and demanded, 'What is this?'

Gemma had her answer ready. The tray was neatly laid with toast, orange juice, coffee and four boiled eggs, all standing proud in egg cups. She smiled sweetly at her passenger. 'I thought I'd give you a choice, madam. If you don't like one, then try another. We do like to keep our passengers happy.' The woman was speechless and Gemma made good her escape, chuckling to herself once she was outside the cabin door.

That evening, Gwen the stewardess who'd taken care of Gemma on her first day, called at her cabin. 'I'm going for a trot around the shops to do a bit of window gazing and wondered if you would like to come along?' she said. 'After that we can go back to my place for a drink and meet a couple of the other girls.'

Gemma was delighted to accept.

They ascended the grand public staircase to the promenade deck, passing several passengers decked out in their finery who were making for the various restaurants and bars. Gemma's eyes were wide with wonderment at some of the beautiful gowns worn by the women. Never had she seen such creations, and never in her wildest dreams could she have envisaged some of the jewellery she saw – encrusted diamond necklaces and earrings, bracelets, and mink wraps slung carelessly over arms and shoulders. It was her first experience of great wealth. Her Cabin-Class passengers had nothing to match those who travelled First Class.

The shopping centre on the promenade deck was another eye-opener, and both girls pored over the beautiful china, the clothes, and jewellery, spending imaginary money between them. As they moved from shop to shop, a familiar figure caught Gemma's eye. Walking down the staircase was Nick Weston in his evening uniform, with a beautiful woman on his arm, both laughing as they talked.

'Our illustrious First Officer is doing well for himself,' remarked Gwen who had followed Gemma's gaze.

'I wonder who she is?' murmured Gemma.

'Some wealthy female, out for a bit of sport, no doubt. Some of these women have a high old time whilst they're on board. And let's face it, I wouldn't kick Nick Weston out of my bed . . . would you?'

'No,' said Gemma slowly. 'I certainly wouldn't.' But she wondered why Nick would want to take her out in New York when he could have someone like that?

Gwen took Gemma back to her cabin where she met some of the other stewardesses. They seemed a jolly bunch and she enjoyed their company, but the nicest thing that happened was that Gwen offered to take her ashore shopping, as it was her first trip to New York.

'I can show you how to get around. The city can be a bit daunting the first time. It's an exciting place and there's plenty to see, and the shops are great. But I warn you, it's noisy and frantic.'

'I can't wait,' said Gemma.

Docking day came at last. All the baggage was outside the cabins ready to be taken down to the Baggage Master. And Gemma, on deck briefly, saw for the first time the Manhattan skyline with its stunning skyscrapers. The sight of the Statue of Liberty took her breath away. The tall green statue was far larger than she'd ever imagined, with a torch held in one hand. She now knew for certain she was in America! Her dream was fulfilled. Coming back to earth, she rushed below to finish her work.

She said goodbye to her passengers, all of whom gave her either cash in her hand or an envelope – with the exception of Mrs Myers. Charlie sidled up to her. 'Did you get anything from the Myers?' he asked quietly.

She shook her head. 'Not a bean.'

'Neither did I, mean bastards. Never mind, I've fixed them.'

She looked puzzled. 'Whatever do you mean?'

He gave a sly wink. 'I took all the labels off their luggage before I took it away. It'll take them ages to locate them.'

'Charlie! How could you?'

'Easily, my dear. People like that deserve to be taught a lesson. They'll be on the dockside standing under the letter M for a very long time. Maybe the next voyage they take, they'll remember to do the right thing.' He wandered away to talk to another steward.

Later, as Gemma was taken across the dock to the American Immigration to be registered, as this was her first entry into the States, she heard a voice she recognised, raised in anger. Under the letter M, she saw Mrs Myers, puce with anger, having an argument with a customs official – and she smiled to herself.

Back on board, Gemma and Charlie were working flat out, stripping the beds of dirty linen, ready to make them up again for their next passengers, when they decided to stop for a refreshing cup of tea. As they sat in the pantry ready to enjoy this respite, they were interrupted.

'Hi, Charlie. How you doing?'

Charlie looked round. 'Vince! Come on in. This is my new stewardess. Gemma, this here is Vince Morelli, one of the gang bosses of the longshoremen, or stevedores as we call them back home.'

Gemma looked at the tall young man with dark hair and

smiling brown eyes. 'Hello,' she said.

Vince stepped inside the pantry. 'Well, and hello to you, gorgeous.' To Charlie he said, 'Now this lovely gal is a hell of a sight better than the old dragon you used to work with.' He turned back to Gemma and stared steadily into her eyes. 'I think I'm in love,' he said softly. 'Will you marry me? I'll get a special licence, take you away from all this. What do you say?'

She was highly amused. 'I'd need to know you just a little better before I'd contemplate marriage to you.'

Vince continued to gaze at her. 'Don't she talk pretty, Charlie?' He didn't wait for an answer. 'Now sweetheart, that makes real good sense. I think we should spend some time together, get to know each other. How about a date tonight, then I can find out if you can cook, if you want children – I want at least three – and we have a whole lifetime to plan so we need to talk about it.'

'I'm sorry, Vince, I already have a date tonight.'

'How can you say that? You're already being unfaithful to me. I'm gonna kill myself!'

Gemma was convulsed with laughter. 'That's a bit extreme, isn't it?'

He placed his hand on his heart. 'You don't understand. This is love at first sight. I've never proposed to any other woman – that makes you real special. And you're going to walk out on me already. How could you?'

Gemma rose from her stool. 'And I'm going to walk out of your life right now. I've work to do . . . but I expect you'll recover,' she said dryly as she left the pantry.

'I'll come on board tomorrow and we'll talk again,' he called after her. 'Remember, I love you madly!'

A couple of stewards she knew walked by and heard him. 'You don't waste any time, do you?' one teased as they passed.

With a smile and a toss of her head she said, 'Well, you know how it is when you're irresistible!'

As they finished their work for the day, Gemma asked Charlie about Vince. 'Who is that crazy Yank I met this morning?'

'Crazy? Not really, I can assure you. He's one of the sharpest bosses on the dockside. His gang is one of several who unload the cargo from the ships. I've seen him work his men. He can be a tough bastard, but he has the right connections. He gets me tickets for the best seats in Madison Square Garden when there is a big fight on, and they are like gold dust. Beneath all that banter is a real sharp cookie, believe me.'

As she walked back to her cabin, Gemma was stopped by a bellboy.

'Miss Gemma Barrett?'

'Yes.'

He handed her a message. As he walked away she opened the envelope. Inside was a card from Nick. *Meet me at the dock gates at eight o'clock. Wear a disguise! Nick.* She chuckled quietly. It would serve him right if she did. A yashmak, perhaps.

Once inside her cabin, Gemma took a fistful of dollars from her uniform pocket and several envelopes. She was amazed as she counted out just over a hundred dollars – more than forty pounds. A small fortune to her. How wonderful! And she had a return trip yet to make. Thrilled with such bounty, she picked up the notes and threw them into the air, squealing and giggling with delight like a schoolgirl as she picked them up from the floor.

Whilst getting washed and changed before meeting Gwen, she wondered about Vince. With all his brashness there was something likeable about him. His sense of humour appealed to her and she thought he'd be fun to go out with, but there was no question of that. She had a date with Nick. Where would they go, she wondered. And what of his glamorous lady friend? Was it someone he had just met on board or was it something more? She knew so little about him. Perhaps this evening, she'd learn more.

Gemma was taken by surprise at the humidity as she and Gwen walked down the gangway. Across the road from pier 90, Gwen pointed out the market diner. The low building had a bar to one side and an eating-house on the other, for fast food to eat in or take out, she was told. Nearby was a newsagent's shop, where apparently you could purchase English papers.

They took a bus and Gemma caught her first sight of the shabby, rusting, rundown tenement buildings near the docks.

'Don't ever think of walking around here,' warned Gwen. 'Always get a bus back to the ship or a cab, especially at night. Central Park, too, is safe during the day but don't ever go there after dark.'

'What about the centre of the city?' asked Gemma, somewhat anxiously.

Gwen assured her. 'I'm not trying to scare you. You'll be quite safe walking around the shops and at night along Broadway and the theatre district, but like all major cities, there are danger spots. What are your plans for this evening?'

'I have a date.'

Gwen looked at her and with a sly grin said, 'My, but you don't waste any time.'

'It's with someone I know.'

They alighted from the bus and Gemma just stood there, staring up at the skyscrapers all around her until she had a crick in her neck. 'My, God, if you jumped off one of those you'd be a bit of a mess.'

'What a morbid thought,' said Gwen.

'And look at the policemen . . . they're wearing guns!'

'All the police in New York are armed. Guns are more readily available here than at home. But never mind them. Let's do some serious shopping!'

New York was a revelation to Gemma. The city was all bustle. The air was filled with the aroma of hot dogs and pretzels being sold on the street from stands. Yellow cabs sped along at a hectic speed, honking furiously at anything that got in their way. Gemma learned to wait at intersections until a green traffic signal said *Walk*. She was almost run over as she went to step off the sidewalk, forgetting the traffic was on a different side of the road.

They spent hours in Macy's, the largest department store in the world. Gemma was overcome with the size of it and the wondrous fashion displays, the shoes, the clouds of scent emanating from the huge perfume department. Everything you could want was here and she searched eagerly for a smart dress to wear that evening.

They moved on to Bloomingdales store on Lexington

Avenue and Gemma spent her time in the department selling household goods and fripperies, thinking how she could cheer up the council house. Readymade curtains and cushions would transform the dull abode. She could scarcely contain her excitement.

They stopped at a Howard Johnson's restaurant for lunch. 'I'm dining out later,' Gemma said, 'so I'll just have a sandwich,' but when her toasted chicken sandwich arrived it was like a full meal, served on an oval platter with salad and coleslaw as an accompaniment.

'This is some snack,' she said to her companion.

'Look at the size of that then,' said Gwen, indicating another table where a huge portion of strawberry short-cake was being placed before a rather large lady.

'She'll never eat all that.'

The girls watched in amazement as the woman devoured every crumb.

Gemma looked at Gwen and said, 'Eating here is a health hazard,' then as she tasted her succulent chicken, 'but wonderful.'

When the girls arrived back on board they were exhausted. They'd bought a carton of coffee each at the diner in an effort to lift their flagging energy.

'Thanks for taking me ashore, Gwen,' said Gemma.

The other girl brushed her thanks aside. 'One of us always takes someone new ashore to show them the ropes. Now you'll feel confident of going alone next time.'

Gemma sat on the day bed shaking her head in wonderment. 'Today has been amazing. A fulfilment of a life's dream. You have no idea.'

'I think we all feel a bit like that the first time,' said

Gwen. 'Now I must go as I have a heavy date too. See you tomorrow.'

Alone, Gemma examined her shopping. Underwear for herself, a glamorous turquoise petticoat for Eunice, heavily trimmed with lace, a smart beaded black top for Eve which she hoped her mother would like, some new towels as theirs at home were very thin, and some stockings. What a great day! Now she'd get ready to meet Nick. Life couldn't be more perfect.

Chapter Seventeen

Nick Weston waited impatiently on the dockside, hoping that Gemma wasn't one of those women who were always late. It was something that really annoyed him. But just one minute after eight o'clock he saw a female walking towards him. She was wearing a figure-hugging black dress with a low neckline. On her feet were emerald-green shoes with high heels. He was unable to identify her as around her head and across the lower part of her face, an emerald-green stole covered her features. She stopped in front of him.

'Is anyone looking?' she whispered. 'Or shall we make a run for it?'

The corners of his eyes crinkled as he smiled at her. 'No, Gemma, everything's fine. You can come out now.'

She slowly removed the stole and rearranged it around her shoulders. 'Good evening, Mr Weston,' she said with a beguiling look. 'Am I allowed to put my arm through yours, or should we stay two feet apart?'

'I can see I'm going to have trouble with you this evening,' he said, as he hailed a cab. Once settled inside the vehicle and on their way he looked at her and said, 'You look stunning.'

'I feel like Mata Hari,' she chuckled. 'You realise I shall be after all your secrets over dinner, don't you?'

'I thought she did that from the bed,' he answered.

She chuckled softly. 'Really? Another of life's disappointments for you, then. Where are we going?' she asked.

'To the Tavern on the Green, on the edge of Central Park. I think you'll like it.'

When they arrived, the waiter led them through the restaurant to the rear garden, where tables were set beneath trees which moved gently in the cooling night breeze, making the coloured fairy-lights amidst the branches twinkle. Table lamps lit the area in a soft seductive glow, which was enhanced by the street-lamps placed at intervals beyond.

'This is absolutely delightful,' said Gemma as the waiter held her chair for her.

'I thought it would appeal to you,' Nick said, pleased.

They ordered from the extensive menu. As they waited for their food, Nick asked, 'How was your trip?'

'Fine,' she told him. 'After the first couple of days, I began to find my way around, and Charlie, my bedroom steward, is a lovely man. How was yours?'

He shrugged. 'All right. No problems.'

'You looked as if you were having a good time when I last saw you,' she said archly.

'Really? When was that?'

'A couple of nights ago. I was on the promenade deck looking at the shops and you were walking down the staircase with a *very* glamorous woman.'

'Oh yes,' he said. 'That was Mrs Van Housen. One of the more tiresome duties of the senior officers is to entertain the important passengers at dinner.'

'I could see how that would be a burden,' she said cheekily. 'We all have our crosses to bear.'

'Well, some passengers are easier than others,' he said with a laugh. And Gemma wondered if the officers' duties finished when the ship docked, but she supposed that they did, or why would he be here with her?

'We are old friends,' he added, which only served to confuse her thinking, but Nick didn't elucidate further. Although Gemma felt she couldn't continue to question him, she did, however, ask about his family.

'My father is a Captain with the Furness Withy Lines, but he's on the New York to Bermuda run.'

'Your mother doesn't see very much of him, then.'

'On the contrary, they live in Bermuda, which suits them both. When he retires, they'll have to decide where they'll live out their retirement – Bermuda or England. But as they have a nice home in Hamilton, and neither of them like the British winters, I expect they'll stay where they are.'

Gemma couldn't help but silently compare their family backgrounds. His couldn't be more different. But she decided quickly that for just an evening spent together, it simply wasn't important.

After their meal, Nick took her by cab to the Latin Quarter, a celebrated nightclub where they sat at a ringside table over drinks and enjoyed the cabaret and the dancing girls, bedecked in fabulous feathers and scanty beaded costumes, who performed on the raised horseshoe-shaped stage beside them.

Gemma became really excited when halfway through the performance, Errol Flynn arrived with two beautiful young women and sat just three tables away from them.

'Oh my God, I don't believe this!' she exclaimed. 'I used to have his pictures all over the wall of my bedroom and there he is, in the flesh.' At that moment, the film star looked up and met her gaze. He removed the long cigarette-holder from his mouth, picked up his glass and raised it in salute to her. She beamed back at him, much to Nick's amusement.

'You're not going to faint on me, are you?'

'No, don't be silly . . . but my knees are shaking. I couldn't stand up if you asked me to! My friend Eunice adores him, she even asked me to get his autograph if ever I saw him. Little did I think I would.'

'We could always stop by his table on the way out.'

She looked horrified at the idea. 'I couldn't do that.'

'Of course you could. These people thrive on adoration.'

'No, I really couldn't.'

When the cabaret had finished, Nick looked at his watch. 'It's after midnight,' he said. 'Time to be getting back.' He picked up two post cards that were on the table, advertising the club, and much to her dismay as they drew level with Errol Flynn's table, Nick held Gemma firmly by the arm and stopped.

'Mr Flynn,' he said, in his beautifully modulated voice, 'Gemma here is a great fan of yours, so is her friend back in England. Would it be too much of an imposition to ask you to sign these cards?'

The star rose from his seat and took Gemma's hand in his. 'A beautiful name for a beautiful woman,' he said, and kissed her hand. Then he proceeded to write on the cards. 'What's your friend's name?' he asked.

'Eunice,' she managed to say.

He handed the cards back to her. 'My pleasure,' he said. 'Goodnight, Gemma.'

Clutching the cards in her hand, in a daze, she felt Nick lead her towards the exit. Outside he took her into his arms.

'I'd better hold on to you,' he joked. 'I'm afraid your legs might give way.'

She held out her hand. 'I'll never wash it again,' she cried.

Still holding her firmly, Nick looked into her shining eyes and said softly, 'Dear Gemma, you are such a child.' And then he kissed her.

She felt her senses reel as his mouth moved expertly over hers. His strong arms gathered her even closer, and she entwined hers around his neck and returned his kisses eagerly.

Reluctantly they drew apart. He didn't speak but he gazed into her eyes for what seemed an eternity. At last he said, 'We'd better get a cab.'

The doorman, who had been standing at a discreet distance now stepped forward and flagged a passing car. Nick tipped him and helped Gemma into the vehicle. Once inside, he put his arm around her shoulders until she was nestled cosily against him and they were driven back to the docks.

At pier 90, they climbed out of the vehicle and Gemma waited whilst Nick paid the driver. Just as they were about to walk along the dockside, she heard her name being called and looked around to see Vince Morelli. He was not in his working clothes but wore a neat pair of lightweight trousers and a shirt; over his shoulder he had casually slung his jacket, which he now threw into the back of an open red sports car parked nearby. He ambled over to them.

'Hi, Gemma. My, but you're a sight for sore eyes,' he said with a disarming smile. He looked at Nick. 'I hope you took care of this young lady because one day I'm going to marry her!' With that, he turned on his heel, climbed into his car and drove away, grinning broadly as he did so.

'Who the hell was that?' asked Nick, although he thought the man looked vaguely familiar.

Gemma wasn't sure if she was bemused or embarrassed. 'Vince Morelli. He's one of the gang bosses of the long-shoremen. I met him today for the first time . . . and he proposed to me,' she said, trying to keep a straight face.

Nick frowned. 'You be careful,' he said. 'The New York docks are far more dangerous than ours in Southampton,' and mindful of what Gus had told him, he added, 'You never quite know who these people are.'

'Oh, Vince is harmless enough,' she said. 'Like all Americans, he's full of bull.'

They walked up the gangway together. On duty at the top was a master-at-arms, who saluted Nick. Turning to Gemma, Nick said, 'Let's take a walk around the deck before turning in, shall we?' Without waiting for an answer, he took her hand and led her away.

They stood at the rail of the Cabin-Class deck at the after end of the ship and looked out over the Hudson River. It was a clear night with the stars high in the heavens and the moon shining on the water. Without preamble, Nick took Gemma into his arms and lowered his mouth to hers once again. He caressed her back as his mouth demanded her response. Her fingers found the soft hair in the nape of his neck as her lips opened to return his kisses.

As they paused to catch their breath, he looked deeply into her eyes and said softly, 'You really are a delightful little minx.'

She gazed back at him, at his full sensuous mouth, and said, 'Do you think this is wise?'

'What do you mean?' he said as he buried his face in her neck and nibbled her ear.

'The master-at-arms saw us together.'

He stroked her cheek. 'He knows when to turn a blind eye. Come here.'

He drew her even closer as he rained kisses on her neck, her eyes and her mouth. She felt his hand move to her breast as she kissed him back, wallowing in the passion of the moment.

Never had she been kissed so expertly or so passionately. She felt the tip of his tongue in the soft cavern of her mouth. It made her legs turn to jelly and she clasped him even tighter.

Eventually he let her go. 'Time for bed,' he said.

'What?' she said, startled by his words.

He chuckled softly. 'I'm not inviting you into mine, Gemma, although at this moment the idea is very appealing. Come along. Do you want me to walk you to your quarters?'

She shook her head. 'No, I'm fine and that really would be very unwise, wouldn't it? Thank you for a lovely evening.' She ran her finger over his mouth. 'I'll see you on the next Captain's inspection,' she added mischievously.

'Can I see you in Southampton?' he asked.

'Yes, if you like. Where?'

'Come to my hotel, the same one as before, at eight o'clock and we'll take it from there.' He kissed her briefly and led her back inside, where they went their separate ways.

Her cabin door was locked, and when she entered it was to discover that Sally hadn't returned. Gemma took off her dress, and hung it up. She put her hand to her mouth as she could still feel the imprint of Nick's kisses. The trip home would be very frustrating knowing he was on board. So near but so far, she thought with a wry smile. But at least he had asked to see her again.

She looked at the signed cards, thinking that Eunice would go mad when she received hers. Gemma would never have had the nerve to ask, but Nick had done it with such ease. The same ease with which he'd kissed her. And she'd enjoyed every moment. She'd also enjoyed the look of consternation on his face when Vince had called out to her. He too was good-looking, especially out of his work clothes. Not in the same classy way that Nick was, but enough to allow her to enjoy the meeting of the two men. After all, every woman likes to be admired, she thought. It had been a great evening, but she was still curious about Mrs Van Housen. Did Nick kiss *her*, she wondered.

The alarm woke Gemma from a deep sleep. As she climbed down from her bunk, she saw that Sally's bunk hadn't been slept in. At that moment her cabin-mate arrived. 'Good morning,' she said. 'I've brought us some coffee from the diner. I thought we would probably need a shot of caffeine to get us going.'

Gemma took hers gratefully. 'Have a nice evening?' she asked.

Sally shrugged. 'It was all right, but he was a lousy lover. Some men just don't know their way around a woman's body. Did you have a good time?'

With a sigh Gemma replied, 'It was everything I had hoped it would be.'

'Well, at least one of us was satisfied,' Sally said. 'Right, I must spend a penny.'

Gemma stared after her. Sally obviously thought she'd had a sexual encounter. Remembering the way that Nick had kissed her, and his soft caresses, she wondered what sort of a lover he would be. Experienced, of that she was certain. *He* would know his way around a woman's body. She wondered just for a second, if he would ever get to know his way around hers.

Sally returned and as the girls dressed, she said to Gemma, 'There is one man on board who I really fancy. I would sell my soul to the devil to spend a night with *him*.'

'Really?' said Gemma, interested. 'And who would that be?'

'Our gorgeous First Officer, Nick Weston. Have you seen him?'

'Oh yes,' said Gemma, hiding a smile. 'I've seen him.'

'Now there's a real man and he's single, not that that makes any difference. Although I did once hear a rumour that he was engaged to some American heiress, and what do you know? She travelled with us last trip. A tall willowy blonde. I wonder if they've made it up? Given the chance, he could have my body any day . . . or night!' She chuckled. 'Who knows, with a bit of luck and a following wind, maybe I'll get the opportunity to find out what sort of a lover he is. Come on, we'll be late.'

Gemma followed her out of the cabin. Was the blonde she'd seen with Nick his ex-fiancée? He'd been somewhat reticent about the woman, and yet he'd spent the evening with Gemma. It was all very confusing.

On the quayside, preparations were being made for sailing. On the dockside, Gus Carter watched Vince and his gang load the *Queen Mary* with stores and baggage. He had to admit that the man was good at his job: the gang worked quickly and efficiently under his supervision. However, Gus was still puzzled by the part Morelli played in the organisation. He wasn't just a longshoreman. Anyone who had an occasional meeting with top man, Tony Anastasio, had a role to play. He was certainly no mere gang boss.

Embarkation was well under way and Gemma had been busy settling in her passengers. She said to Charlie, 'That couple in cabin two twenty-three.'

'Yes, what about them?'

'She's years younger than him.'

'So what? Many older wealthy men have young brides. In any case, maybe they aren't married.'

Gemma glanced at the passenger list. 'They're travelling as Mr and Mrs Fellows.'

He pulled a face. 'Doesn't mean a thing. That's the way he booked the cabin. As long as her papers are in order, he can call her what he wants.' He looked at Gemma. 'What is it that's bugging you?'

She was thoughtful for a moment. 'I don't know, I just have a feeling that something's not quite right there. Wealthy he may be, but he looks a brute, and she's so young and lovely. Why would she marry a man like that?'

'Oh, come on, love. Money is the best aphrodisiac of them all, you know that.'

'But she looks scared of him.'

Charlie looked at her and said, 'Now you listen to me, young lady. The longer you work on board, the more you'll see, and the one thing to remember is that whatever goes on between your passengers is nothing to do with you. You serve them their meals when required, you make their beds and look after their cabin. You *do not* . . . I repeat *do not* . . . get involved with their marital problems.'

'But Charlie—'

'No buts. Remember the three wise monkeys? Hear no evil, speak no evil, see no evil. That's us. Now get on with your work.'

Not long after, Vince arrived with an extravagant box of chocolates tied in gold ribbon. 'Here you are, honey,' he said to Gemma. 'A golden bow for a golden girl, although I'm not sure you deserve them after standing me up for another man last night.'

She took the chocolates and said, 'Thank you, but you shouldn't have.'

'When we're married, I'll smother you in diamonds. How does that sound?'

'Like a tall story,' she said.

Charlie came over. 'Now then, Vince, leave her alone, we've got work to do.'

Vince put an arm around Charlie's shoulder. 'If you plead my case with this beautiful woman until you get back next trip, I may have some tickets for you for the big fight.'

'That's blackmail,' Charlie accused.

Vince grinned at him. 'Sure is, buddy.' He turned to Gemma. 'Think how Charlie will suffer and my heart will break if you don't let me take you out next time. You wouldn't like either on your conscience, would you?'

'Now stop messing about, Vince, and let me get on with my work or I won't be ready for my passengers. And thanks for the chocolates.'

He cupped her face gently in his hands and kissed her softly on the mouth, taking her by surprise. 'You really are so cute. I'll see you next trip. You take care of her, Charlie. Remember I have an interest in her well-being. She's the future Mrs Morelli!' With a smile and a wave, he walked away.

Charlie looked at her and said, 'You've certainly made a hit there, girl. Just be careful.'

'What do you mean?'

'A little flirtation is one thing, but just make sure it doesn't get out of hand, that's all.'

Later, having seen that all her passengers were settled and everything was in hand, Gemma said to Charlie. 'I don't think we have any Myers types on the homeward journey.'

'Thank heavens,' he said. 'What do you want for your lunch?'

'I'm not hungry,' she said. 'I'll grab a sandwich later, but

I would like to go on deck for some fresh air, blow the cobwebs away and watch us leave New York.'

'Off you go,' he said. 'Everyone is in the dining room, there's no one in their cabins. Twenty minutes, all right?'

Nick Weston, standing on the wing of the bridge next to the dockside, watched as the last ropes were released and the ship slowly moved away. He cast a glance along the dock and recognised the American who had spoken to Gemma last night. He was gesticulating angrily to one of his men as he verbally berated him. Nick couldn't hear what passed between them but he could recognise the anger on the gang boss's face. A frown creased his brow. He hoped that Gemma didn't get too friendly with him. A pleasant manner could easily be misinterpreted by some men, and from that came trouble. He wouldn't like to see her in a situation she couldn't handle. He went inside the bridge to continue with his duties.

As the mighty liner sailed down the Hudson River, Gemma once again stared at the Manhattan skyline. Now she knew what the city was like, she couldn't wait to go back again. She thought of Jack her father and wished things were different. Nothing would have given her greater pleasure than to have shared with him the thrill of her first voyage. She was momentarily saddened when she thought it would be such a long time before they met again. She wondered too how Eve had fared during her absence. Despite the cruel things her mother had said to her, she couldn't help but be concerned for her; however, now she had made the break, she was determined to lead a life of her own. With one last lingering look, she made her way below.

★ ★ ★

Later that night, in a bar in Little Italy, Vince was in conversation with one of Anastasio's top men, and had Gus been able to listen in, he'd have soon learned the young man's position in the organisation. Albert, brother of Tony, powerful head of the syndicate, was hearing rumours that Gene Bender, a member of the family run by Vito Genovese, another Mafioso, was looking to take over from him, to build his own organisation. He was envious of Anastasio's grip on the unions. But Albert wasn't looking for a gang war. He knew, however, that some gesture on his part was needed to show his strength, enough to convince Bender that it would be unwise to step out of line. He'd had a meeting with his brother Tony to hatch a plan and now Vince had been called in to orchestrate it.

As he listened to what was required of him, Vince knew that to succeed would be to secure a certain place of importance in the organisation. Move him up the ladder, nearer the top, where he wanted to be. In time, he figured, he would be living a life of luxury, with men of his own and who knows, maybe one day he would be top boss himself. Such was his arrogance.

But Tony Anastasio was a wise and clever man. He'd studied his fellow human beings over the years and knew that for a while, young Vince Morelli would be a vital cog in his wheel. He had that necessary ruthless streak. But there would come a time when his ambition made him a danger, as those before him had been . . . but what none of them ever realised was that they were expendable. But Tony knew it, and that was all that mattered.

Chapter Eighteen

The return trip was without incident, apart from the occupants of cabin 223, Mr and Mrs Fellows. They were not demanding or difficult, but Gemma sensed an atmosphere whenever she was summoned to the cabin. Fellows was a man in his fifties, silver-haired, well-dressed and not a person to make conversation with the crew, except to order either drinks or snacks in an authoritative tone. Gemma noticed he scarcely spoke to his wife. She also noticed bruising on the beautiful girl's body one morning before Mrs Fellows hurriedly put on a negligée.

The ship always called in at Cherbourg before finally docking in Southampton, and all the baggage was put ready outside the cabins to be collected and taken to the Baggage Master with appropriate labels for either port.

Gemma saw Mr Fellows leave the cabin and assumed he was going to one of the bars before dinner, as was his habit during the voyage. His wife always joined him later. Gemma saw the light on outside the cabin door summoning a steward, shortly afterwards, and made her way there.

Once inside, Mrs Fellows asked her to take a seat. Curious, Gemma did so.

The young woman looked somewhat harassed and Gemma asked, 'What can I do for you, madam?'

'I want to get off at Cherbourg,' she said.

With a frown Gemma said, 'But you're due to leave the ship at Southampton.'

'I know. Can you arrange for my baggage to be put ashore in France, without Mr Fellows knowing?'

'Yes, that could be arranged. We'd just have to change the label. I don't think it would be a problem. But your husband?'

'He's not my husband,' she said. 'Look – I want to get away from him and this is the only way I can think of. Will you help me, please?'

Seeing the anguished expression in her eyes, Gemma said, 'Yes. I'll go and arrange it now.'

The woman took a hundred-dollar bill from her wallet and pressed it into Gemma's hand. 'I can't thank you enough.'

Gemma held out the money. 'I can't take this.'

'I want you to have it,' she insisted.

'How will you get away from your . . . Mr Fellows?'

The girl smiled for the first time. 'It shouldn't be too difficult,' she said. 'I'll make an excuse when he's in the bar. He's not that interested as to my whereabouts as long as we dine together and I'm here in his bed,' she said bitterly.

Rising to her feet Gemma said, 'I'm sorry for your trouble, but don't you worry. I'll get the labels changed, if I have to do it myself! Good luck.'

Once outside she went in search of Charlie. He was in a nearby cabin, turning down the beds for the night, and looked up as she rushed into the room.

'Charlie, come with me.' She took him by the hand to their pantry where she told him what had transpired. He looked sceptical as he listened to her. 'Now don't you dare tell me not to interfere,' warned Gemma. 'I've seen bruises on that woman's body – not where they would show, of course. If you won't sort it out, I will. We dock late tonight, so we have to get a move on.'

'I was just going to start on taking the baggage down,' he said. He looked at her. 'You really want to do this? What about when Fellows comes looking for her?'

'By then it will be too late. He stays in the bar for hours, anyway.'

'We'll have to tell him if he asks about her,' said Charlie. She was horrified. 'What do you mean?'

'If we don't, he's liable to have the ship searched if she's missing, and we don't want that.'

'So, I'll just tell him and say I assumed that he knew. What can he do? Nothing.'

Charlie shook his head. 'I don't believe I'm doing this.'

Gemma kissed him on the forehead. 'You are a darling.'

'You finish turning down the beds,' he sighed, and left the pantry.

By the time the ship docked, Gemma was off duty, but she was on pins, wondering if the woman would get away. Charlie had sorted out the problem of the baggage and then told her to stay clear. 'I've warned the night steward in case Fellows raises the alarm before the morning. He said he'd be happy to tell him his wife had gone. Apparently he's had a run-in with the man, and he doesn't like him.'

But when the ship docked in Cherbourg, Gemma

couldn't rest, so she put her coat on over her uniform and went on deck where she could see the cabin passengers disembark. The dock was well lit so she was able to see everyone and she didn't take her eyes off the gangway. Her patience was finally rewarded when she saw the woman she knew as Mrs Fellows step onto the dockside and hurry towards the customs shed. 'Good for you,' she whispered. She knew how it felt to be in a destructive relationship and felt justified in helping somcone escape from such a situation. She returned to her cabin well pleased with the outcome.

Mr Fellows, it appeared, was not so happy. When he asked the night steward if he had seen his wife and was told she had left the ship, he complained to the purser, who in turn sent for Charlie, who explained the whole situation. On telling Mr Fellows that his wife, or the young lady travelling as his wife, had insisted on leaving the ship in France and that she was free to do so, the purser was met with abuse. Mr Fellows had to be escorted to his cabin by the master-at-arms.

Charlie related all this to Gemma when she came on duty the next morning. 'So we'll get no tip from him,' he said wryly.

Gemma handed him a fifty-dollar bill. 'This is half of what she gave me,' she explained.

'Well, that sweetens the pill a bit,' he said, grinning at her. 'But please, no more midnight rescues. My nerves won't stand it!'

The ship sailed up Southampton Water at last, early the next morning. Gemma gazed out of the porthole and saw the lush English countryside. It looked so quiet and peaceful, and although she was happy to be home, she experienced the familiar flutterings of apprehension at the thought of seeing her mother. She'd packed her bag the night before, carefully placing the gifts she'd bought, hoping that Eve would like her present.

When at last she left the ship, Gemma caught a taxi to Duke Street, paid the driver and put her key in the door. To her surprise, Eve was sitting at the table, neatly dressed and made-up, drinking tea. Gemma looked at her watch. 'I thought you'd be at work.'

'It's my day off,' lied Eve. 'So, how was your trip?'

Delighted that Eve had asked, Gemma reached for a clean cup and saucer and poured herself some tea from the pot on the table. Then she began to tell her mother of her experiences.

'The *Queen Mary* is huge. I didn't think I'd ever find my way about and a few times I got lost . . .' Gemma told her about Mrs Myers and the débâcle of the woman with Fellows, about Charlie and the shops in New York. She stopped and eagerly opened her suitcase, taking out her gift for Eve. 'I bought this for you, I hope you like it.'

Eve was battling with mixed emotions. She was full of resentment, listening to Gemma's escapades, jealous that her daughter and not she herself had escaped from the dreary docks and found a new way of life. She was frightened that Gemma would discover she'd been sacked from her job, worried about her debts, yet at the same time strangely pleased to have her daughter back home. The past days had been a nightmare. Work had been her salvation and without it, she'd been on a downward spiral of drunkenness. She'd pulled herself together for the day Gemma docked, only because she needed to survive. She'd spent all the money from her allotment and didn't have enough to cover the rent. She didn't know how she was going to get round to asking her daughter for money, without giving away her secret.

She took the beaded top and held it up, knowing how much Gemma desired her approval. 'It's lovely,' she said. 'I'll wear it to work tomorrow evening, or perhaps we could go somewhere this evening and I could wear it then.'

'I thought you'd be working,' said Gemma, dismayed. 'I've made arrangements to go out.'

The smile died from Eve's countenance. 'I see.'

Torn by guilt and wanting to appease her mother, Gemma quickly picked up a bag of groceries she'd bought from a store on the dockside and produced cans of ham, fruit, and the towels she'd purchased in Bloomingdales. 'Look,' she said, 'these will look good in the bathroom, and these cans you can put in the pantry.' She took thirty pounds from her wallet and placed the notes on the table. 'Here, Mum. Put this toward something. I'll be able to help you more financially now.'

Inside, Eve felt a surge of relief. Thank God, it was more than enough to cover the rent, but still seething with resentment, she said nastily, 'You can't buy me off, you know.'

'Buy you off?' Gemma suddenly flared. 'How can you say such a thing? You are my mother and all I'm doing is trying to help, but of course if you prefer that I don't, I'll know in future, won't I?' She picked up her case and went upstairs.

Eve closed her eyes and thanked God that Gemma hadn't removed the money, but she was surprised at the ferocity of her daughter's anger. Being away had changed her already. She was learning to stand on her own two feet, which didn't sit well with Eve. She felt the control she'd always had slipping away. She'd have to be careful.

In her room, Gemma was furious. Nothing changes, she thought. She still couldn't do anything right as far as her mother was concerned. Then she remembered all the hurtful things Eve had said in the past and the anger made her strong. She was filled with determination now not to let Eve interfere with her life. She'd tasted freedom and she liked it; for her there was no going back. She took the gift she had for Eunice and went downstairs.

Eve, trying to make amends for her own sake, went to speak but Gemma walked straight past her and said, 'I'm going out.'

With her newly found confidence, Gemma swept into Cussons, the store where she used to work, and made for the jewellery counter. Eunice saw her coming and greeted her warmly. 'You look terrific,' she said. 'I thought about you every day. I got your letter from New York. It all sounds so exciting. I can't wait to have a chat.'

Looking at her watch Gemma asked, 'What time's your lunch-hour?'

'In ten minutes.'

'Right. Meet me in Mayes' Restaurant and I'll treat you to lunch. I'll go over now and grab a table and order. Anything special you want?'

Eunice grinned with delight. 'I'll leave it to you.'

Over their grilled sole, the girls exchanged their news. When Gemma told her friend about meeting Nick Weston again, she was dumbfounded.

'And he took me out to dinner in New York!'

'Oh Gemma, you lucky devil. Did he kiss you?'

'Yes, and it was lovely.'

'Are you seeing him again?'

'Yes, I'm meeting him this evening. Here.' She handed over her gift. 'This is for you.'

Eunice took off the wrapping and went into raptures when she saw the slip. 'It's so glamorous. I should wear it over my dress, it's such a pity to cover it up.'

Then Gemma handed her the card from the Latin Quarter. 'Oh, by the way, Errol Flynn sent this to you.'

Eunice's eyebrows rose in astonishment, then she looked at the card. *To Eunice with love and best wishes, Errol Flynn.* 'Oh, my God!' she breathed. 'Is this real?'

Gemma nodded. 'He was sitting three tables away. He kissed my hand.'

'Which one, show me!'

'Don't be ridiculous. It doesn't look any different,' Gemma said, laughing at her friend.

Eunice sat back in her chair, speechless, looking at the card. 'Errol Flynn actually held this in his hand.' She clutched it to her bosom. 'Oh Gem, what an exciting life you are leading. Tell me about New York, I want to know everything.'

The minutes sped by quickly and before they knew it, it was time for Eunice to go back to work. 'Write to me, won't you,' said Gemma. 'It's so nice to get mail from home.'

'I will, I promise,' said Eunice as she rose from her seat. As she went to leave she added, 'Keep your eyes open for Clark Gable, will you?'

Gemma's next stop was at the Seaman's Mission. Uncle Ted was thrilled to see her and hear her news, but he wasn't so happy when she told him about Jock MacTaggart. 'You have any trouble with him, you report him,' he said.

She assured him that she would. 'I doubt I shall bump into him again. It was pure chance he had to come to my section that time.'

'It sounds as if your bedroom steward is a good man. If you have any worries about MacTaggart, tell this Charlie. Have you heard from your father?'

She shook her head. 'Only when he wrote and sent his new address.'

'Write to him, Gemma. He is your father, and it would be a great pity to lose that family tie. He wasn't a bad chap and he did have a lot to put up with. How is the Duchess by the way?'

'Same as ever. I must go. There are a few things I need to get before I sail, and then I've got a date.' She beamed at him. 'With the First Officer!'

'Bloody hell, you are moving up in the world.'

'He's very dishy,' she said. 'I just love my life now. To be honest, Uncle Ted, I can't wait until we sail again tomorrow.'

He hugged her. 'You're a chip off the old block, all right. You take care now.'

After shopping, Gemma returned home and bathed and changed for the evening. Eve wasn't around and for that she was grateful. As it was a nice evening, she decided to walk up to Nick's hotel. She was early and didn't want to appear too eager.

She gazed into the shop windows as she walked up the High Street and round the Bargate, the old remains of the city gates which straddled the road. As she looked in at the window displays, she thought how different the atmosphere was here, compared to the frantic buzz of New York. The traffic was so much lighter, there were no brash neon signs advertising goods. There was a feeling of gentle reserve about the place. Of peace and tranquillity. The local parks as always were immaculate, the trees turning different shades of gold in the autumnal air, ready to shed their leaves in the coming month.

When she arrived at the hotel, there was a message for her at the reception desk to go to Nick's room. She was shown to the elevator and given his room number. She found it easily enough and knocked on the door.

He opened it and immediately apologised. 'I'm sorry about this,' he said, 'but I was caught up in a meeting and I'm late. Come in.' He was wearing his trousers, but his torso was bare. Laid out on the bed, Gemma saw his clean shirt and tie.

She was a little embarrassed to see the broad bare shoulders, the powerful chest, but at the same time it gave her a frisson of desire. 'I could have waited downstairs,' she said.

He drew her into his arms. 'I couldn't have kissed you downstairs.'

As his mouth covered hers, she put her arms around him, feeling the warm naked flesh beneath her fingers. She ran her hands across him as she eagerly returned his kisses, aware of the desire beginning to course through her.

As he kissed her, Nick lifted her off her feet and laid her on the bed. 'Oh Gemma,' he murmured, 'I don't think you realise the effect you have on a man.' She was relieved that Nick didn't know the effect *he* was having on her. She lay nestled in his arms. 'I've missed you,' he said softly as he slowly undid the buttons on the front of her dress.

She didn't stop him, didn't want to. She caressed his face. 'Did you? I missed you too. You didn't come round on inspection.'

'I'll make up for it now,' he said, cupping her breast, as his mouth closed over the pink nipple, standing proud.

'Oh Nick,' she whispered as he raked his teeth gently over the tip. His mouth once more closed over hers and there was a certain frenzy in their kisses, until suddenly he stopped.

'What's the matter?' she asked.

'If I don't stop now,' he said, 'this is going to get out of hand.' He got up and went over to the washbasin in the corner, and rinsed his face with cold water. Then he turned to look at her, laid out on his bed. He crossed over, pulled her open dress together and said, 'You'd better do up those buttons or I won't be responsible for my actions.' He picked his shirt up and put it on. 'Have you eaten?' he asked.

Wordless, she shook her head.

'Then let's go down to the dining room. I'm starving. I've had nothing since breakfast.'

There was a strange feeling of intimacy watching Nick finish dressing as she combed her hair and freshened her make-up. It was as if they were a married couple, Gemma thought, and the idea lingered as they made their way to the dining room.

She gazed at him as he ordered from the menu and wondered just how it would have been if he hadn't stopped kissing her when he did. And she knew that part of her wished he hadn't.

Chapter Nineteen

In New York, Gus Carter was called from his bed in the early hours of the morning to look at two bodies. As he approached the crime scene he asked the police officer standing by what he'd found.

'These two stiffs were dumped here about an hour ago from a car, according to one of the local residents,' he explained.

'Do we know who they are?'

'Yeah, Lieutenant. A couple of hoods that belong to the Genovese family.'

Gus frowned. Vito Genovese was head of one of the most powerful Mafia families. Surely this wasn't the start of a gang war? That was the last thing the NYPD needed.

'They're reasonably small fry,' said the officer. He pointed to one of the corpses whose eyes stared vacantly towards the sky, with a bullet hole in the middle of his forehead. 'This guy is a runner in the numbers racket and the other is one of Genovese's bodyguards.'

Gus's eyes narrowed. 'Seems to me as if a message is being sent here. But who by, I wonder?'

Lou Masters appeared by his side. 'Hi, Gus. I've

questioned the woman in the tenement who saw the car, but she couldn't tell me much. She just saw the bodies being pushed out on to the sidewalk from a black sedan. She'd been to the bathroom and heard the squeal of brakes as the car stopped and looked out to see what was going on.'

Gazing at the two men Gus remarked, 'This is another professional hit. Clean and neat . . . like the guy in the warehouse we saw a while back.' He shook his head. 'No doubt the bullet will match the ones they found on these bodies. Let me know if anything else turns up. I'm going back to bed.'

But when he returned to his apartment, sleep eluded him. He was getting nowhere with his investigations. Despite the watch being kept on the docks, nothing was forthcoming. Young Vince Morelli was leading a quiet life these days; even his womanising had almost stopped. Occasionally he took some dame out to dinner and back to his place, but his carousing seemed to be at an end for the moment and Gus wondered why. Morelli was obviously keeping a low profile and people only did that when they had something to hide. Well, it was up to him to find out exactly what it was.

In a side street off Broadway at four o'clock in the morning, Vince stood at the window of his apartment and looked out. The streets were quiet at this hour with just the occasional sound of a police car or the whine of an ambulance to disturb the peace. He drew on his cigarette and blew out the smoke slowly, then took a sip of coffee from the cup in his hand. There was an expression of satisfaction on his face. Another job well executed. He smiled to himself. That was an apt way of putting it. Two hits in twenty-four hours. Not bad. Not bad at all.

The first one had been easy. He knew the guy visited his old mother in the evening of the first Monday of every month. He'd followed him at a discreet distance, waiting for an opportune moment. It came when the man had stopped off at a small store on the way. When he emerged carrying two bags of groceries, Vince caught him with a bullet as he went towards his car. He then bundled the dying man into his own vehicle, the goods scattered over the sidewalk. There had been a few people about, but they quickly disappeared. No one wanted to hang around when they saw a gun. The body had been put into the trunk of the car later, to await disposal, but Vince had one more appointment first.

Vince knew that target number two would be playing poker at a certain club this particular evening, because he himself had arranged the invitation, knowing the man in question was an inveterate gambler. When he left, in the early hours, the guy didn't know what hit him. The last thing he would remember was his name being called from the dark doorway next to the club entrance. Even now, Vince could see the look of surprise on the man's face as he saw the muzzle of the silencer on Vince's gun pointing at him.

He had half-carried his victim to the vehicle he was driving nearby, making out he was drunk to any passer-by. It had been so easy to put him in the passenger seat, his hat low over his eyes. In a side alley away from prying eyes, the body in the trunk had been heaved out and placed in the back seat near the door. Both had been pushed out in a quiet street in the early hours of the following morning. The car – stolen – had then been driven into the Hudson River.

Tony Anastasio would be pleased, Vince knew. He always showed his appreciation with a sizable bonus – and there would be more work in the future because Vince was reliable and knew how to keep his mouth shut. He wasn't one to brag about his deeds as some fools did. He'd heard them, trying to prove how tough they were, and he'd seen their demise. He didn't need to do that. Besides, the only person he wanted to impress was the top man himself, and he'd already done that or he wouldn't have been given this job. Things were on the up and up, and that was just how he liked it.

Lou Masters rushed into Gus Carter's office at the 52nd Precinct, waving a piece of paper. 'Good news!' he exclaimed. 'I lifted a cup Morelli had had his coffee in from the Market Diner the other day and the fingerprints match some we found at the warehouse on the docks.'

'I knew it,' snapped Gus. 'Anywhere else?'

Lou shook his head. 'No, Lieutenant.'

'It's not enough,' said Gus. 'All that tells us is that he was there. We need more evidence, this doesn't prove a thing.'

'Maybe, but it puts him at the scene of a crime. Do we still tail him?'

'Damned right. He'll slip up at some stage and I want to have someone behind him when he does.'

Gus sat back in his chair and scratched his balding pate. There had been rumblings that Vito Genovese, *capo* (boss) of one of the most powerful Mafia families, was getting greedy, which made Frank Costello and Albert Anastasia, heads of two of the five Mafia families, very jumpy. Things at La Cosa Nostra were generally edgy, especially as at this time, Costello was on trial for tax evasions.

Vince too had heard the rumours. Maybe this would be the moment for him to rise from his position. In times of need, his skills would be invaluable, he thought. After all, he'd made his bones (killing on instruction) a long time ago. He was the main man all right.

The more he thought about it, the more he wondered just how he could make himself indispensable to Tony Anastasio. The fact that Tony ran the Brooklyn and New York dockyards, among other things, would make his turf really attractive to Genovese, whom he suspected of wanting to be *capo di tutti cappi* – boss of all bosses. Power was what drove these men . . . and if he was honest, that was what he wanted too. He'd nose around quietly; maybe he'd come up with something, some vital clue as to what was going on. Something that would make his boss realise his true worth to the organisation. He'd start tonight.

Through nefarious dealings and careful questioning in the right quarters, Vince had discovered that although Vito Genovese was not beyond plotting to take over from the Anastasio brothers, this was not on his immediate agenda. However, one of his top men, Gene Bender, had ambitions to establish his own Mafia family, and it was he who was trying to muscle in on the brothers. Bender was already quietly recruiting his own band of soldiers. As yet, Genovese was unaware of this. Vince saw it as his big chance, but he had to make his plans carefully. Nothing was to be done in a hurry. He'd let Bender dig himself into a ditch so deep, that eventually he, Vince, could ride to the rescue and be a big hero. His future would be secure in the organisation. He would be a king among his peers.

Carried away with dreams of the good life, he drove to the Waldorf Astoria Hotel barbershop where he knew that Frank Costello did all his business, wanting to get the feel of being top dog.

He lay back in the chair and let the barber shave him, a manicurist do his nails and then he had his hair cut. As he was shown the finished result in the mirror, he smiled to himself. This all felt so good. He over-tipped the staff and left.

Vince wasn't the only one to discover the ambitious plotting of Bender. Gus Carter, through a reliable inform-ant, also knew, and Bender was under constant surveillance by members of Carter's team. In the squad room, Gus held a meeting to gather the latest reports and to plan their strategy.

'It's now quite obvious, based on information received, as to what's going on,' said Gus, standing facing his men. 'What we have to do is find out which of the brothers he's going to hit first.' He scratched the top of his head. 'For my money the guy's putting a noose around his own neck – unless he plans to take them both out together.'

'But then he's going to have Genovese after him, surely?' said Lou. 'It doesn't make sense. He's not powerful enough to stand against Vito.'

Gus stood ruminating over things, then said, 'Maybe he's trying to be smart, paving the way for *his* boss to take over, then expecting to be given a family of his own, as a reward.'

'Jesus! He's taking a lot for granted. And what the hell is Morelli doing, hanging around all of a sudden?'

'I wish I knew,' muttered Gus. 'Unless Tony Anastasio has heard something and Morelli's watching out for him.'

'Shall we pull him in for questioning?' someone asked.

'About what?' shrugged Gus. 'The guy hasn't broken any laws. We'll just have to wait and see what happens. But I don't like it one bit.'

When the *Queen Mary* docked in New York, Vince was one of the first up the gangway. He was heading for B deck to see Gemma. She was rushed off her feet seeing to her departing passengers, and when Vince said, 'Honey, I want to talk to you,' she told him he'd have to come back later.

Gemma was feeling frustrated. She'd hoped to see Nick during the trip, but when the inspection party passed through, he was not among the officers. She was wondering if he would be seeing her in New York after their amorous encounter in Southampton, but as yet she'd heard nothing. A couple of hours later when her arms were full of dirty linen, Gwen came along to see her.

'You'll never guess who I've just seen leaving the ship,' she said.

'Who?' asked Gemma.

'Remember that glamorous blonde with the divine Nick Weston we saw that night when we were window shopping upstairs?'

Gemma felt her heart sink.

'I've just seen them going off the ship together! What do

221

you know? I thought she was a married woman, but that doesn't seem to make any difference; he had his arm around her and he gave her one of his smouldering looks. I wish a man would look at me like that,' Gwen said as she departed.

Gemma felt sick. Never before had she allowed any man such intimacy as she had Nick Weston. At the time it had seemed right, but now she wasn't so sure. Was this woman Nick's ex-fiancée? The woman seemed to fit the description Sally had given her and she had been on board last trip. Perhaps she wasn't married as Gwen thought; maybe she and Nick were getting back together again. If so, why had he invited her out? It was quite obvious now that he wouldn't be seeing her in New York. Gemma was swamped in misery.

She was sitting alone in the pantry, drinking a cup of coffee when Vince returned. He bounded in but took one look at her face and said, 'Whatever is wrong? You had bad news from home or something, honey?'

She took a deep breath and forced a smile. 'No, I'm just tired.'

He put a comforting arm around her shoulders and said, 'Why don't you let me take you out this evening? We'll have a couple of drinks, a meal somewhere. Come on, what do you say?'

Had he been behaving in his usual brash manner, she would have dismissed him, but he was being quiet and gentle, as if he really cared, and before she could think twice about his offer, she heard herself say, 'I'd like that, Vince. Thanks.'

His expression of delight made her pleased she'd said

yes. It wouldn't do any harm and it would be better than spending an evening alone, wondering what Nick was up to with the glamorous Mrs Van Housen.

Charlie arrived as Vince was leaving. When he heard him say he would meet Gemma on the docks at seven-thirty, he frowned and when they were alone he looked at her and said, 'Did I hear right? Are you really meeting Vince this evening?'

'Yes,' she said with a note of defiance. 'He's taking me out to dinner.'

With a look of concern, Charlie said, 'It's none of my business, but you should be very careful. These longshoremen are a pretty tough lot and into a lot of dodgy deals. Are you sure you know what you're letting yourself in for?'

'I'm just going out for a meal, Charlie. That's all. That's pretty harmless.'

He didn't say any more, but she could see he wasn't very happy about it.

Gemma went ashore alone that afternoon, and caught the bus to the city centre. She wandered around the shops making her purchases without any real enthusiasm, stopping off here and there for a coffee or a sandwich. It was easy to be anonymous in a big city and she was grateful she didn't have to make conversation with anyone, other than shop assistants.

She decided to wear the same outfit that evening as she'd worn when Nick had taken her out. She didn't want to go to the expense of buying another.

At the allotted time she walked along the dockside and saw Vince leaning against the bonnet of his shiny red sports car, waiting. He was wearing a smart lightweight beige suit, cream shirt and tie and highly polished shoes. With his dark hair neatly combed and his tanned features smiling at her as she approached, she had to admit that in his own way, Vince was just as handsome as Nick. He let out a whistle of appreciation.

'Wow! You look sensational.' He held her by the shoulders and kissed her lightly on the mouth. He opened the door to the passenger seat and helped her into the vehicle.

'You look very smooth yourself,' she said.

'I don't always look a bum,' he replied, grinning at her as he started the car.

It was pleasant driving in the open-topped automobile in the autumn evening, with the breeze blowing through her hair, and Gemma felt a sudden sense of elation. But she could scarcely believe it when he drove up and parked outside the famous Copacabana nightclub. He helped her from the car, then threw the keys to a waiting doorman. 'Don't scratch the paintwork,' he warned him.

Inside, they were shown to their table where Vince ordered champagne, then studied the dinner menu. During the sumptuous meal, to Gemma's astonishment, Nat King Cole appeared as the cabaret. He bowed to the audience, sat at the piano and sang all his popular songs, finishing with one of her favourites, 'When I Fall in Love'. She was thrilled and enthralled.

Vince looked at her and said, 'You look happier now than when I saw you on board.'

'Oh Vince, how could I not be happy? Here at the Copa, with Nat King Cole singing. Thank you for bringing me here.'

Across the table he took her hand gently in his. 'You

could have come here a lot sooner if you hadn't stood me up.' He was overcome with the freshness and innocence of the beautiful young woman sitting opposite him. The women he usually dated were so crude in comparison. Out for a good time, not too intelligent and certainly not unspoilt, like this girl. She was genuinely thrilled to be here and it made him feel like a hero.

He bought her a corsage of orchids from a girl selling them in the club. 'I just wish the *Queen Mary* stayed longer in port. There is so much of the city I could show you. We'd have such a great time together.'

The small band started to play and he led her on to the dance floor. She was surprised to discover he was an accomplished dancer. 'I think we should wait to have children,' he said.

'What!'

He grinned at her. 'When we're married, I mean.'

She looked at him in surprise. She hadn't expected him to continue with this pretence, but seeing the amusement reflected in his eyes, she said, 'Why is that?'

'We should have some time together first. Really get to know one another. I want you to understand my way of life.'

'How do you live?' She was suddenly curious. 'What do you do in your spare time?'

He chuckled softly. 'I'm pretty busy, I have a few deals going. I'm going to make it big, honey. You stick with me and you'll see.'

'I don't understand. How are you going to make it big?'

He winked at her. 'You'd be bored if I told you, but believe me, I'm heading for the top.'

As they sat chatting and drinking coffee, a man walked over to their table. Vince immediately jumped to his feet.

'I see you still manage to pick up all the good-looking broads,' the stranger said.

Gemma looked up at him. The man was wearing evening dress. He smiled at her but she noticed the smile didn't reach his eyes. She felt a cold chill run down her back.

'Gemma, this is my boss, Tony Anastasio.'

'How do you do,' she said.

He raised an eyebrow. 'A limey, and classy with it.' He shook her hand firmly then walked back over to his table. Gemma saw three men standing waiting. They all sat down when the man joined him. He sent liqueurs over to them and as Gemma looked across when the drinks arrived, he nodded in her direction. There was something ruthless about him, she felt, but she didn't know why.

'Now *that* is a powerful man,' Vince told her. 'One day I'll be like him.'

Gemma hoped not. There was a warmth about Vince, for all his brashness, but Tony Anastasio was a very cold fish.

Eventually it was time to head back to the ship. The doorman went for the car and Vince gave him a five-dollar bill.

'Thank you, sir. The paintwork is still just fine,' he said.

When they arrived back at pier 90, Vince got out of the car and assisted Gemma from her seat. He held her in his arms and said, 'That was the nicest evening of my entire life,' then he leaned forward and kissed her on the mouth.

As she felt Vince's mouth on hers, Gemma thought guiltily of Nick. It was his arms she wanted to feel around her, not this stranger's, but Nick wasn't available, perhaps would never be again. Vince's kiss was strangely gentle, not demanding, but lingering and Gemma kissed him back. After all, he had given her a wonderful night out, he'd treated her with respect and she'd enjoyed his company. 'Thank you for a lovely evening,' she said sincerely.

He kissed her forehead and held her close. 'I'll come on board before you sail,' he promised. 'Will you be all right now to get back to your cabin?'

She assured him that she would, at which he kissed her again. As he did so, Gus drew up in his car. He got out of one side and Nick Weston got out of the other. They both stared at the couple nearby, locked in a warm embrace.

'Well, I'm damned!' exclaimed Nick.

'What is it?' asked Gus, watching Vince Morelli for his own reasons.

'That girl there, Gemma Barrett – I've been seeing her. What the hell is she doing with *him*?'

'That's what I'd like to know, too,' muttered Gus as Vince climbed into his car and drove away.

As the red automobile disappeared out of sight, Gus stood chatting to Nick who only vaguely heard what he said. He'd been distracted and shaken by the sight of Gemma in another man's arms. What sort of game was she playing? He watched her as she walked up the gangway, unaware of his presence. He wanted to run to her and demand an explanation, but Gus was rambling on.

Nick couldn't help but compare Gemma with Greta Van Housen. Greta with her sophistication, elegance and wonderful self-confidence, and Gemma . . . unspoiled, amusing and, he had thought, innocent in a beguiling sort of way. However, after seeing her tonight, he wondered if she really was the same girl he had pictured in his mind. Turning to Gus, he made his excuses and returned to his cabin.

Chapter Twenty

When Gemma entered her cabin, she was grateful that Sally wasn't around as she didn't feel like company. Although she'd enjoyed herself this evening, she was deeply unsettled. After feeling so very close to Nick when they were together in his hotel room in Southampton, she really thought there was something special between them and that he felt the same way . . . but now she didn't know what to believe. With his devastating good looks, women probably flocked around him. Was she just a little amusement until some older, more sophisticated female came along? Was she being, after all, very naïve? Nick Weston attracted her like no other man. When he held her in his arms and kissed her, she was lost. She knew that if he'd asked to make love to her in his hotel room, she would have denied him nothing. With a deep sigh, she climbed into her bunk and tried to sleep.

In his cabin, Nick was still seething. When he had seen Gemma in the arms of that longshoreman, he had wanted to drag her away and thump the Yank! He wearily rubbed his eyes. What was happening to him? A woman on a permanent basis was not part of his plan – well, not for a while yet. When he first met Gemma, she was a pleasant distraction, but as he grew to know her a little more, she somehow got under his skin. He loved the way her blue eyes shone when she was happy and flashed when she was angry. He enjoyed her quirky sense of humour; when you were with her, you were never quite certain what she would say or do. Her unpredictability made her interesting. She had also got under his skin in other ways. When they were together in his hotel room in Southampton, he had wanted to make love to her so much, the ache in his loins had been almost unbearable.

It worried him that she had been in the company of the American. No doubt he had a certain charm, but who was to know what his background was? Nick remembered going into the dockside bar with Gus and Lou, seeing all the longshoremen with criminal records. He frowned. He would ask Gus to look into this Vince character, for Gemma's sake.

The following morning, just before embarkation, Vince breezed into the pantry on B deck in time to catch Charlie and Gemma drinking a welcome cup of coffee, before their passengers arrived.

'Hi, Charlie. How's things?'

'Fine, and you?'

Vince put an arm around Gemma's shoulders. 'I'm the luckiest man on God's earth. This beautiful creature allowed me to take her out to dinner last night.'

'I trust you took good care of her?'

There was just a note of terseness in his tone and Vince

shot a sideways glance at him. 'Of course I did. In fact, if you can spare her for half an hour, I'd like to take her across to the diner now for a coffee and a chat.'

Charlie looked at Gemma. 'Embarkation doesn't start for half an hour, it's up to you.'

'I won't be long then,' she said, ignoring the look of concern on her colleague's face.

As they walked along the working alleyway towards the crew gangway, Gemma saw Jock MacTaggart standing talking to another man. He gave her a baleful look and she stiffened. Vince, who was holding her arm, felt her tension and followed her gaze. 'What's the matter, honey?'

'It's that electrician,' she said in a low voice. 'I had a run-in with him when I worked for my uncle at the Seaman's Mission in Southampton. I'm not exactly his favourite person.'

Vince turned and looked over his shoulder, and saw they were being watched closely by the man. 'What's his name?'

'Jock MacTaggart – why?'

He shrugged. 'No reason. Has he given you any trouble?'

'Not yet.'

'What do you mean, not yet? Are you scared of him?'

She nodded. 'He saw me on deck one evening and told me how easy it would be for someone to fall overboard.' Glancing at Vince she was startled to see how angry he looked. 'It's nothing to worry about, Vince. He just likes to put the fear of God in people.'

'Anyone gives you trouble like that, you let me know. I'll soon sort them out.'

Although he was half-smiling, the ice-cold look in his eyes reminded her of Tony Anastasio. He'd worn the same expression, and just for a moment Gemma felt uneasy.

The café side of the market diner was buzzing with customers and the short-order cook was besieged by calls from the waitresses. 'Two eggs on a raft, sunny side up,' called one. Gemma knew that meant two fried eggs on toast, yolk side up. The food was good and the service quick.

The two of them sat over toast and coffee, chatting. Vince gazed into her eyes. 'You are so beautiful,' he said. 'I could sit and look at you all day.'

'That would be a waste of time for such an ambitious man,' she quipped, embarrassed by his compliment.

'Ambitious I certainly am.' He caught hold of her hand and held it to his lips. 'I told you I'm going right to the top.'

'You are already a gang boss, what's the next step up from there?'

'What I have in mind will take me off the docks. One day we'll live in a big apartment on Park Avenue, and maybe a place on Long Island.'

'What do you mean, we?'

He grinned at her broadly. 'Gemma, honey, are you forgetting already we are to be married?'

'Vince, for goodness sake behave,' she laughed. 'Someone might hear you. That's how rumours get started.'

He stared into her eyes and said softly, 'Would it be such a bad idea? Wouldn't you like to come to New York to live with me? Be Mrs Vince Morelli?'

For a moment all she felt was panic.

As if sensing he'd gone too far, he chuckled. 'Gee, honey, don't look so scared. A guy can dream, can't he?'

She felt immense relief. A joke was one thing, reality another. She'd never for one moment taken him seriously and for a second the intensity of his gaze and the serious tone of his voice had scared her. His flirting made her feel good, and he was great company. He also had a certain charisma about him that was totally American and fascinating, but marriage was definitely out of the question. As he didn't make more comments in that vein, she relaxed and finished her coffee – unaware that their every movement was being monitored by one of Gus Carter's men, sitting at a table behind them.

Vince looked at his watch. 'We'd better go or Charlie will be after me, and I have to get my men together.'

As they walked back along the dockside, Vince insisted on buying her an extravagant bunch of yellow roses. 'To remind you of me, until you hit the Big Apple again,' he said. At the bottom of the gangway he bade her goodbye with a lingering kiss. 'You take care,' he said. 'I'll come on board as soon as you dock next time.'

'Are you sure you haven't a wife and kids tucked away somewhere?' she asked playfully.

He laughed loudly. 'Me? Christ no! I've been saving myself for someone like you, baby.' Still laughing, he walked off down the quay.

As he strolled along the dock, Vince smiled to himself. What a great girl Gemma was. He had enjoyed taking her out, showing her the bright lights, treating her right. It made a pleasant change to be in the company of a lady. He thought of their conversation in the diner. He hadn't meant to be serious about marriage, but as he was talking, he had kind of grown to like the idea. He knew he'd spooked her. The look of panic in her beautiful blue eyes stopped him. But he would think about it. Marriage hadn't been on his agenda at all, he'd been teasing Gemma when he'd mentioned it before, but now, if things were going well for him in the organisation, it would be just great to have someone to share his good fortune with. Jeez! He must be going soft! But the idea still had a certain appeal.

He rounded up his men and got them started on the stowing of the baggage. Work was always frantic when a ship docked or sailed and he prided himself on being efficient.

Pier 90 was busy. The passengers were arriving, cargo was being loaded in the hold. Baggage was being shipped on board along moving conveyor belts. Ship's stores were taken on board, stewards rushed around in their white coats, the magazine stand was doing a fast trade, as much from the members of the crew as the passengers. The crew were buying American candy bars and comics to take home to their kids.

Eventually the time came for the mighty liner to sail. The gangways were taken away and the roar from the *Queen Mary's* funnels heralded her departure. Gold-braided uniformed figures peered over the side of the docking bridge, shouting orders. Hawsers were let loose by the longshoremen. As the tugs got to work, Vince stood and watched the *Queen Mary* slowly move away from the quayside.

Behind Vince, but way back, stood Gus Carter. His man had reported the trip to the diner by Vince and a young stewardess. Vince Morelli didn't have a police record, he'd checked, but he had a gut feeling about this young man. He would be watching him even more closely now that his cousin Nick's girl was involved.

On the other side of the Atlantic, in a police station at Southampton's Civic Centre, Eve Barrett had spent a night in the cells. This morning she was being charged with being drunk and disorderly. She sat on a wooden bench feeling deeply ashamed. Her head was pounding and she needed a wash. Her mouth felt like the bottom of a birdcage.

The sound of the cell door being unlocked made her look up. A police sergeant whom she'd known since he was a constable on the beat entered, carrying a tray with a cup of tea and some buttered toast. He placed it beside her, then to her surprise, he sat down.

'It breaks my heart to see you in this state, Eve, it really does.'

She couldn't answer him, she was so humiliated.

He leaned back against the brick wall. 'You know,' he said, 'I remember you years ago, on the stage of the Empire Theatre, sitting in a mocked-up aeroplane, wearing a flying jacket and a leather helmet, dressed as Amy Johnson, and I thought you were the most beautiful girl I'd ever seen.'

Tears filled her eyes as she looked at him.

He pushed a tendril of her hair away from her face. 'You still have what it takes, you know, if only you'd pull yourself together. When you leave court this morning, I want you to go home and sort yourself out. I don't *ever* want to see you in here again.' He handed her a card. 'Here. This is the address of the local Alcoholics Anonymous.' He saw the horror reflected in her eyes and added, 'You need help, my dear. Do yourself and me a favour – and go.' He rose from his seat and left her alone, locking the door behind him.

Wiping away the tears that spilled down her cheeks, Eve held the cup to her lips with difficulty as her hands were shaking, and sipped the hot liquid. Someone still remembered her. Someone could see in her the woman that she wanted to be. She looked down at the card. Maybe he was right . . . she did need help. She needed something to stop this downhill spiral. She only vaguely remembered the events of the previous night. She'd made a round of the pubs, and at closing time she must have tried to stagger home. She remembered falling off the pavement and landing in a gutter. When a police constable had helped her to her feet, she'd struck out at him. God! What a mess. Jack had told her she would end this way. She emptied her cup. Well, the only place from here was up. She couldn't sink any lower.

In court, later that morning, the magistrate fined her. She asked for time to pay; to her relief it was granted. When finally released, she walked home, her head bent low, filled with shame that she now had a police record. How could she aspire to emulate the Duchess of Windsor now? She had used the similarity between them to feed her ego. To look so much like a famous figure had made her feel important and she loved it when people looked at her, remarking on the likeness.

As she made her way home, Eve asked herself why she should try to be like someone else anyway? She would be her own woman. She had to get her life organised or go under. If her jailer could still see some kind of attraction about her, even in the state she was in, there was sufficient reason to try. She took a deep breath. If she was going to do that, she would do it as Eve Barrett, not as Wallis Simpson!

Eve hadn't had a drink for twenty-four hours, and she was suffering. She had tried to make an effort after her overnight incarceration. She'd had a bath, washed her hair, and with a pair of dressmaking scissors, had cut it shorter. It looked a mess! As she gazed at her reflection in the mirror, she could have wept. Apart from her hair, her skin was pallid and the laughter lines around her eyes had deepened. Huh! Laughter lines, she thought. There had been very little to laugh about since the day Jack had walked out on her.

She made her way downstairs to put the kettle on for yet another pot of tea when her taste buds were crying out for a drop of gin. From the mantelpiece she took down the card the police sergeant had given her and looked at the address. There was an afternoon meeting that very day. Should she go? *Could* she go? Once you stepped through those doors, everyone would know your secret. With a wry smile Eve acknowledged that her addiction couldn't possibly be a secret any longer. Too many people would have seen her staggering home from the pub night after night. Who was she kidding!

She made herself a piece of dry toast – her stomach turned if she thought of anything else – dressed, applied her make-up and brushed her ill-cut hair vigorously. Then, straightening her back, she stepped out into the street and made her way to the meeting.

She stood across the road from the small church hall and watched the various figures enter. There were more men than women, she noted, but they seemed to come from all walks of life. They were certainly not the dregs of the earth, which was what she had expected. Eventually, taking a deep breath, she crossed the road and entered the hall.

Eve sat in the back row of the chairs that had been laid out, trying to look inconspicuous. One man took the meeting, facing his audience, standing behind a lectern. He looked a decent type, dressed in a suit and tie. He was well spoken and Eve was surprised when he eventually gave his name and declared, 'I am an alcoholic. I have been dry for ten years.' He opened the meeting, welcomed any new-comers and he invited anyone who wished to do so, to speak. Then he sat down.

Filled with horror that she might have to talk to a room full of strangers, Eve looked down at her tightly clasped hands, staring at the knuckles, which were white from the strength of her grip. She heard a man's voice and looked up.

'My name is Bert, and I am an alcoholic. I haven't had a drink for two weeks.'

There was applause and remarks like, 'Well done. Good on you, mate.' Then another stood. He hadn't had a drink for three months. Loud shouts of encouragement. Then a woman rose to her feet. She looked shabby in an old grimy jacket, she was in dire need of a bath, and her hair was dishevelled. 'I haven't had a drink for ten hours,' she said pitifully. The speaker walked over to her and took her arm. 'Well done, Nelly,' he said. 'You'll make it, I know you will.'

Eve looked at the woman and almost cried. Is that how she would look if she didn't beat this addiction? She gazed at the pathetic creature and tried in vain to picture her as she might have been before . . .

Suddenly, Eve couldn't stand it in there a minute longer. She rose quickly from her seat and fled. Once outside, she took a packet of cigarettes from her handbag and tried to light one, but her hands were shaking too much.

Beside her, a man's voice said quietly, 'Here. Let me help you.' The stranger steadied her hand and held a match to her cigarette. She drew deeply on it.

'Your first time, is it?' he asked.

'Yes,' she said, feeling nauseous.

'Scares the hell out of you, doesn't it?'

She was surprised at his understanding and looked at him properly. He was a few years older than her, with dark brown hair, thinning on top and flecked with silver at the sides. He was dressed in a pair of decent trousers with a smart, if slightly worn, sports jacket. But what impressed her was the kindness which shone from his grey eyes.

'How did you know how I felt?' she asked.

'Because I felt just the same my first time.'

Her eyes widened. 'You are an . . .' She couldn't bring herself to say it.

'An alcoholic? Yes, I am.'

'How long . . .?'

'Five years.'

'You haven't had a drink for five years?' She could hardly believe it.

He gave a chuckle. 'I fell off the wagon a couple of times,' he explained, 'but I've been dry for four years now.'

'And you still come?'

His smile was sweet. 'Oh yes. Every week when I can and sometimes more, if I feel the need.'

Eve closed her eyes to hide her despondency. God, after five years he still needed help. What chance did she have then? Did she have the will to survive without a drink? She doubted it.

He placed a hand gently on her arm. As she opened her eyes he said, 'Why don't we go and have a cup of tea somewhere? You look as if you need a drink.'

She burst out laughing at the incongruity of his remark. 'Tea?'

A wide grin spread across his features. 'Definitely tea.'

'I've drunk so many cups today, I'll probably drown if I have another,' she said.

'Then it will have to be coffee. Come on.'

She felt herself being led towards a small café along the road. The stranger seated her at a table in a corner and returned with two cups of coffee. He sat opposite her and said, 'My name is Daniel. Danny. Danny Hooper.'

'Eve. Eve Barrett.'

He pushed the sugar bowl towards her. 'Here. It's good for shock.'

'It shows that much, does it?'

'I'm afraid so, but it also shows you have courage, Eve. It takes guts to accept you have a problem, but it takes real courage to do something about it. Congratulations!' He held his cup up to salute her.

'Cheers!' she said with a cheeky grin.

It was the best afternoon that Eve could remember for a

very long time. She and Danny didn't stop talking. They took a walk together along the waterfront, strolled around the Royal Pier, played with the penny slot machines and sat in deck chairs, exchanging life stories. Danny had been a salesman, travelling the country, dealing in machinery. But staying alone in guesthouses had been his undoing, until eventually his marriage broke up.

'You see,' he explained, 'I started drinking out of loneliness, but when I came home to my wife, I couldn't stop. She got fed up with me in the end, and I don't blame her.'

'Where is she now?'

'Happily married to a man with no drinking problems. A veritable saint, according to her.'

'How very dull,' remarked Eve, which made him laugh.

She told him of her unfulfilled ambitions, her bitterness towards Jack. 'I suppose I too was lonely, with Jack being away so much. Then when he came home, I made his life hell.'

'Do you have any children?'

'A daughter, Gemma. She's a stewardess on the *Queen Mary*.'

'You must be very proud of her.'

Eve frowned. 'I suppose I should be . . .'

'But?'

She let out a deep sigh. 'I was a bitch to her too.'

He shook his head sadly. 'Unfortunately we can't turn back the clock.' He gazed intently at her. 'But we can have a better future.'

'Can we? Do you really believe that?'

'If I didn't, what's the point of going on?' he said.

'I'm not at all sure I've got the determination to carry it off, but I honestly don't like my life at the moment.'

'Then change it! No one can do it for you, Eve.'

They got up to go their respective ways.

Before they parted, he gave her a leaflet that listed all the AA meetings in the town. 'I'll be at the same one next week, but you may feel the need to go to another before then. A week is a long time without a drink to begin with.'

'Any tips on how to succeed?'

'Keep busy. Fill your time until you're so tired all you want to do is sleep.' He shook her hand. 'I'll look forward to seeing you next week. I've enjoyed talking to you, Eve. And good luck, because it won't be easy.'

'I'm sure it won't. And thanks.'

When she returned home, Eve changed into old clothes and set about cleaning the small house from top to bottom. She scrubbed the kitchen floor, threw out the empty bottles she found at the back of the cupboards she'd turned out. Cleaned the windows, stopping only to eat the contents of a tin of soup she'd bought on the way home. She turned out the two bedrooms, washed the curtains, changed her bedding, and eventually had a bath to remove her aches and pains, then she fell into bed, exhausted. As she lay in her clean sheets she thought of Daniel, of the people at the meeting. 'I am Eve Barrett,' she whispered. 'I am an alcoholic and I haven't had a drink for two days . . . But how I would enjoy one right at this moment,' she added as she turned over and tried to sleep. The last thing she remembered was seeing a vision of the old woman at the meeting, standing with her back to her, but when she turned, her face was Eve's.

Chapter Twenty-one

It was without any real enthusiasm that Gemma opened the front door of her mother's house, after the ship had eventually docked in Southampton. She was tired from the busy voyage and still feeling upset about the mystery woman in Nick's life. He hadn't been to see her during the voyage so she was no nearer solving her problem. And as he hadn't arranged a meeting between them in their home port, she could only believe that he had used her and that was the end of it all. She was both angry and unhappy. All she wanted was a bit of peace and quiet and this was probably the last place she would get it. Yet when she opened the door, she received an unexpected surprise.

Her mother, beautifully dressed, with a new, shorter hairstyle, and obviously sober, rose from her chair and came forward to greet her. 'Hello, Gemma, you look weary. I'll make you a cup of tea.' So saying, she walked into the scullery.

Gemma looked around the room. It was spotless. Every conceivable surface shone. The unfamiliar smell of furniture polish wafted in the air. The brass ornaments gleamed and on the sideboard was a small vase of flowers. For a moment it seemed as if she'd stepped into the wrong house. This was her home as it used to be before Eve took to the bottle. Since then she'd become careless about her house-keeping and the smell that usually invaded your nostrils when you entered had been of stale tobacco and alcohol. To this day, Gemma hated the smell of Booths gin. Even the atmosphere was different. There was not the usual tension, it all seemed very calm. She couldn't understand it, but nevertheless, she was grateful. Putting down her suit-case and carrying a box of groceries she'd bought over the threshold, she sat in one of the two easy chairs and kicked off her shoes.

Eve soon returned with a tray all set out with cups and saucers, a teapot and a plate of cakes. 'Did you have a good trip?' she asked.

Gemma was looking at her mother trying to make out what it was that was so different about her. Then she realised. Eve no longer emulated the Duchess of Windsor. It took some getting used to, this new creature. As long as she could remember, it had been like living with an image. Now it was gone. Instead, there was this new woman . . . almost a stranger to her.

'Well?'

'Well what?'

'Did you have a good trip?' Eve repeated.

'Oh. Oh yes, but it was very hectic. The passenger list was full . . . You look well,' she added.

'Different is what you mean, isn't it?'

'Certainly different,' agreed Gemma. She smiled as she studied her mother. 'It suits you. Is that a new dress?'

'No, I've had it for ages, but I never wore it. It wasn't my

244

style, I thought.' There was a note of uncertainty in Eve's voice as she asked, 'Do you think it looks all right?'

It looked just fine, Gemma thought. The dress was less severe in style than the ones Eve usually wore. It was emerald green, with a nipped-in waist and full skirt. 'It makes you look younger,' she said.

'Really? Not too young – not like mutton dressed as lamb?'

This unexpected vulnerability was even more strange, and rather touching. 'No, Mum. You look really nice.' And sober, she thought. It was almost too good to be true. What on earth had brought this about, she wondered. It made her very wary. What was Eve up to now? She could be so devious that you were never quite sure of her motives. 'Shouldn't you be at work?'

Casually Eve answered, 'No. I gave in my notice.'

'Why was that?' asked Gemma, who was by now completely mystified.

'I want to better myself, that's why.' At the look of surprise registered on her daughter's face she said defiantly, 'After all, Jack has gone off to live a new life, you've changed yours, and I don't see why I can't change mine.'

'I think it's a splendid idea,' was Gemma's enthusiastic reply. 'How are you going to do that?'

'I haven't quite made up my mind,' Eve said. 'It needs a lot of thinking about.' And this was true. She had originally planned to get a job as a barmaid in a hotel, but now she realised that a bar was the last place for her to be, and she wasn't at all sure what else she could do. What's more, she was still battling with her need for a drink. It was now five days since she had tasted alcohol, but the longing was still there, despite a visit to another meeting of AA. She was edgy and bad-tempered, and in her heart she knew that at the moment, she was incapable of holding down any job.

'Why don't we go out for a meal to celebrate this new you?' Gemma suggested.

Eve's eyes narrowed. 'Aren't you seeing anyone?' she asked. She heard the flat tone in Gemma's voice as she answered.

'No. I don't have any plans this evening, but I do need to have a bath and get changed first.'

'Take your time, I'm not going anywhere,' said Eve.

Later, the two of them left the house and made their way into the town centre. They chose a restaurant and settled at a table, studying the menu. When they had chosen from it Gemma asked, with some trepidation, 'Would you like some wine, Mother?'

Eve hesitated for a moment and then quickly said, 'No. I don't feel like it. Just a glass of water, please, but you have some if you like.'

Gemma decided against it, thinking if she had some, Eve might change her mind and she didn't relish the conse-quences. 'No, I'm too tired to drink,' she said and left it at that.

Eve looked at the Dover sole on her plate and wondered if she would be able to consume it. She was finding eating somewhat difficult these days. Her stomach turned at anything heavy. She gazed across at the steak on Gemma's plate and felt quite ill. She quickly averted her gaze.

The meal was a rather stilted affair as far as conversa-tion went. It had been a very long time since the two women had been in such close social proximity and they both felt under a strain. Gemma was too cautious to question her mother closely and Eve was not at ease with her daughter. She had been so filled with antagonism towards her over the years, that she found she was incapable of idle chit chat, so they didn't say a great deal. It was a relief to both of them when they finished their meal and left the restaurant.

'That was very nice,' said Eve, trying to make conversation as they walked home.

'I'm glad you enjoyed it. I'm also glad you've decided to take control of your life, Mum.'

Immediately on the defensive, Eve said, 'And what do you mean by that?'

'Just that you have so much to offer. You've still got your looks. You might meet some man who could make you happy.'

'That I don't bloody well need, thank you very much! Men are too selfish. I got rid of one, I certainly don't need another.' The bitterness she felt about being left by Jack hadn't diminished one bit, Eve realised as she spoke. But she knew she carried a great share of the blame for the breakdown of their marriage. She looked at her daughter. 'You're probably finding out a few home-truths about men yourself, working with them.'

Gemma cast an angry glance in her direction. Her mother's casual remark had hit a sore point, but she said nothing.

Before she went to bed that night, she gave her mother thirty pounds as she had done the trip before. This time, Eve didn't berate her but quietly said, 'Thanks. With my not working at the moment, this will be useful.'

'How do you fill your evenings now?' asked Gemma. 'Before you were working at night, so you might feel rather lonely.'

For Eve, the evenings were the worst time. It was then she really had to battle with her craving for alcohol. Once or twice she'd actually put her coat on to go to the pub, but she thought of Danny Hooper telling her it would be a difficult week and took it off, she didn't want to meet him again and have to tell him she'd failed miserably. 'I listen to the radio, and I try to read a bit.'

'You hate reading.'

'What else can I do?' snapped Eve. 'I don't always want to go to the pictures.'

There was a desperation in her voice that didn't escape Gemma's notice, and for a moment she seemed to tune into her mother's anguish.

'What if I rented you a television set from Redifusion before I join the ship in the morning?'

'A TV? Gracious!' Eve was startled by the idea, but she also looked pleased and interested.

'Well, it certainly would keep you company. It would fill the hours until you went to bed.'

'We don't have an aerial.'

'No, we don't, but I can get one set up. What do you say? Do you think you'd like one?'

'It would certainly be good entertainment.'

For the first time in years, Gemma had done something that had met with Eve's approval and it gave her great satisfaction. 'I'll see to it first thing. I'll get it installed tomorrow. Make sure you are at home.'

'I won't go out at all,' said Eve. 'Ooh – I can't believe it.'
She sounded really satisfied when she added, 'I'll be just
like Jack's sister, Freda. Snobby bitch. She was always
ramming it down my throat that they had a set.'

Gemma hid a smile. Eve hadn't altered, fundamentally,
after all. She made her way to bed, still bemused by the
changed atmosphere of her homecoming.

The following morning, she rushed out and visited
Redifusion, the local television rental shop and paid a
deposit then arranged for the set to be installed, complete
with aerial, that afternoon.

Eve looked delighted with the prospect. 'Will they show
me how to make it work?' she asked.

'Of course they will,' Gemma assured her. 'And if anything goes wrong, all you do is go to the call box and ring
them and they'll come and fix it. It won't cost a penny.' Her
mother looked thrilled but she hadn't changed that much;
she didn't enthuse vocally, Gemma noted. But then she
asked herself, what was she hoping for – a miracle?

As she made her way back to the ship, Gemma was
happier than she'd been for years in many respects. Eve had
made her life so grim at times, that moments like this were
to be cherished.

Once on board the *Queen Mary*, Gemma was as usual
rushed off her feet, except for the break, first thing, when
the Staff Captain inspected the assembled section of the
crew for a boat drill, checking they knew what the fire
alarm sounded like and the position of their boat stations
in case of emergencies. Nick Weston was with him, but he
never once glanced in her direction. Gemma's heart was

beating frantically as he came closer.

Nick walked along the line of female staff, stopping to see that their life-jackets were tied properly, then he stood in front of the stewardess next to Gemma and asked her if she knew how to work the fire extinguishers that were placed around the ship. Gemma held her breath and listened closely, for she had no idea how to operate one, thanking her lucky stars he hadn't asked her, for she would have felt a fool.

When they had been dismissed, she went back down to her section, stopping to read the instructions on one of the extinguishers, making sure that if she was ever asked, she would be able to give a confident answer. She'd felt very strange standing in a line with Nick doing his job. In uniform he was like a stranger, a million miles from the ardent lover who'd held her in his arms against his bare chest as he kissed her passionately.

Back in her section, she removed her life-jacket, stowing it in the pantry until she could slip away to her cabin.

'Pass muster, did you?' enquired Charlie.

She grimaced and told him how she had nearly been caught out.

'And what would you have said if he'd asked you this morning?'

'Well, it isn't something you can fake, is it, Charlie? I would have said, "I'm sorry, sir, I don't know but I'll make sure I find out as soon as we leave here, I promise"?'

Charlie smothered a smile. With her lovely face, bright blue eyes and cheeky manner, she might well have got away with it too. 'A lot of bloody good you'll be in a fire then.'

'You're wrong. Now I do know, so when you burst into flames, I'll be happy to put your fire out!'

'Listen, love, the last time I felt that hot was a great many years ago.'

She patted him on the face and said, 'You poor thing. It must be really sad to get that old.'

'You saucy young devil! The trouble with all you young 'uns is that you forget that one day you'll be old too.'

'Not me, Charlie boy. When I reach twenty-nine, I'll stay there. Then when I get to be a middle-aged twenty-nine, I'll lie back on a couch and have virile young men peel me grapes and wipe my fevered brow.'

'Yeah, I know, tell you how beautiful you are.'

'That's right. And at night I'll count my money because I'll have married an old millionaire who will have died happily in my arms and left me all his cash.'

'I can see you haven't grown out of fairy stories anyway.'

Gemma said wryly, 'Well, it's better than real life, you must admit.'

That evening, after the night steward had taken over their sections, Gemma, at Sally's invitation, walked around the boat deck to get some fresh air.

'Haven't you got any plans for this evening?' asked Gemma as they stood at the ship's rail, looking out over the ocean.

'Well, not for this evening anyway,' said Sally with a sly grin, 'but I'm working on it.'

'What do you mean?'

'The other evening I went to look at the kennels and who should be there but the glorious Nick Weston.'

'Really? And how was he?' asked Gemma, filled with curiosity.

Sally turned and leaned back against the rail, stretching her long slim body like a cat. 'He was just delicious.' She glanced at Gemma beneath her long eyelashes. 'It's really very private up there, you see. Tucked away nicely. Realising you can't be observed removes any inhibitions, if you know what I mean.' She turned back towards the sea.

Gemma's heart sank.

So now Nick was playing around with Sally, too. Sally, who would be only too eager, she felt, to please any man who took her fancy. Well, now she was under no illusion at all. With all his charm and education he was no different from all the other men who just wanted a good time. She felt tears prick her eyes and was angry with herself. No man was worth the salt in a woman's tears . . . so why did she feel so very wretched?

The two girls walked on in quiet contemplation, lost in their own thoughts. It was peaceful on deck with a slight breeze on the air. Jack, her father, came into Gemma's mind and she wondered how he was. She'd written to him from New York after much consideration. After all, as her uncle had said, he was her own flesh and blood and she felt she understood a little more about him, since she had been at sea. For both of them it seemed, it had eventually been an escape from Eve. But more than that, she could understand the hold the sea could have on a person. Once she stepped on board, she was in a different world, one she loved. One that gave her satisfaction and pleasure – except for her love life! The fact that the work was hard, the passengers demanding and the hours long – none of that was of any consequence. But to walk the decks of this magnificent liner in the moonlight, to feel the swell of the ocean beneath her was a wondrous feeling. She now fully understood why Jack had been unable to give up his way of life for any woman.

She was still bemused at the change in her mother, but couldn't bring herself to trust her, and wondered what she would find on her return next time.

Chapter Twenty-two

The *Queen Mary* was lying quietly at anchor on pier 90 in New York after docking that morning. It was now late afternoon and Jock MacTaggart downed the last of his beer in the bar of the market diner, ready to make his way back to the ship. Just then, he noticed Gemma go into the cafeteria side of the diner and order something to take out. He lingered in the doorway of the bar until she emerged, clutching a brown paper bag containing her purchases. He'd had enough beer in his belly to make him belligerent, and the sight of the young whipper-snapper who to his mind had put him in the cells for the night in Southampton, enraged him. He followed her, a little unsteadily, back to the ship, keeping his distance so as not to alert her to his presence.

Gemma had been shopping and was tired. She'd not seen or heard from Nick, and Vince had been on board for just a second when they docked to say he'd return to make arrangements for them to go out that evening, but he hadn't been back to see her as yet and she was in a quandary. They were supposed to be meeting, but when? She didn't really want to go out. The heat today had been intense and the humidity even worse. Every time she emerged from an air-conditioned store, the humidity seemed to wrap itself around her like a damp blanket and drain her of all energy. She would be content to eat her sandwiches, have a shower and stay quietly on board, reading, recharging her batteries for the return trip.

She half-shut the door, leaving it on the hook to let a little air in and started to unpack her shopping. She heard footsteps but thought nothing of it, assuming they belonged to one of the other girls returning to their cabin after shopping as she had just done. She was therefore stunned when the door to her cabin was kicked open, breaking the slender hook which held it. Framed in the doorway, swaying on his feet, was Jock MacTaggart . . . and her mouth dried with fear as she saw the expression in his eyes.

'I warned you to keep looking over your shoulder,' he said menacingly. 'I told you one day I'd catch up with you.' He leered at her when he saw the scared expression on her face.

Gemma recovered quickly from the shock and bravely faced him. 'What the hell do you think you're doing in the female quarters? You're not allowed in here. Now get out!'

He chuckled. 'Oh, feisty little thing, aren't you? No, lassie, I'm not going anywhere until I pay you back for getting me locked up.'

She moved back to try and get away from him, but the cabin was narrow and she felt the edge of the bunks trapping her.

Jock stepped inside the door.

'Don't be so bloody stupid,' she snapped at him, trying

to keep control of her fear. 'If anyone finds you here, you'll be out of a job. Go back to your cabin and I won't say anything. You've been drinking, you don't know what you're doing.'

He moved even closer. 'I know exactly what I'm doing. I've waited for this moment ever since I saw you when I fixed the light on your section.' He grabbed her by the wrist. 'By the time I've finished with you, you won't be able to work.' Then he lifted his fist and hit her.

Gemma screamed as she ducked. His blow landed on her shoulder. She cried out with pain, as she valiantly tried to defend herself and push him away. It was like trying to move a mountain with one hand.

He laughed at her efforts as he raised his fist again.

She yelled at him to stop.

Suddenly a figure bounded through the doorway and grabbed the Scot by the raised arm, twisting it viciously up his back until MacTaggart was the one to cry out. 'Let go, you're breaking my bloody arm!'

'Vince!' Jenny gasped with relief.

He didn't reply, but forced the electrician out of the cabin and into the alleyway. Producing a small revolver from the back of his belt, he pressed it against the Scot's temple.

Jock MacTaggart stared at Vince in terror.

'Now get moving or I'll blow your fucking brains out!' hissed Vince.

MacTaggart moved along. Vince replaced the gun and marched him away, muttering, 'Any mention of the weapon and it will be the last time you speak.'

Gemma collapsed on the day-bed, rubbing her sore

shoulder, shaking from head to foot. Tears filled her eyes as she realised just how close she had come to being seriously hurt. When Vince reappeared a few minutes later, she flung herself into his arms and sobbed.

'There, honey, everything is all right. That crazy man has gone. I promise you, he won't bother you again.'

At first she couldn't speak, then when at last she'd collected herself, she asked, 'Where is he?'

Vince told her he'd handed him over to the master-at-arms who was on duty at a nearby gangway.

'What will happen to him?'

'What the hell do you care! You're holding your shoulder. Here, let me look at it. I want to see if you need hospital treatment.'

'I'm fine,' she assured him but when he touched it, she winced with pain. 'I don't want to go to the ship's hospital and have to explain how I got this,' she pleaded. 'I've only recently joined the ship and I don't want any trouble. I might lose my job. The fewer people who know about this the better. What did you say to the master-at-arms?' she asked anxiously. 'You didn't tell him what had happened, did you?'

'No. I just said he'd been making a nuisance of himself, being drunk and out of control. I didn't want to get you involved without your say-so. I can take care of MacTaggart in my own way.'

'Whatever do you mean?'

'Forget it,' he said shortly. 'Just leave this with me. Now get yourself ready and I'll take you out for something to eat.'

Gemma shook her head. 'I don't think I could face it,' she said.

But Vince was adamant. 'The last thing you need, honey, is to sit here all evening, thinking over what's happened. We'll go somewhere quiet and I'll bring you back early.'

She made to argue but he pushed her protests aside. 'I'll give you half an hour. I've got some business to see to then I'll be back.' He left before she could say any more.

As it transpired, she was pleased he had been so insistent. When Vince had collected her, he first of all took her to a doctor he knew who examined her shoulder and said it was just badly bruised, but prescribed some painkillers, which they got at a pharmacist's. Then Vince took Gemma to a sedate restaurant on the east side of New York and made her eat. His brashness had gone and she found him to be a compassionate and understanding man, which was most unexpected and very endearing.

After they had eaten he drove her back to the ship and escorted her to her cabin, making sure she was safe. Sally wasn't there and Gemma invited him inside for a moment.

Vince gathered her into his arms and kissed her gently. 'You had a rough time today,' he said softly. 'Do you think you'll be able to work tomorrow?'

'I've got to,' she said.

'Then I'll come on board in the morning and make sure you're all right. I'll have a word with Charlie.'

'Don't tell him what happened,' she cried. 'If you do, it will become complicated. I'll have to report Jock MacTaggart.' She looked uncertain. 'At least during the trip he won't dare come anywhere near me.'

'I'll have a word with him before you sail,' said Vince. 'He won't bother you again, I promise.'

She looked uncertain. 'When he's had a few drinks, he goes mad.'

He cupped her face in his hands and kissed her. 'Trust me, Gemma. He won't bother you in the future.' He held her close, mindful of her injured shoulder and smoothed her soft curls. 'I'll see you tomorrow morning. Try and get a good night's sleep.'

The following morning, Gemma was in a lot of discomfort with her shoulder which was painful and stiff. Charlie saw immediately that something was wrong.

'What have you done to yourself?' he asked.

'I tripped over my shopping in the cabin and banged my shoulder.'

'Has the doctor seen it?'

'Yes. He said it was only bruised.' Well, she wasn't really lying. She *had* seen a doctor, not the one he was alluding to, but he wasn't to know that. I've got some painkillers,' she added.

He was most concerned. 'Now don't you try to pick up anything heavy, I'll do that.'

'Thanks, Charlie. I'll be careful. I'll be all right, honestly.'

'You're not the only one in the wars this trip,' he remarked as he pottered about the pantry.

She looked puzzled. 'What do you mean?'

'One of the electricians was badly beaten up late last night. They found him on the docks. He's in a bad way, in the ship's hospital. Apparently he's got broken ribs, a broken nose and a fractured collarbone.'

Gemma felt the blood drain from her and her stomach churned.

'You all right, girl? You've gone as white as a sheet.'

'Who was it, do you know?' she asked. But she already knew the answer.

'Yes, big Jock MacTaggart. Nasty piece of work at the best of times.'

'Does anyone know what happened to him?'

Charlie shook his head. 'No, but the *Mauritania* is in port too. You know how it is, there's often a punch-up between the crews from time to time. He probably upset one of them. Come on, love, we'd best be getting stuck in.'

As Gemma proceeded with her duties, she was uneasy and suspicious. Vince was behind this, she was sure. Didn't he tell her he'd make sure MacTaggart wouldn't trouble her again? She was shocked at the thought that Vince might have been responsible for causing such injuries, yet she found it hard to picture him using such violence; after all, yesterday he had been so gentle with her. And strangely, she felt pity for the Scot.

When Vince came searching for her later that morning, she stared at him for a moment. His expression was one of concern. He caught her gently by the arms. 'How are you today, sweetheart? I've been so worried about you. Did you manage to sleep?'

'Yes, I did. I took some painkillers. Vince, did you beat up Big Jock last night?'

He looked shocked at her suggestion. 'What are you talking about?'

'Charlie told me Jock's in the ship's hospital with various broken bones. They found him in a bad way last night.'

Vince held up his hands in surrender. 'That wasn't my doing, honey. I was certainly going to find him this morning and have a word with him, but I've been real busy.' He looked at her quizzically. 'After what he tried to do to you, I'd say he had it coming, wouldn't you?' At her hesitation he said, 'Don't tell me you feel sorry for the miserable bastard.'

She pulled a face. 'No, I don't. In fact if I'm truthful, I'm glad to know he's out of the way. But he's quite badly hurt, by all accounts.'

'And what sort of state would *you* be in now, if I hadn't happened on the scene?' Vince demanded. 'Ask yourself *that*, Gemma. It might have been you in that hospital bed, in a far worse state. So don't waste your sympathy on someone who doesn't deserve it!'

For a moment she was shaken by the anger in his tone, then she had to admit that he had a point. She didn't like to think of the consequences, had Vince not intervened when he did. 'You're right,' she whispered.

He kissed her cheek. 'You must learn to be a bit tougher if you want to get by in this world. OK, honey, I have to go now. I'll try and get back before you sail, but if I can't get away, you take care, you hear?'

She smiled softly. 'I will.'

'Come here,' he said, and took her into his arms. He kissed her longingly. 'I'll see you next trip,' he said and walked away. Seeing Charlie along the alleyway, hauling luggage out of the elevator, he stopped. 'Take care of my girl, Charlie,' he said. 'She's hurt her shoulder and isn't feeling too good.'

Putting down the baggage, Charlie said, 'Yes, so she told me.'

'She fell over going up the gangway. Anyway, keep an eye on her. I'll see you next trip.'

Charlie watched him walk away and frowned. Fell up the gangway, tripped over her shopping in the cabin . . . two different stories. What's going on, he wondered.

Vince returned to his gang on the dockside and continued working, barking out orders to the men. Jeez, women were strange creatures, he mused. How could Gemma feel any sympathy for the guy in hospital after what he had tried to do to her? He himself was totally satisfied. He'd passed the word to the right quarter, stipulating the victim was not to be killed, just hurt, but badly enough to put him out of action . . . and his orders had been carried out to the letter. He would have happily put a bullet in the guy's gut, but he had the sense to know this was one job he had to leave to others. He'd been in a club when it happened, with witnesses to prove it. He was no fool. Besides, he had other business to attend to. Bender was laying his plans very carefully and he was with him, all the way.

Gus Carter came on board and managed to see Nick for a few moments.

'Look,' said Gus. 'Have a word with your girlfriend, will you? Stop her seeing Vince Morelli, for goodness sake. He's mixed up with some seriously bad company and I don't want her involved. I've got enough to worry about as it is.'

Nick looked uncomfortable but he was also concerned. 'I haven't seen her and I'm not sure that I will in the near future.'

Gus glared at him. 'You like her, don't you?'

'Well, yes, since you ask.'

'Then put your damned injured pride away! She could be in danger if she continues to see him. Understand?'

'Yes, of course.'

'Then do it!' He left without another word, leaving Nick to work out how he was going to handle this delicate situation. He'd steered clear of Gemma, apart from seeing her on boat drill, ever since he'd spotted her kissing Vince on that last trip in New York. He'd been so angry he hadn't contacted her since. Now what the hell was he going to do? But he was called to the bridge as the ship prepared to sail before he had the chance to think of a solution.

Chapter Twenty-three

Eve Barrett dressed with extra care. She was off to the AA meeting where a week ago she had first encountered Danny Hooper, and she felt decidedly nervous. At the same time, she was pleased with herself. She had managed, eventually, to get through the week without taking one drop of spirits, but she had bought a couple of bottles of Guinness one night at the off-licence, and enjoyed them. However, she quickly realised that although she had told herself Guinness was good for you, it was just an excuse. It hadn't been easy. In fact, it had been painful. Her stomach and liver had been abused for so long, she had suffered, but at least she was able to pick up a cup of tea now without her hands shaking so much.

She made her way to the church hall and sat at the back as she had done before. She gazed around the room, but Danny was not there. When the meeting began and he still hadn't arrived, she felt suddenly deflated. She barely listened to the other members telling of their successes and failures. She did, however, realise that old Nelly wasn't in attendance and wondered if she had fallen by the wayside.

265

Looking around she was struck by the earnest expressions on everyone's face. How sad they all looked, she thought. At least with a drink inside you, you had a feeling of euphoria, for a time. She was restless. She didn't want to be here. Why the hell was she putting herself through this ordeal? Life was too short. I'm getting out of this place, she thought. But just as she was about to get to her feet, Danny slipped into the seat beside her with a muttered apology for his tardiness. She sat back and relaxed.

At the end of the meeting the speaker made an announcement. 'I'm sorry to tell you that Nelly passed away a few days ago. Let's have a minute's silence to remember her. She had such a struggle in life, but now at last, she's at peace.'

As the members stood together, heads bowed, Eve was filled with sadness as she recalled the woman and she wondered what had happened to her. She had this awful picture of poor Nelly curled up in a drunken stupor in some gutter, alone. She hoped this wasn't the case and that someone had been with her during her final hour. Everyone was silent as they left the building.

Danny took her by the arm. 'Tea?' he offered.

'That would be nice.'

They made their way to the same small café as before. As they sat sipping their hot drinks he said, 'I'm sorry I was late.'

'That's all right,' said Eve flippantly. 'It's not as if we were on a date or anything.'

'I got the feeling as I arrived that you were about to leave,' he said, gazing steadily at her.

She looked away. 'I was.'

'Why?'

Slowly she raised her head and looked at him and for once in her life she didn't want to lie. 'I was disappointed you weren't there and suddenly I wondered why I was. It all seemed so pointless. Everyone looked so bloody miserable I honestly didn't think it was worth the effort. I was off to the pub.'

'I'm glad that I arrived when I did then. What sort of a week have you had?' he asked.

'Awful. This has been the longest seven days of my life.'

'Did you have a drink?'

She nodded. 'A couple of bottles of Guinness. I didn't think you could call that drinking.'

'Mine was a bottle of Halls Wine or Wincarnis in the old days – a tonic, it said on the label, which seemed a good enough reason. But I soon found one bottle was not enough.' He sighed. 'An alcoholic can always find an excuse, Eve.'

Her mouth tightened. 'I'm not an alcoholic. I can give it up any time I want.'

'Can you?' he asked softly. 'Do you really think it's that easy?'

His tone was gentle, he wasn't being judgemental, she knew that. Eve shook her head. 'No, of course it isn't. It's just that I *hate* the word.'

'Alcoholism isn't a stigma, my dear. It's an illness. If you had broken your arm and it was in plaster, you wouldn't mind that, would you?'

'No, of course not.'

'If you were ill in bed with influenza, you wouldn't mind that either, would you?'

'I know what you're trying to say,' she said, 'but being a drunk is so undignified.'

He burst out laughing. 'You mean it doesn't fit your image.'

She grinned at him. 'Exactly.' Then she started to laugh too. 'Ridiculous, isn't it?'

'No,' he said. 'Just very feminine.'

After they had finished their tea, Danny suggested they might go to the pictures together. 'There's a good film on at the Forum,' he said. 'We could have a bite to eat after – if you would like to, that is.'

'I'd like that very much,' she said.

They enjoyed watching the film, *Genevieve*, and laughed at the antics of the stars trying to get from London to Brighton driving old cars of yesteryear, or 'the old crocks' race' as it was affectionately known. Eve particularly enjoyed the part in the film where Kay Kendall got drunk and played the trumpet in a nightclub, then passed out in front of everyone. She leaned towards Danny and whispered, 'So undignified!' She heard him chuckle.

They went to a small restaurant when the programme had finished, and ate. Danny was a good conversationalist and with him Eve was at ease. Here was a man she hardly knew, who knew about the worst side of her, yet treated her with kindness and respect. It was a nice feeling. One she hadn't had for a very long time.

Danny had a stillness about him somehow. A feeling of calm that seemed to rub off on her as they sat opposite each other and chatted. They talked of many things. The state of the country, the coronation of the young Queen

Elizabeth, earlier in June, the awful Christie murder trial – and how they would like to live the rest of their lives. Danny's needs were simple.

'I'd like a little house somewhere with a garden,' he told her. 'I quite fancy growing my own vegetables.'

She looked at him with surprise. 'Is that all?'

'Isn't it enough? I've had so many ups and downs in my life, Eve. I want to spend the rest of it peacefully . . . and dry. For years I've seen the world through an alcoholic haze. Now I can see the blue of the sky, the vibrant colours of the flowers in the parks. The hazel flecks in your green eyes. It's enough for me, is a life of peace.'

Eve had not changed that much. 'I still want to be someone.'

'You *are* someone. You are Eve Barrett, a good-looking woman with potential.'

She became irritated. 'What's the good of having potential if you don't use it?'

'The trouble is that so far you don't like who you are, whereas I'm content with being me.'

'Well, bully for you! So tell me what you've got to be so happy about? Do you do anything else but go to AA meetings?'

He laughed loudly. 'I work.'

'You do?' Eve was surprised.

'Of course I do. How do you think I survive financially?'

She shrugged. 'How should I know?'

'My brother and I have a small engineering works.'

'And this is how you spend your day off, is it? Consorting with drunks?'

He smiled at her. 'Oh dear, I can see that you are going to be a handful all right.'

She looked uncertainly at him. 'What do you mean?'

'I have this philosophy that people come into our lives for a reason. Now as far as you are concerned, I'm not sure if you have arrived for my benefit or the other way around. But I think it's going to be interesting finding out, don't you?'

Her eyes narrowed slightly as she gazed at him. No, he wasn't teasing her, he seemed serious. Did he imagine that they would continue to see each other? It certainly sounded that way, and that gave her hope, but she was still a little apprehensive.

'We'll have to wait and see, I suppose.'

Danny chuckled. 'You really have got to learn to trust people,' he chided. 'I'm not out to hurt you, only to hold out a helping hand – if you need it.'

'To stop me drinking, I suppose,' she grumbled.

'Good heavens, no. Only you can do that. But a bit of companionship can help along the way.'

'Mm,' was her only reply. She didn't understand this man at all.

On board the *Queen Mary*, Nick Weston was trying to think of a way of approaching Gemma about consorting with the American. He could hardly walk up to her and tell her to stop seeing him. Gemma was likely to tell him where to go! It was impossible to have a serious conversation with her until the ship docked in Southampton. It would be better if they met for a drink, but not at his hotel, somewhere else on mutual ground . . . but would she meet him if he asked? He was frustrated with the whole thing. Women! Why did they have to be so difficult?

The following morning he made his way to B deck and found Gemma alone in the pantry, washing up. He stood in the doorway and coughed. She looked round and her eyes widened with surprise when she saw him. 'Hello, Gemma,' he said softly. 'Look, I desperately need to talk to you. Would you meet me in the bar of the Dolphin Hotel at seven-thirty on docking day? Please. It's important.'

Gemma felt confused. Nick was the last person she had expected to see, and now he was asking to meet her. Well, she wasn't going to jump to his tune. 'I can't think you have anything to say to me that would be of any interest,' she said tartly.

Immediately his hackles rose. 'I have been asked to pass on some information to you and I promised I would do so. I suggest you meet me, Miss Barrett. It may have a bearing on your personal safety.'

There was something compelling about his tone of voice and she realised that this was no flippant invitation.

'Yes,' she said reluctantly. 'All right.'

'Good. I won't waste any more of your time. I'll see you in Southampton.'

As she listened to his retreating footsteps, Gemma poked her head around the door and watched the tall figure until he turned a corner and was out of sight. What was it about a uniform, she asked herself. She was always impressed when she saw Nick in his. He was a handsome man normally but his uniform seemed to add to his stature and presence. The sensuous mouth that had given her so much pleasure had been tightened in anger today and she couldn't imagine what he wanted to talk to her about that was so important. He hadn't been near her and she had thought she would only ever see him again when he was on duty . . . and now this! Well, she would know soon. Whatever it was, she at least would spend some time in his company, and she wanted that very much – which made her furious at her own weakness.

A little later, Charlie came rushing up to her and asked, 'Have you heard about one of your stewardesses?'

She frowned. 'Who?'

'I don't know her name, she works in the Tourist section.' He gave a knowing grin. 'She was caught last night coming out of the cabin of one of the catering officers, wearing only a raincoat and a pair of high-heeled shoes. Underneath she was as naked as the day she was born.'

'No! What about the catering officer?'

'He did at least have a towel around his middle. He's up before the Staff Captain this morning and so is the girl.'

'Bloody hell! What will happen to them?'

'He'll be reprimanded, probably fined and moved to a smaller ship most likely. She'll be off the ship when we dock and out of the company.'

'That hardly seems fair.'

'Oh, don't you worry, he won't get off scot free. He'll have to tell his wife.'

'He can always lie – men usually do. They get away with murder.'

'No, love, it won't work. If you are a member of any fleet, every misdemeanour is heard of eventually. Everywhere he goes, this little escapade will follow him. It will be the scandal of the month, and go on his record. Someone will be bound to tell his missus the truth at some time or other. He'll be better telling her himself . . . then the shit *will* hit the fan!'

'I don't envy them in front of Captain Matthews,' she muttered. 'He puts the fear of God in me when he's on inspection.'

'He's a tough bastard,' Charlie agreed. 'They'll know it too, when he's finished with them.'

'Who will run the girl's section?'

'She will, of course,' said Charlie. 'She's not going to be put in irons, for goodness sake, but come the end of the voyage she'll be packed off. They don't like their female staff becoming involved with married men.'

'I know,' said Gemma. 'The lady super made that very clear at my interview.' She started to put away the clean crockery in the wooden racks. 'I hope the girl in question thinks it was worth it.'

By now the ship was buzzing with the gossip and when Gemma returned to her cabin after she'd finished for the day, Sally was there, laid out on her bunk, smoking.

'I suppose you've heard about that girl,' she said.

'Yes I have, as a matter of fact.'

'Stupid idiot!' she exclaimed. 'Imagine getting caught like that.'

Gemma looked at Sally and said, 'You'd be more careful, I suppose.'

'Well, I haven't been caught yet, but then I haven't been foolish enough to go to the Bridge Officer's cabin.' She took her towel and toilet bag and went to the bathroom.

The Bridge Officer Sally was alluding to no doubt was Nick. She wondered just where they held their secret meetings and felt sick in the pit of her stomach.

When the ship docked in Southampton, Gemma made her way home. Eve was getting ready to go out and barely acknowledged her return. She just glanced at her daughter and said, 'I can't talk or I'll be late.'

'Late for what?'

'I'm going to the New Forest with a friend and I've got to meet him in half an hour.'

Gemma raised her eyebrows. 'Him?' she queried.

Defiantly Eve said, 'Yes, him. I'm going out with a man.'

'And who is this man?' Gemma asked with concern, in case he was like some of her mother's previous escorts.

Eve stopped brushing her hair. 'You're not my keeper, Gemma. I'm free to go out with whom I like – just as you are.'

'Of course. It's just that I'm worried in case he's not good enough for you.'

Eve's cheeks flushed angrily. 'We all make mistakes. You'll make a few in your lifetime, then perhaps you'll be a bit more understanding.' She walked to the alcove by the door and took down her jacket. 'I don't know what time I'll be home,' she said as she left.

Gemma sat at the table feeling like a small child who had been reprimanded. 'Welcome home, Gemma,' she said. 'Did you have a good trip?' She took a cigarette from her handbag and lit it. 'Oh well, you can't win 'em all,' she said. At least Eve was sober and that was something.

She looked at her watch. She had time for a sandwich and a cup of coffee before she got changed to meet Nick. She picked out a smart suit she'd bought in New York, with a mustard skirt and a boxy yellow white and mustard check jacket, which suited her blonde colouring and was very stylish. She wanted Nick to see her looking her best. She wanted to show him just what he was missing, but she was also feeling nervous.

Chapter Twenty-four

When she arrived at the Dolphin Hotel, Gemma walked into the cocktail bar and saw Nick sitting on a high stool at the counter, talking to the barman. He looked as immaculate as ever. He turned and she felt her heart beat that little bit faster.

'Gemma!' He rose from the stool and led her to a table and chairs at the side of the small room. 'What would you like to drink?'

'A gin and tonic would be nice, with ice and lemon, please.'

As he stood at the bar and waited, she admired his broad shoulders, looked longingly at the hair in the nape of his neck and fought the urge to get up and run her fingers through it. Oh Nick, she thought, what happened to us?

He carried the drinks over to the table, sat beside her and said, 'You look charming,' but he didn't smile.

Always the perfect gentleman, she thought, but although she felt he'd played with her affections, she couldn't deny the chemistry that had been between them. Yet where was it now? Now he seemed cold and distant. 'I'm so glad you agreed to come tonight,' he began, 'but to be honest I don't quite know how to say what I have to.'

That was completely out of character, she thought. Nick always seemed in control of every situation. It was a trait she had particularly admired in him.

'It's about that American, Vince.'

Immediately Gemma felt herself on the defensive. 'What about him?'

'I'm worried about you going out with him. He's not a very desirable person, you know.'

'How can you sit there and criticise someone of whom you know nothing!' she retorted.

'Gemma, please don't be angry. These are not my observations alone. Lieutenant Carter, my cousin in the New York Police, asked me to have a word with you. He's concerned for your safety if you continue to see this man . . . and so am I.'

She didn't believe him. He was using his association with the police to his own ends. But she would play along. 'What did he say, then?'

'He said that Vince was mixed up with a lot of unsavoury people and it would be most unwise of you to continue to see him.'

Gemma immediately thought of her meeting with Tony Anastasio.

Nick leaned forward and said, 'Gus and his partner took me into a dockside bar one day in New York, one that is frequented by the longshoremen. Most of them have crime sheets and they all look like criminals . . . and some of them work for gangsters.'

'Oh, for heaven's sake, Nick! You've been watching too many American movies. Besides, even if all you say *is* true, it doesn't follow that Vince is one of them.'

He looked furious. 'If it isn't true, why on earth do you think I've taken the time to see you?'

She thought he was jealous. It was all right for him to have his women but his pride was hurt, knowing she was seeing another man. 'I can't imagine. You have no interest in me whatsoever.'

'I am concerned for your safety, you little fool.'

'How very touching. Well, I can take care of myself, thank you.'

He leaned forward and gripped her wrist. 'I am being serious. This is no joke. Vince Morelli is bad news.'

She shook off his hold. 'You just object to me seeing him, that's all. Well, let me tell you, he's a perfect gentleman in every way. He has never taken advantage of me, like you did.'

His gaze was like ice. 'I assume you are referring to our meeting in my hotel room. I don't remember taking advantage of you, Gemma. I was under the impression you enjoyed every moment.'

'And I was under the impression that you were a gentleman.'

He leaned closer. 'Believe me I am, otherwise things would have gone much further, I can assure you.'

She flushed with anger and embarrassment. 'Perhaps you realised I was different from the other women you know.'

He raised his eyebrows and gave her a sardonic look. 'Oh, you are, my dear. Most definitely.'

She rose to her feet. 'Thank you for the advice but there really was no need. Your concerns are misplaced. Vince

Morelli is no gangster. He may not have your sophistication, but he is honest and that's more than I can say about you.' She turned and walked away before he could answer.

Gemma strode angrily along the High Street. How dare Nick take it into his head to dictate to her who she should see and who she shouldn't! Not that she hadn't been a little alarmed at what he'd had to say, but she didn't for one moment think that Vince was a criminal, despite her concerns about Jock MacTaggart. Vince had been adamant that the Scot's injuries had not had anything to do with him. And how could anyone who was supposed to be of a violent nature have been so gentle and caring as Vince had been when Jock had attacked her? She dismissed all doubts about him and went home.

When Gemma put her key into the front door and opened it, she found that Eve was already there, with a guest.

'This is my friend Danny,' she said somewhat sharply. 'This is Gemma, my daughter.'

Danny shook her hand. 'I'm delighted to meet you,' he said.

Gemma took note of the fact that Danny and Eve were drinking hot chocolate. 'Did you enjoy your trip to the Forest?' she asked.

'Yes,' replied Danny. 'It was a very pleasant ride out there. We had a walk round, looked at the ponies, had a meal.'

Gemma could feel the hostility oozing from her mother so she decided to make herself scarce. But she couldn't help getting in a little dig at Eve.

'Oh, by the way. How's the new television?'

'Yes, it's fine,' answered Eve casually. 'I watch it occasionally.'

Careful, Mother, she thought. Don't sound too grateful. The shock would be too much for a poor girl to bear! 'I'll say goodnight then.' She smiled at Danny. 'Perhaps I'll see you again.'

'I certainly hope so. Have a good trip.'

When they were alone, he said to Eve, 'Why are you so cold towards your daughter? She seems a nice girl.'

Eve felt her hackles rise. 'What on earth has it got to do with you?'

'Absolutely nothing. It was just an observation, that's all.'

'Then keep your damned observations to yourself.'

Danny didn't argue, but sipped his chocolate, wondering just what was behind Eve's attitude. She was indeed going to be a difficult challenge . . . but he felt he was up to it.

Before he left the house a little later he said, 'I really enjoyed this evening. I hope you did too?'

All the tension in Eve had gone and she said, 'Yes, I did. It's years since I went to the New Forest. I'd forgotten how beautiful a place it is.'

'What would you like to do next time?'

'Is there to be a next time?' she asked coyly.

'I don't see why not, do you?'

'No, I don't.'

'Good, I'll be in touch.' He leaned forward and kissed her softly on the mouth. 'Take care,' he said, and left the house.

Eve closed the door and leaned against it. She felt like a young girl again, being taken out for her first date, and she liked it. Putting out the lights she made her way upstairs to bed.

Gemma heard her pottering about in her room, and listened to Eve singing, softly. She tried to remember the last time she'd heard her do this and couldn't. It's amazing what changes love can bring when it's going well, she mused. And how painful it can be when it isn't. She wished now that she had refused to see Nick tonight. It had been upsetting being so close to him but feeling such a deep divide between them.

Two days after Gemma had sailed, Eve was really struggling to stay dry. Her guts ached at times and she craved the taste of alcohol. She played with the idea of going to an AA meeting, but without Danny sitting beside her, she found the meetings depressing.

She had a headache and felt tense and miserable. She decided to walk along the Esplanade to try and clear her head, thinking the sea breezes would blow away the devils that were tempting her, but she eventually gave in to her cravings and bought two miniature bottles of Booths gin and a bottle of tonic water. She hurried home, clutching them in her pocket to prevent them from rattling, not wanting her neighbours to know what she was carrying.

Her hands shook as the anticipation inside her grew whilst she unscrewed the top of the first miniature and poured the contents into a glass. The rising vapour of the spirit that reached her nostrils was as satisfying as the most expensive perfume on the market. She added a splash of tonic and sat in an armchair, slowly sipping the drink. It was pure nectar. She lit a cigarette and drew deeply on it, expelling the smoke from her lungs slowly and deliberately, then took another sip of her gin. Somehow the two things together felt almost erotic. It was more satisfying than sex, she thought, and it wasn't as if she'd really fallen off the wagon. A miniature wasn't big enough to count.

She opened the other bottle soon after, added some more tonic water, switched on the television and sat back in her chair. All her tension eased and she felt more content than she had in weeks. Yes, she thought, I can handle this. A couple of miniatures a night won't harm me. But three nights later, when she opened the door and saw Danny standing there, she was swaying on her feet.

He took one look at her and said, 'Oh, Eve! And you were doing so well.' He led her to a chair and seated her, then went into the scullery and made her some black coffee, sugaring it liberally. 'Here, drink this,' he urged, handing her the cup.

Eve looked at him with glassy eyes. 'I only had a few miniatures,' she said plaintively.

'I know. I saw the empties in the waste bin.'

She shot him a baleful look. 'Been poking your nose round, have you?'

He shook his head. 'No. I threw away an empty cigarette packet.'

She eyed him suspiciously, but sipped reluctantly at her coffee. 'I suppose you're going to lecture me now,' she said irritably.

'Why would I do that? Remember, I've been down the same road.'

She stared into space. 'I don't like the journey,' she

whispered. 'It's too difficult. I'm never going to make it to the end.'

He took a firm hold of her hand. 'You can, if you want to,' he insisted. 'But you really have to want to.'

She looked at him and met his gaze. 'I'm not sure that I do.'

'I don't believe you. You don't want to end up like poor old Nelly, do you?'

Remembering the pathetic creature she said raggedly, 'No, but I can't manage this alone.'

Danny put his arm around her. 'You won't have to, I'll be here to help you. Finish your coffee and let me put you to bed.' At the sudden anxious expression on her face, he added, 'I'll stay here if it's all right with you. I'll sleep on the sofa.'

With a look of relief she asked, 'Will you be here in the morning?'

'Of course I will. Come along, let me help you upstairs.'

Once Eve was settled, Danny took the empty bottles from the scullery and put them outside in the dustbin. Then he made himself comfortable. I knew she'd be a challenge, he thought. But I'll get her through this, one way or another.

Chapter Twenty-five

Things were getting pretty tense in New York at the 52nd Precinct of the NYPD. It was now quite obvious to the Department that Gene Bender was planning to take out the two Anastasio brothers when the family gathered to celebrate their mother's eightieth birthday, in a New Jersey hotel, in a month's time.

'All the information we've received points to this,' said Gus. 'It's the perfect opportunity, with the brothers together. Bender has already got several of his men on the staff of the hotel. By the time the party takes place, they will have been recognised members of the hotel for some weeks.'

'But if he fronts this, he'll have to go into hiding – then what will happen? He won't be around to protect his own family,' one of the operatives commented.

'He won't be there in person, you mutt,' Gus said impatiently. 'He'll be in full view somewhere else with lots of witnesses. Somewhere near Vito Genovese, so he can go to his godfather and tell him what a clever boy he's been.'

'So what's the plan, Lieutenant?' asked Lou.

Grinning all over his face, Gus said, 'We can just sit back

and let them blast themselves to hell and do nothing, or we can be nearby and still let them blast themselves to hell, which will rid us of a few of the scum . . . then pick up the perpetrators as they make their getaway. Someone may turn States evidence to save their neck. We can certainly pick up some of the small fry – and who knows, with a bit of luck, we could get someone at the top.'

'I like the sound of that,' said Lou.

'Well here, I've drawn up a plan of action,' said Gus. 'This is how I see it going down and here is where I want you men. So take a copy each and let's sit round a table and discuss it.'

'Do we need to bring the Feds in on this?' asked Lou with a grin, knowing how Gus hated having to deal with the FBI.

'Nah. We can manage on our own. This one will be down to the Department. We don't want Washington getting involved.'

The others agreed – with great enthusiasm.

One thing was giving Gus real cause for concern – Nick's young lady friend and her association with Morelli. He still didn't know quite where exactly Vince fitted in with current developments in the underworld, and it bothered him. Morelli was a loose cannon – just what you didn't want when you were carefully laying plans. He had a gut feeling that the man was bad news . . . and that didn't bode well for the young English girl.

Vince Morelli was making his plans too. He obviously couldn't let Bender's men rub out his boss and his brother, that would spoil his finest moment. His big problem was when to take out Bender. He had to wait long enough for the man to implicate himself sufficiently so that he, Vince, could show Tony Anastasio just what Bender had been planning. Timing was of the essence. He had to keep on top of his target's every movement. He had a couple of men working for him whom he could trust, yet they were unaware of the real reason behind their stake-outs. He, himself, still had to put in an appearance at the docks, making everything appear normal. But when it came to the hit, it would be Vince alone who knew about it. He didn't trust the others to that extent. Besides, he always worked by himself.

He also wanted to be in New York when the *Queen Mary* docked so that he could see Gemma. He was keen to show her an especially good time this trip after her bad experience with that bum of an electrician. Still, MacTaggart was out of the way now: there would be no further trouble from *him*. It would be weeks if not months before that son of a bitch would be fit to work again.

As he drove down to pier 90 that morning to unload the cargo from the *Queen Elizabeth*, Vince was feeling pretty pleased with himself. Things were going to be just fine. After he'd sorted Bender, he'd move up in the organisation, and he had a great woman in his life. What more could a guy want!

When the *Queen Mary* docked a week later, it was Gus who was first up the gangway. He made his way to B deck and asked Charlie the name of the girl who worked with him.

'Who wants to know?' asked Charlie suspiciously.

With a grin, Gus showed him his badge. 'I'm also a

distant cousin of Nick Weston, the First Officer,' he said.

'That's a relief,' said Charlie. 'When a Lieutenant of the NYPD comes asking, you wonder what's up. I'll go and get her.'

Gus waited beside the pantry and saw Charlie enter one of the cabins. Gemma followed him out, carrying some dirty linen.

'I'll take that,' said Charlie. 'This cop wants to see you.'

Gemma's heart sank. She immediately thought of Jock MacTaggart and wondered if things had come out into the open, something she had been dreading. She hadn't told anyone, apart from Vince, about Jock, but she wondered what the Scotsman might have said to the police when he had recovered.

'I'm Lieutenant Gus Carter. Nick Weston is a distant cousin of mine.' He saw her frown.

'Come into the pantry,' she said. 'I'll make you a cup of coffee.' She grinned broadly. 'I promise it will be drinkable. Despite what you Yanks say, we do know how to make it.'

With a soft chuckle Gus said, 'It'll be a first if you do.'

'Would you rather have tea?'

'Certainly not. I'll take my chance with the coffee.'

He sat on a stool and watched her. She was a bright young thing, he thought. Lots of personality, quick and capable. What in hell's name was she doing with the likes of Vince Morelli?

'I believe you and Nick used to go out together a while back.'

'Yes, that's right.'

'I asked Nick to have a word with you about Vince Morelli, but when I called him on the phone, he seemed to think you didn't believe a word he said. Is that right?'

'Yes, that's right,' she replied uncertainly, eyeing the detective anxiously.

'Just what is your relationship with Morelli?' he asked.

She glared at him. 'Now look here, Lieutenant, you may be a relative of Nick's but that doesn't give you the right to ask such personal questions.'

He noticed that her nostrils flared when she was angry. 'I'm afraid that it does. You see, I'm here on police business.'

'You are?'

He noticed the sudden scared quaver in her voice.

'What do you know about Morelli?'

She shrugged. 'Not that much. I know about his job on the docks and how he's hoping to change it in the near future.'

This interested Gus. 'In what way?'

She sipped her coffee. 'To be honest I don't know. It must be pretty big. He talks about getting an apartment in the future on the East Side of Manhattan.'

'That takes a lot of dollars,' remarked Gus.

'He seems to think he'll have it with some kind of promotion. But that's all I know.' Gemma was beginning to feel really nervous. Although this man seemed friendly, his eyes bored into her and she felt he would see through any lie.

Gus held her gaze and asked, 'And where exactly do you fit into these plans?'

'Me? Nowhere, I can assure you.'

His eyes narrowed. 'Is that the way he sees it?'

Gemma felt herself becoming flustered beneath such

close scrutiny. 'He jokes about us getting married.' She saw Gus's expression change. 'But it's all in fun.'

'Are you sure about that?'

'Yes, of course. He told me we were going to be married within two seconds of our meeting. Ask Charlie. It's a kind of running joke. Does that answer your question?' Why would an officer of the NYPD be so interested in Vince, she wondered. She challenged Gus. 'Is there something I should know?'

He pursed his lips. He couldn't give too much away. He couldn't risk her repeating his comments to Vince, but he had to try to warn her somehow.

'When he's taken you out, has he ever shown any signs of violence?'

'What!' She was horrified by the question but, after the initial shock, her thoughts returned to the electrician. 'No, of course not. Why do you ask? What are you trying to tell me, Lieutenant? I wish you would stop beating about the bush and come to the point!'

He smothered a smile. This girl had spirit, and that was good. But he still had to be careful. He relaxed and smiled and changed the official tone in his voice. 'I guess I'm trying to get you out of a hole before you get in too deep.'

She eyed him suspiciously. 'You are not being entirely truthful, Lieutenant. You're keeping something from me.' She cursed her own foolhardiness. What if Vince *had* been the one to attack Big Jock? She had to find out what was behind these questions. If it was about Jock, she might as well know the worst.

'You're quite a girl, Gemma. *You* certainly couldn't be accused of beating about the bush. Fine. Here goes.

Morelli mixes with some pretty heavy-duty guys – so it would be very unwise for you to become involved with him. And it wouldn't be very clever if he knew about this conversation.'

Gemma could feel a sense of panic building up inside her. 'You're really frightening me, Lieutenant.'

'Jesus, I hope so, Gemma. You really want out of this situation.'

'I'm going to see him tonight.'

'Are you in love with the guy?'

'Good heavens, no. He's kind and amusing, but to tell you the truth, I only went out with him to spite Nick.' She ran her hand around the back of her neck. 'Stupid, wasn't it?'

He just raised his eyebrows. 'I would advise you to bring this friendship to an end – tonight.'

'You're not telling me all this on Nick's behalf, are you? He didn't like me seeing Vince and I wondered if he was jealous,' she said hopefully.

'Look, Gemma, Nick is big enough to fight his own battles. How can I make you understand that a friendship with Morelli is a very dangerous thing for you. You need to tell him goodbye!'

Looking at the grim expression on his face she said, 'All right. I will.'

'Just be very careful how you tell him,' advised Gus.

'What do you mean?'

'Listen, Gemma. No guy likes the brush-off. Pick your words carefully. Leave him some dignity.'

'You know you're making me very nervous, Lieutenant.'

'Gus, please. All I'm saying is to take care. Have you led him to believe that you care for him?'

'No, I have not. We've just had fun. He's a really nice man, I enjoy his company.'

He took hold of her arm. '*Finish it!*'

'There's more to all this than you're telling me, isn't there?'

His gaze didn't waver, but he didn't answer.

'If Vince isn't to know about this conversation,' said Gemma, 'you'd better go. He comes on board early on docking day.'

'I know.'

She looked sharply at him. 'Are you watching him?'

'I'd better be off,' he said, and left the pantry.

Gemma stood there, stunned by the conversation. What had she become involved in? She cursed her stupidity for agreeing to go out with Vince in the first place. So lost in her muddled thoughts was she, that she wasn't aware of his approach until a pair of arms encircled her waist and his lips brushed the back of her neck.

'Hello, gorgeous. How's my girl?'

She was startled, but tried to act naturally. 'Hello, Vince. How are you?'

'Better for seeing you.'

He bent forward to kiss her, but she wriggled out of his embrace. 'I can't stop now, I have my cabins to see to.'

He caught hold of her arm and asked, 'Is something wrong?'

'No, should there be?'

'You seem mighty tense . . . distant. Aren't you pleased to see me?'

'I'm tired, Vince. We've had a busy trip.'

He released her. 'Of course, how dumb of me. Look, I'll

pick you up at eight-thirty. OK?'

'Yes, of course. Now I must go or Charlie will be after my blood.' She hurried out of the pantry and went to find her colleague.

'So you're not being carted off to the pokey!' joked Charlie when she found him.

'No. You don't get rid of me that easily,' she retorted.

'He said he was a relative of our First Officer.'

'He told you that?'

'Well, when a stranger asks to know the name of my stewardess, I want to know who he is and why.'

She grinned at him. 'My protector.'

'No, love. Common-sense. I wondered if his visit was anything to do with Vince.'

'Why would you think that?' she asked carefully.

With a frown he said, 'I don't know, just a gut feeling I have about that man.' He stared at her, but didn't say any more.

'You don't like him, do you?'

'No, you're wrong. He's a likeable chap, it's just that there's something about him that worries me, and I can't put my finger on it. I do get concerned when you go out with him.'

She patted his cheek. 'You are a dear, but you won't have to worry about me any longer. After this trip I won't be going out with him again.'

Charlie looked anxious. 'He's been treating you right, I hope?'

She reassured him. 'Absolutely. He's good company, but he's not my type really, and I don't want to get too involved. It's not fair on him.'

Charlie looked grave. 'He's not going to like it,' he stated.

'Why? What do you mean?'

'Vince is a man who's full of confidence, cocky even. He won't take kindly to the idea that you don't want to see him any more.'

Gemma felt the muscles in her stomach tighten, because she too was worried about Vince's reaction. She would have to tread carefully, come up with a good reason, one that he would readily accept. But what on earth could she say to him? What excuse could she give?

Chapter Twenty-six

Vince didn't make Gemma's predicament any easier for her when he picked her up later that evening. He was so obviously pleased to see her. He paid her extravagant compliments, gave her a beautiful corsage and said he had a really nice place to take her to dinner. One that he felt sure she'd enjoy.

'I thought we would just have a drink together,' she told him. 'I'm really tired after such a busy trip and I would like an early night.'

'Jeez, honey, I'm starving. I haven't eaten all day. I don't want to drink on an empty stomach.'

What could she say?

He took her to the Four Seasons – an expensive restaurant, with large frescos on the walls depicting Spring, Summer, Autumn and Winter. As the waiter seated them, Vince smiled at her and asked, 'Well, what do you think, honey? Do you like it here?'

'It's lovely.' And it was. But it made the task ahead of her all the more difficult.

Vince ordered a steak which covered his plate when it arrived. Gemma's chicken salad was enough to feed an army, but it was beautifully arranged in a round glass bowl, and looked delicious.

'I can't possibly eat all this!' she exclaimed.

'Just tuck in and leave what you don't want,' he said.

The waiter arrived and poured the wine. When they were alone, Vince looked at her with real affection and said, 'I can't tell you how much I looked forward to seeing you this trip. I want to make this evening real special, to make up for last time. How's the shoulder? Is it all healed?'

'Yes, thank you, I'm fine now.' Her curiosity got the better of her. Gus seemed so interested in Vince's plans of which she knew nothing, that she thought she'd do a little digging. 'So what have you been up to since I last saw you?'

'Much of the usual. Moving the freight around, keeping the docks flowing smoothly.'

'What of your promotion? How's that going?'

He looked somewhat surprised and a little wary. 'Nothing's certain yet,' he said carefully. 'In a few weeks' time I should know for sure.'

'If you won't be on the docks when you're promoted,' she said, 'what will you be doing?'

'I always think it's unlucky to speculate. How's your chicken?' he asked, changing the subject.

'Delicious,' Gemma answered, realising it would do no good at all to question him further.

At that moment three men and a woman were escorted to a table across from them and she noticed that Vince sat up, suddenly alert.

'Who are they?' she asked. 'Are they friends of yours?'

'No, no. They're just in the same business as me.' He smiled knowingly. 'The opposition, if you like.'

Gemma studied the people carefully. One man, sturdy, tough looking despite his expensive light blue suit with matching shirt and tie, was the superior being of the bunch. This was obvious as the other two men treated him with deference. She heard one call him 'Mr Bender.' The woman, with smartly coiffed hair, a black dress with an expensive-looking brooch pinned to one side, looked bored. The men spoke together in low voices. It looked for all the world as if they were plotting something, thought Gemma.

Although Vince kept talking to her, she was conscious that his mind was elsewhere. But never once did he cast a glance in the direction of the others.

Gemma declined a dessert, saying she was far too full, but agreed to have a coffee and a liqueur, thinking that this was the perfect opportunity to tell Vince she wouldn't be seeing him again. But he scuppered her plans.

'Look honey, I'm sorry but I have to go somewhere, real important. When you've finished your coffee, I'll put you in a cab and send you back to the ship.'

'I don't understand,' she said. 'You didn't mention this when we came out.'

He reached across the table and took her hand in his. 'I didn't want to spoil our evening,' he said. 'I wanted to see you so badly.'

'But Vince, there was something I need to tell you.'

'I just don't have the time. I'll come on board in the morning. You can tell me then.'

'But, Vince,' she protested.

'Gemma, honey. Please!' His tone brooked no argument. As he bundled her into a cab, he kissed her goodnight.

297

'I'll make this up to you, I promise,' he said. He told the driver where to go and handed him a five-dollar bill. 'You make sure she gets on board safely.'

'Yes, sir,' said the driver, pleased with his fare. 'I sure will.'

Gemma sat back in the cab, feeling disgruntled. She hadn't solved anything and now she would have to face Vince in the morning and tell him then. It wasn't how she had planned it at all. There was little privacy on sailing day, which would make things very difficult.

After he had put Gemma into a cab, Vince waited outside the restaurant for Gene Bender and his party to leave. His heart was beating faster and he felt the adrenaline pumping. This was the man who was going to be the means of him becoming an established and important part of the syndicate. His death would breathe new life in the affairs of Vince Morelli. He chuckled to himself at the metaphor.

As Bender's party left the restaurant and pulled away in their large automobile, Vince saw another vehicle pull out and follow at a distance. His men were doing their job well. He himself jumped in his car and followed them all to the Taft Hotel.

When Bender and his companions walked through the swing doors and disappeared into the foyer of the hotel, Vince got out of his car and went over to the other waiting vehicle.

'What's going on?' he asked.

The occupants of the car looked startled at his sudden appearance. 'We're not quite sure,' one of them said. 'Bender has been all over the city, talking to small gatherings of his men. He's obviously getting organised for the hit.'

'Are you sure?' asked Vince.

The driver of the car smiled at him. 'Yes, Mr Morelli. We managed to hijack one of his men one evening. A little gentle persuasion soon loosened his tongue. It's the birthday party in New Jersey for sure.'

'And the stool pigeon?'

'He ain't gonna talk to no one again,' the man said with great satisfaction.

'Did he tell you anything else?'

'Yeah. He said that Bender was going to a concert at Carnegie Hall next week. On Thursday night.'

'Carnegie Hall?' Vince exclaimed.

'It ain't a symphony concert, but there is one night dedicated to the music of George Gershwin. It seems that he's a fan.'

'Thursday night, you say?'

The other man nodded.

'Let me know if anything else comes up,' said Vince. Then he strolled back to his own car and drove away.

The following morning was a nightmare for Gemma. Apart from preparing the cabins for her passengers and the work that entailed, her nerves were tighter than a drum waiting for Vince to appear. She knew now she would have to face him amid the chaos that was sailing day. Would he be angry? Would he cause a scene? Would she be able to handle him if he did – and if she couldn't, what would happen then? Would she have to call the master-at-arms . . . and if she had to go to those lengths, what would the consequences be?

She was a nervous wreck by the time the ship sailed . . . and Vince hadn't shown up. She felt enormous relief as the liner moved away from the dock, but she knew it was only delaying the inevitable. And Gus would not be pleased.

When eventually she and Charlie had the chance to sit down for a few minutes' break he said to her, 'Now I suppose I won't be getting any more tickets to Madison Square Garden.'

She frowned. What on earth was he talking about?

Seeing the puzzled expression on her face he said, 'Vince . . . tickets. He didn't come on board this morning so I assume you gave him the old heave ho last night.'

'Oh, Charlie. I wondered whatever you were on about. No, I didn't get a chance to tell him, I'm afraid. He had to rush off before I had the opportunity, but he did say he'd be on board this morning. I can't imagine why he didn't come but I'm secretly relieved that he didn't.'

'You realise that your love life is seriously interfering with my social life, don't you?'

'I'm really sorry,' she laughed.

'Well, young lady, you'll have to make it up to me with your next boyfriend. There will have to be something in it for me.' He cast a sly look in her direction. 'What about the First Officer?'

'Why do you ask?'

'Well, you know, his cousin coming round . . . and you did say he was a good kisser.'

Her eyes twinkled with devilment. 'And if he was my boyfriend, how would that be of use to you?'

'If I got into trouble, he could save me going up to the bridge in front of the Staff Captain.'

Gemma started to laugh. 'You're too old to get into trouble.'

'You're never too old, love. Ask the wife!'

'I'm sorry to disappoint you, but at the moment I'm not seeing anyone.'

'You're no bloody good to me then,' he grumbled as he left her.

On the following Thursday night, Vince Morelli mingled with the audience entering the doors of Carnegie Hall, clutching his ticket. He lingered in the foyer, watching carefully, not knowing just where Bender would be sitting. Eventually he saw him arrive with two of his henchmen and the same bored-looking woman, tonight bedecked in jewels and a mink stole.

He followed them at a distance until he saw where they were seated, then turned back to find his own seat at the back of the auditorium. He might as well enjoy the concert, he thought. He preferred jazz himself, but Gershwin wrote good music.

During the interval, he made his way to the bar and stood sipping a scotch on the rocks, watching out for his prey, but Bender was nowhere in sight. They were probably in another bar, he guessed.

To his surprise, he enjoyed the concert. He especially liked the music from *Porgy and Bess* and *Showboat*. 'Old Man River' was particularly stirring, sung in low rich tones by a black male singer. The finale of the concert was a wonderful arrangement of *Rhapsody in Blue*, played by the full orchestra. Vince found to his amazement that he was deeply moved by the music.

He stayed in his seat as the audience started to leave, knowing that Bender would eventually come up the aisle beside him. As he saw the group approach, he rose from his own seat and filtered in behind them. This was going to be a piece of cake!

With so many people milling around, the bodyguards were having difficulty keeping close to their boss and a sudden surge in the crowd as they reached the foyer gave Vince the opportunity he was waiting for. Hidden by his programme, he produced his revolver, already fitted with a silencer, from his pocket, rammed it into Bender's back . . . and pulled the trigger.

The density of the crowds carried Bender forward for a few seconds before he fell, giving Vince time to wander away. He could hear the screams of a woman as he left the hall, a smile upon his face.

Gus Carter and his sidekick Lou heard the commotion from outside and looked at each other. Police cars began to arrive and they leapt out of their car and ran into the hall. Gus flashed his badge at one of the officers and asked, 'What the hell is going on?'

'Gene Bender's been hit,' he said.

Lou and Gus looked at one another and together said, 'Morelli!'

They knew he'd been at the concert as they'd been following him, but with the crowd milling about, they hadn't seen him leave. They made their way further into the foyer. There on the floor, lying in a pool of blood, was Bender, a blonde woman beside his body, weeping. The two bodyguards were standing by, looking nervous and worried.

An ambulance was called and the body taken to the morgue after a doctor had proclaimed Bender dead. The police took the names and addresses of the two men and the woman.

'He's my husband!' she screamed at them. 'Instead of asking all these questions you should be looking for his killer!'

How many relatives of Bender's victims had said the very same thing, thought Gus. He felt no sympathy for her. She must know what her husband did for a living – now it had been his turn. As far as he was concerned it was one less piece of scum off the streets of New York. He walked away and let the officer in charge do his job.

As they got back into their vehicle he looked at Lou and said, 'Well, that screws up everything.'

'What do you mean, boss?'

'All our plans are kaput. Now there won't be a hit on the Anastasio boys. Bender's men won't go ahead without him.'

'So what happens next?'

'Christ knows.'

'What are we going to do about Morelli?'

'We'll go and question the bastard. Search him and see if he's carrying the gun he shot the mobster with.'

They drove to Vince's apartment, but he wasn't there. 'We'll wait,' snapped Gus.

Vince drove to Grand Central Station, parked his car and wrapping up his revolver in a cloth, put it in a left-luggage compartment, locked it and pocketed the key. You couldn't be too careful. When he got into the car, he slipped the key under a mat at his feet. Then he drove home.

As he was about to unlock his front door, Gus and Lou came up behind him. 'Morelli! Got a minute?'

He turned quickly with a look of apprehension which faded as he saw their badges. 'What do you want?'

'Where were you this evening?' asked Gus.

'Carnegie Hall,' answered Vince calmly. 'It was a Gershwin concert.'

'You into that kind of music?' asked Lou.

'Nah! I like jazz but someone gave me a ticket. It was good,' he said. 'Why are you asking?'

'A man got shot coming out of the concert.' Gus watched his expression closely. Vince didn't flinch or show any reaction except surprise.

'You don't say. I never heard a thing, but then it was pretty crowded.'

'You didn't hear the sound of a shot?'

Vince shook his head.

Gus stepped forward. 'Put your arms against the wall and spread your legs,' he ordered.

Vince just raised his eyebrows and complied.

He was carrying a gun, but Gus smelt the barrel. It hadn't been fired recently. 'You got a licence for this?'

'Of course I have,' said Vince.

'If I check and find you're lying . . .' Gus began.

'Why would I do that? Come in and I'll show it to you, if you like.'

Gus wanted to strike him. The arrogance of the man got to him. To think young Gemma was involved with this punk – it made the hairs on his neck stand up. 'That'll be all,' he said, and walked back to the car.

'The bastard has stashed it somewhere,' he muttered as they drove away. 'Unless we can find it, there's nothing we can do.'

But what Gus Carter and Vince Morelli didn't know, or Bender for that matter, before his sudden demise, was that in Brooklyn Heights in an exclusive hotel, a meeting had been arranged between the Anastasio brothers and Vito Genovese.

Chapter Twenty-seven

During the return voyage Gemma had her first experience of rough weather as the ship caught the edge of a storm. The *Queen Mary* rolled from side to side. Crockery in the pantries crashed to the deck. The tablecloths in the dining rooms were damped down with water to stop the dishes from sliding across the linen, and storm ropes were put up across open square to allow the passengers something to hold on to, to help them keep their balance. Many of them were seasick.

The ship's doctor was kept busy visiting those who had taken to their bunks; he went from cabin to cabin handing out seasickness tablets and comforting words. Stewards were busy cleaning up in various alleyways where some unfortunates hadn't made it to the nearest toilets in time. It was an exhausting period for everyone, including the Captain, who ignored the pleas from some of the passengers to slow the ship's passage, remaining on the bridge in the evening instead of joining them at dinner.

In her pantry on B deck, Gemma lodged herself between a small cupboard and the sink in a desperate effort to keep steady. She shot out a hand to catch a tray she had prepared as it started to slide off the worktop, and caught it just in time, but she was too late to stop a cup and saucer from crashing to the floor.

Picking up the tray, laid for breakfast, she carried it along to the passenger's cabin, leaning against the roll of the ship to maintain her balance. She knocked on the door, and walked in.

'I'll place this on the floor, madam,' she said. 'If I put it on the table, you'll lose it.'

The passenger, one of the few who was not unwell, was looking out of the porthole. 'Have you seen the sea out here?' she asked.

Gemma hadn't had time, but she walked over and peered out. Huge waves met her startled gaze. They looked so menacing as they rose to great heights, then crashed away into deep troughs. She shivered, and wondered what the scene looked like from the bridge.

As Gemma continued to rush around administering to her passengers, she wondered if Nick was on duty and hoped they would soon be sailing in smoother waters. This continuing battle against the elements and the chaos it was causing was extremely tiring.

That night, she and Sally pushed their life-jackets down the small storm boards along their bunks, to stop them falling out as the ship rolled. Before going to bed, they had put away anything that was sitting on a shelf and hadn't already fallen to the deck.

At one time, the ship rolled over, shuddered and continued to roll in the same direction. For one awful moment, Gemma didn't think it would right itself, but eventually it did. She lay back on her bunk, her heart pounding in terror.

'Have you known it to be this bad before?' she asked Sally.

'Not quite as bad, but don't worry, it'll pass in time.'

'I suppose with your boyfriend Nick Weston up on the bridge, we're in safe hands,' said Gemma in biting tones.

'Of course,' was the noncommittal reply, which Gemma put down to the drama of the moment.

The following morning the forecast was that the ship would be clear of the storm by the afternoon, which was a relief to everyone.

'Bloody hell, Charlie,' Gemma said tiredly, as she carried a tray into their pantry, 'we can do without this.'

He gave a lopsided grin. 'It's part and parcel of sea life, love. But at least you've got your sea legs.'

And she realised that she had, as her uncle had predicted. Without even thinking about it, she'd naturally leaned against the motion of the ship as it rolled, keeping her balance, although it made the calfs of her legs ache . . . and she hadn't been sick.

In Southampton, Eve's relationship with Danny was suffering an equally stormy passage, and as yet, there was no sign of it abating. She had kept off the bottle, with his help, but she soon reverted to her carping ways, and he would have none of it. One evening they had an almighty row.

'I thought it was the drink that made you an embittered woman,' he said, 'but sadly, I can see that this is the real you.'

'What do you mean?' she demanded.

Without raising his voice he said, 'You are a completely selfish person, Eve. You think of no one but yourself. In the weeks that I have known you, I have yet to hear you say a nice word about Gemma, and I know she does a great deal for you.'

'Oh, really!'

'Yes, really. She brings you something home every trip. She stocks your larder, buys you clothes, she even rented a television for your enjoyment and no doubt she helps you financially.'

'And why shouldn't she? I'm her mother.'

He slowly shook his head. 'You are a taker.'

'Whatever do you mean?'

'There are two types in this world, Eve, takers and givers. You give nothing to anyone else, you take all the time.'

'And what have I taken from you?'

A slow smile crossed his lips. 'From me, nothing. I have *given* you my time – because I wanted to. In the beginning, there was a vulnerability about you that was somehow endearing. Not now, alas. I had hoped that maybe we could have a future together, but now I'm not so sure. Unless you change, you would try to destroy me, as you do with everyone, even your own daughter. It is such a shame.' He rose from his seat. 'I have done as much as I can – the rest is up to you. You can make a life for yourself, but you have to learn to give, to put others first.' He placed his hand on hers. 'And there is so much that is good, buried under all that bitterness, if only you would dig deep enough.'

Eve's face was white and she felt panic rising inside her. 'Won't I see you any more?'

'That depends on you, really. I can't be your crutch any longer. Now *you* must decide where you are going . . . who you really are. It's time to stand up and be counted, as they say.' He walked towards the door. 'If you can find that woman who is buried inside and bring her out, get in touch with me. You know where you can find me.' He opened the door. 'Good luck, Eve.'

When she was alone, Eve sat at the dining table, tears trickling down her cheeks. She'd done it again. She had driven Jack away, she would soon lose Gemma, she sensed it, and now Danny had gone, too. Dear Danny, who had shown her nothing but kindness, whom she really liked, on whom she had built such high hopes. A man who truly understood her demons because he had faced them also. She had pictured spending the rest of her days with this special man, but once again, her bitterness had come between them. Much as she hated to admit it, he was right.

Dig deep, he had said, there was a lot of good buried inside her, so there was something in her he had seen and liked. She clung to this thought. She didn't want to spend the rest of her life alone. She wanted to be cared for . . . loved. And Danny was capable of all this. She wiped the tears away with the back of her hand. Find that other woman, he had said, then get in touch . . . so he had left the door open. Now it was up to her.

When Gemma came home with the usual box of groceries and a Hermès scarf for her mother she'd bought from one of the shops on board, she was stunned when Eve thanked her.

'The groceries save a lot on my housekeeping,' she told her daughter, 'and this scarf is lovely. What luxury! Thank you, Gemma. Now sit down and I'll make us a cup of tea and you can tell me all about your trip.'

She watched her mother potter about, wondering just what had brought about this metamorphosis. After thinking about it she decided it was all down to Danny's influence, but wherever it came from, it was a godsend!

She told Eve all about the rough weather, but nothing about Vince. It would have been nice to have had a mother in whom she could confide, who would have comforted her over the loss of Nick Weston, but she'd never had it so what did it matter. She was used to having to solve her own problems . . . and maybe it was better that way. But in her heart she knew it wasn't.

Her friend Eunice, however, was a different kettle of fish. When Gemma went to call on her that evening and poured her heart out, Eunice was both understanding and sympathetic.

'Such a shame,' she said. 'He was a good-looking bloke, and nice with it, wasn't he? I envied you, I can tell you.' She put an arm around Gemma's shoulders. 'There will be someone else for you, Gem, you'll see.'

But Gemma didn't want anyone else; she wanted Nick so much, it was unbearable. She didn't tell Eunice anything about Vince either. It would only worry her friend and Gemma didn't want to discuss it anyway. The confrontation to come was making her anxious enough as it was.

Two days after Gemma had sailed, Eve took herself off to the AA meeting and slid into a seat beside Danny. He looked at her and nodded, but didn't say a word. However, at the end of the meeting he waited for her outside.

'Hello, Eve. You're looking well, how are you?'

'Danny, could we go and have a cup of tea? I need to talk to you.'

They went to their usual little café and when the waitress had served them Eve said, 'I owe you an apology, Danny.'

His expression didn't change. 'And how's that?' he asked.

'Over my behaviour,' she explained. 'You are absolutely right, I *am* a taker and I suppose I always have been. I'm not proud of that, but I am trying to change, honestly.'

He smiled softly. 'I'm happy to hear it. How is Gemma?'

'She's fine. She brought me a lovely scarf home and a load of foodstuff. I told her how much of a help it was.'

He looked at her in surprise. 'My word, you have changed.'

'I have a lot of bridges to build with Gemma,' she said. And with a frown she added, 'I'm not sure if I can repair them. I said some wicked things to her.' She looked at him beseechingly.

'Some things are beyond repair,' he said, 'but you can start again and build new bridges. Young Gemma has a lot of love in her heart if only you give her some encouragement.'

She sipped her tea. 'I hope you're right,' she said, and looked up at him. 'Can I build new ones with you, Danny?'

'Why do you want to?'

Taking a deep breath she said, 'Because you are a good man, a dear man . . . and I don't want to lose you.'

He laid his hand on her arm. 'Our bridges didn't

break, Eve. It may have had a couple of broken planks in the middle, but they can be repaired with a bit of new wood.'

She smiled at him. 'I'm so pleased you feel that way,' she said. 'I promise you, you won't regret it.'

'Drink your tea,' he said. 'It's getting cold.'

Chapter Twenty-eight

The meeting in New York between the Anastasio brothers and Vito Genovese was going well. Albert had heard a whisper that there was to be a hit on him and his brother on their mother's birthday and had faced Genovese with this fact, without actually accusing him. Genovese had looked genuinely shocked, which surprised Albert, who was convinced that the other godfather was behind the plot.

Vito, in fact, was shattered by the news. Sure he eventually wanted to take over the territory of the Anastasios, but he wasn't nearly ready to do it yet, and the last thing he needed now was to be at odds with the brothers.

'Who is the person behind this?' he demanded.

Albert told him he didn't know the name, except it was one of Vito's men who was near the top of his organisation.

'I gave no such orders and when I find out who it is, I'll deal with him,' he promised. 'Look, Albert, we are both good businessmen, we don't want trouble. You are doing well, I'm doing well, who needs a war?'

'Not me,' said Albert. His eyes narrowed. 'You are not getting just a little bit greedy, are you, Vito?'

'On my son's life!' he exclaimed.

Eventually the evening ended without further incident. Vito and Albert kissed each other on the cheeks, Italian fashion, promising everlasting loyalty – lying through their teeth.

As Vito Genovese was driven away from the meeting, he exploded with anger. 'Who is the traitor who would jeopardise everything I've worked for?' he asked. None of his men could answer his question. But Vito thought deeply. It was always those near the top who were the most dangerous. Bender hated the Anastasio brothers, that was why he hadn't been informed about this meeting. Could it be him? Albert would haul him in for questioning, because he was determined to get to the bottom of all this. But when Vito arrived home, it was to be told of Bender's death. Another shock. This didn't make sense. Anastasio wouldn't have ordered a hit when they were in such delicate negotiations. He ordered Bender's bodyguards to come and see him.

Vito Genovese had a fearsome reputation and as he sat behind his desk and stared at the men with his deepset eyes beneath bushy black eyebrows, they became increasingly nervous.

'What happened?' he rasped.

He was told how the crowd had separated Gene Bender from them for a fleeting moment, but long enough for the assassin to do his job.

'Did you see who it was?'

The man shook his head then hesitatingly he said, 'I thought I saw Vince Morelli in the crowd, but I couldn't be sure.'

'Morelli?' Vito snapped. 'Who the fuck is Morelli?'

'One of Tony Anastasio's men. He's a gang boss in the docks, but word is out that he's an enforcer for Tough Tony.'

Vito immediately picked up the telephone. 'Tony? Good evening, wasn't it? When I got home I was told the sad news that Gene Bender had been shot at Carnegie Hall.' He listened. 'You just got the news too? I gotta ask if you were surprised.' The men in the office could hear the voice raised in anger on the other end of the phone. 'So you were – that pleases me. We both have a rotten apple in our barrels, it seems. A Vince Morelli was seen at the concert . . . does that name mean anything to you?' He listened, then replaced the receiver.

'A problem solved,' he said. Then once again he looked at Bender's men. 'Now you can tell me all you know about Gene's plan to rub out the Anastasio brothers.'

Two weeks later, Tony Anastasio, back from a visit to Cuba, sent for Vince to come to his office situated near the docks.

He bounced in, full of confidence. 'You wanted to see me, boss?'

Tony smiled at him. 'How's it going, Vince?'

'Everything is ready for the *Queen Mary* when she docks,' he said. 'She's coming up the Hudson River at this very moment. My men are standing by, as usual.'

Tony nodded slowly. 'You do a good job, in other ways as well. You obey orders without question, do what you have to do, and efficiently. You have a good head on your shoulders.'

Vince beamed at him. 'Thanks, boss.'

'You got something to tell me, maybe?'

Suddenly the eyes of Tony Anastasio looked cold, and Vince felt a chill of fear seep into his veins, but only for a moment, such was his arrogance. 'How do you mean?' he asked.

'Do you like good music, Vince? Like George Gershwin, perhaps?'

Morelli relaxed. Somehow Tony Anastasio had learned about his connection with Bender's death. He would be really pleased.

'Yeah. I was at Carnegie Hall.' He grinned broadly. 'I rubbed out that piece of shit for you. Did you know he was planning to hit you and your brother in New Jersey at your Mom's birthday party, Tony?'

'No, I didn't,' he lied, 'but you did – is that what you're saying?'

'Yeah, I knew. I wasn't going to let him get away with that, so I fixed him, but good. You've got nothing to worry about.'

'You didn't think to tell me about it?' His tone was sharp.

'It was something I could handle myself,' said Vince confidently. 'There was no reason to bother you.'

'You didn't think I had the right to know that the closest members of my family could have been killed? There would have been women and children there! *My* wife – *my* children. You didn't think I should know about this?' Tony's face was flushed with rage, as his voice rose. 'You think you're Jesus Christ or someone?'

Morelli's smile faded. This wasn't how it was meant to be. Tony should have been pleased, grateful. Making a place for him in the organisation. He began to feel edgy.

'It wasn't like that at all,' he began.

'Then how was it? You tell me.'

'I wanted to show you how reliable I was, how I could be trusted with your safety, the safety of your family. This was my way of proving I knew my job . . . that I could be an asset to the organisation.'

'But that was never in doubt. I knew that already. The thing that worries me, Vince, is that to prove a point, you put all these lives at risk. What if it had all gone wrong?'

Vince raised his head, unapologetic. 'It wouldn't have, I'd have made sure of that.' He stared at Anastasio and challenged him. 'Are you telling me that by killing Bender, I did wrong?'

'No, Vince, I'm not saying that, but another time, before you make decisions on your own, talk to me first. I like to know what's going down. OK?'

'Sure, Tony, sure. At least now you can be certain that nothing will happen to spoil your mother's party. I'd better get back. Do you want me for anything else?'

'No, go ahead. You've got work to do, and so have I.'

Vince walked along the quayside, whistling happily to himself.

Tony Anastasio stood at the office window and watched him go. Beside him stood his number one man. 'Look at the swagger on him. Thinks he's God Almighty. Before we know it, he'll take out someone else without my say so and one day it might be me. That man is too ambitious.' He turned to his associate. 'See to it. And change the venue of the party.'

★　★　★

Vince was so busy that he didn't have time to call on Gemma, so he sent one of his men along with a message. 'Mr Morelli said to tell you he'll pick you up at eight o'clock this evening,' he told Gemma. 'Is that all right with you?'

She hesitated for a moment, then said, 'Yes, tell him I'll be there.'

The longshoreman smiled. 'He said he was going to take you to his favourite Italian restaurant in Little Italy. They serve real good pasta there, miss.'

Charlie heard the conversation and frowned. 'Is this your last date with Vince?' he asked when the man had left.

Gemma nodded. 'It's better that I tell him somewhere more private than here, on board ship.'

'You don't think it's a mite *too* private? What if he turns nasty?'

'He won't, Charlie. I'll be diplomatic and let him down gently.'

'What are you going to say?'

'I don't know. I'll have to play it by ear.'

'Would you like me to come with you? I will do so willingly.'

She was overcome by his concern. 'You are a brick,' she said gratefully, 'but really, I'll be fine.'

'I wish I could be so sure,' he muttered to himself as he started to tidy a cabin.

Gemma went to Macy's in the afternoon, shopping. Mostly to take her mind off what was before her. She stopped for a quick meal at the diner before she went back to the ship and changed.

It was with some trepidation that she walked along the dock to meet Vince, later that evening. He seemed in high spirits as they drove away. He smiled at her and said, 'Tonight you'll taste real Italian food. Food like my mamma makes.' Listening to him chatting away, she was getting more nervous by the minute. What she was going to say to him would come as a great shock, and she knew she'd been foolish to come at all.

Whilst Vince was driving Gemma to the restaurant, Gus Carter was boarding the *Queen Mary*, praying he would find Nick in his quarters. To his relief, Nick opened the cabin door. He was dressed in casual clothes and had been reading a book.

'Gus! What on earth are you doing here?' he asked.

'Your girlfriend is in grave danger. There is a contract out on Morelli, one of our informants told us, and he knows that Vince has booked a table in this particular restaurant in Little Italy. Now nothing may happen tonight, but I'm real worried about Gemma. My men are tailing them, so she's covered. I thought you'd like to come along for the ride.'

Before he had finished talking, Nick had grabbed his jacket. 'This situation has gone far enough,' he said forcefully. 'Take me there, Gus, and I'll damn well go in and get her myself.'

Vince stopped the car and helped Gemma out. Once inside, the waiter led them to a table and then handed them a menu.

Gemma spoke up. 'Vince, could we just have a drink first, because I need to talk to you.'

'Bring a bottle of Chianti,' he said to the waiter. 'We'll order later.'

He smiled warmly as he put an arm around her shoulders. 'I know, you're going to tell me to set a date for the wedding.'

'Vince, please, this isn't a time for jokes.'

He looked at her and asked. 'What is it, has somebody died? You look so sad. What's happened, sweetheart?'

Just then the waiter brought their wine. She waited for him to leave, then took a deep breath. She said, 'I'm really sorry, Vince, but this is the last time we'll be seeing each other.'

His face fell. 'What do you mean? Are you giving up the sea, is that it?'

'No, I'm not doing that, but before we started going out, I was seeing someone else.'

'That big guy I saw you with? The one I told to take care of you for me?'

'Yes, that's the one, although I don't see him any more.'

'So what's the big deal? What difference does that make to us?'

Gemma hesitated. 'I was in love with him . . . and I still am.'

She was startled by the change in his expression. Suddenly the smile had gone, his jaw was set and his mouth tightened.

'And?' he asked coldly.

'I just think I'm not being fair to you and that's why I can't see you any more.'

He took his arm away. 'In other words you've been taking me for a ride.'

'No, Vince! It wasn't like that at all.'

'Then what *was* it like? I would really like to know.'

She made to touch his cheek but he moved his face away. 'When you first asked me out, I was angry with Nick and that made me accept your kind invitation. I'd like to say, I have really enjoyed your company. I liked being with you.'

'But not enough, is that it?'

'Come on, Vince. We had great fun, but it wasn't serious, you know that.'

He gripped her wrist. 'How do you know what I was thinking and feeling? What makes you think that I'm not in love with *you*?'

Gemma was shattered. This was worse than she had ever imagined. 'But you're not, are you?'

He stared into her eyes. 'To begin with I was joking about us getting married, but lately I've grown to like the idea. I want to settle down and I want to do it with you. Never mind this Nick guy, forget about him. Marry me, Gemma. Be my wife. What's it matter that you love him? I'll make you forget him. I'll be so good to you, honey, we'll have a great life together.'

'Oh Vince, please don't do this. I do like you, you have been a good friend, but I'm not in love with you. I'm so sorry.'

'Don't give me your pity, Gemma, I don't need it!'

'That's not what I meant and you know it.' She held his gaze, frightened by the anger in his eyes. 'Can't we remain friends?'

'Who is the wonderful Nick? Is he on board? What does he do?'

At that moment, Gemma knew real fear. She remembered

Jock MacTaggart. Her blood turned to ice in her veins. 'He's on leave,' she lied.

'And that's that, is it?'

How could she cool his anger, she wondered. 'I'm very flattered that you want to marry me, Vince. That's the greatest compliment any man can pay a woman, and you'd be a wonderful husband.'

'But not yours.'

'You're a lovely man, you deserve a woman who adores you. I'm sorry, but I'm in love with someone else.' As she spoke the words she realised they were the truth. She *was* in love with Nick. 'I won't sit here and argue with you, Vince. I would like to still be your friend, but that's up to you.' She rose from her seat. 'I'll get a taxi back to the ship.'

As she went quickly through the entrance of the restaurant and out on to the sidewalk, Vince came running after her. He caught hold of her arm. 'Wait, Gemma! Don't go rushing off like this. Let's talk some more.'

'There's nothing left to say,' she said quietly. 'We can't go on seeing each other. It wouldn't be fair to you.'

His face was white with anger. He tightened his hold on her. 'You can't just kiss me off like that. You're my girl whether you like it or not.'

'No, Vince, I'm not. Now let me go, you're hurting me.'

'You aren't going anywhere!' Vince caught hold of her shoulders and pulled her roughly towards him. His mouth covered hers in a bruising kiss. As she was trying to struggle free from his grasp, a voice from behind her said, 'Good evening, Gemma. Is everything all right?'

Vince let go of her and she turned and saw Gus walking towards them. At the same time she saw Nick getting out of the back of a police car.

'I want to go back to the ship,' she said, her eyes pleading with him to help her.

'Sure thing.' He looked at Vince and said, 'Remember me, Morelli? Lieutenant Carter. NYPD.' He casually placed himself between them.

Vince looked at Gemma and gave a wry smile. 'You do have friends in high places, honey.' Then he saw Nick walking towards them and scowled. 'And here comes your boyfriend who's supposed to be on leave, arriving like the cavalry!'

Nick came up to them. 'Are you all right?' he asked, a grim expression on his face.

'Yes,' she said, barely above a whisper. This was a nightmare.

'You get on your way, Morelli,' said Gus. 'We'll take the little lady back to her ship. There's no need for you to wait.' He hardly noticed the car that pulled up slowly beside them; it was only as a man climbed out of the back seat that his instincts came to the fore. He shoved Nick and Gemma away, yelling, 'GET DOWN!' Nick pushed Gemma on to the sidewalk and threw himself on top of her, with Lou landing beside him as the stranger called, 'Hey – Morelli!'

Vince, for once, was taken completely by surprise. He was so busy watching Nick with Gemma, that only at the very last minute did he realise the danger he was in. By then it was too late. The stranger aimed the revolver he was holding at Vince and fired three times, then he got back into the car which drove away at speed, as Vince fell to the sidewalk.

Gemma tried to get up to run over to him, screaming, 'Vince! Vince!' but Nick stopped her. Holding her firmly he pulled her towards the police car, ignoring her protestations.

'What are you doing?' Gemma yelled at him. 'Vince could be dying back there!'

Gus spoke to her sharply. 'Do you want to be the centre of a gangland killing, with your name spread all over the papers?'

'What?'

'I can see it now,' he said quietly. '*Queen Mary* stewardess, mixed up with the Mafia.'

'The Mafia!' Her eyes were as big as saucers. 'Are you out of your mind?'

'No, Gemma, I'm not. Vince Morelli is a hit man for the Mafia.'

'Oh my God.' She covered her mouth with a shaking hand. 'Why didn't you tell me?'

'Because I wasn't sure. I tried to warn you. I told you to get out of the friendship, to tell him goodbye.'

She became hysterical and pummelled his chest with her fists, crying, 'You bastard, Gus! I could have been killed.'

He caught hold of her fists. 'You were never, ever alone with him. Everywhere you went, either I or my men were not far away.'

Nick took her by the shoulders. 'My God, you really like to live dangerously, Gemma. Well, I've had enough. I just won't have it, do you hear!' he shouted at her.

Her bottom lip trembled and she started to cry. She

buried her head in her hands. 'This is a nightmare . . . I don't believe it's happening.'

Nick pulled her to him roughly. 'Oh, Gemma darling, I'm sorry. I didn't mean to yell at you, but I love you, you little fool, and for one awful moment I thought I was going to lose you.'

'Come on,' said Gus heavily. 'I'll drive you both back to the ship. Lou can take over here.'

Nick sat in the back of the car holding Gemma in his arms and tried to comfort her as she wept uncontrollably from the shock of the incident.

When they got back to the ship, Nick insisted the three of them went to his cabin where he poured three stiff brandies. 'Here, drink this,' he said to Gemma. She was trembling so much she clutched the glass with both hands. Nick took a blanket from his bed and wrapped it around her. Then he sat beside her and held her close.

She looked across at Gus. 'I have never been so happy to see anyone in my whole life as you, when you turned up tonight.'

'When I saw you going out with Morelli earlier, I was real worried, but you were going nowhere without me or my men. I'm just so sorry you had to see this going down tonight, that's all.'

'It was awful seeing him lying there in a pool of blood.' Tears sprang to her eyes. 'Poor Vince. What a terrible way to die.'

'The man was a killer,' said Gus, 'so don't waste your sympathy.'

'So you say, but I find it very hard to believe, because he

wasn't like that to me . . . until I told him I wouldn't be seeing him again. Then I have to admit, he did scare me.' She sipped her brandy. 'You see such things at the pictures, read about it in the New York papers, but you never expect to be a part of it.'

Nick looked deeply concerned. 'Will the police want to question Gemma? Will she be involved?'

Gemma looked horrified as Gus said, 'Not if I can help it. It's a straightforward gangland execution. Morelli is dead. All anyone will want to know is who was in the car that carried the killers. If the police question the waiter, he won't have seen much. I was on the spot and saw what happened.'

'Won't you get into trouble if you don't mention her in your report?'

'All I need to say, if pushed, was that I was on a stake-out, that I saw a young lady I barely know in an argument and went to her rescue. I don't see a problem – it's just the death of another hoodlum.' He downed the rest of his drink.

'What will I say if they come on board to question me? After all, I have been seen in his company a few times,' Gemma asked anxiously.

'Just tell the truth,' said Gus. 'Look, I'm off now. I'll see you when you're here next trip.' He looked at Gemma and smiled. 'Please stay out of trouble, and keep what happened tonight to yourself.'

When they were alone, Nick gazed at Gemma and asked, 'Are you all right?'

'No, I'm not.' She looked at him. 'I feel very shaky. I can't stop trembling. I was so scared tonight, Nick.'

'I'm not surprised. When I saw you struggling in his arms, I wanted to kill that bastard myself.' He paused. 'I'm sorry, that wasn't very tactful of me, but you know what I mean.'

'You said you loved me,' she said softly.

He cupped her chin in his hand and kissed her gently. 'I fell in love with you the first night we danced together, although I didn't realise it at the time. If anything bad had happened to you tonight, I don't know what I would have done.'

She caressed his cheek. 'I love you too,' she whispered, 'but I don't understand any of this. Why were you there in the first place?'

'Gus came looking for me. He told me you were in some kind of danger.'

'But why would you be interested? What about Mrs Van Housen?' Gemma felt faint; her head was pounding. There were so many questions, so much she needed to know, but oh, how dizzy she felt.

'Come on,' Nick said. 'I'll take you back to your cabin. You need to rest. When we get to Southampton, you and I have a lot of talking to do. This is not the time. The main thing is you're fine, but you've had a terrible experience and you need to sleep.'

Luck was on their side, since no one saw them together. Outside her cabin, Nick kissed her gently but with obvious enjoyment. 'I'll see you soon, darling,' he promised.

As she climbed wearily into her bunk, she was thankful that Sally had not yet returned to the ship. Gemma could scarcely believe the evening's events. Vince was dead. She still couldn't get that into her head, it seemed unreal. But she understood that Nick had said he loved her . . . and he'd called her darling. The rest was a nightmare.

Chapter Twenty-nine

The following morning, Gemma's emotions were still in turmoil. She had slept fitfully, her dreams full of terrible images. She couldn't shut out her last moments with Vince. The sight of him lying in a pool of blood kept invading her thoughts. It was still difficult for her to think of him as a killer; he had always treated her with kindness and after he had rescued her from Big Jock, he'd been nothing but gentle and compassionate. If he could be so sensitive to her needs, how could he kill anyone in cold blood? It didn't make sense, even though she was now certain that he had been behind the attack on Jock MacTaggart. What if the Scot had been murdered . . . how would she have been able to live with that? And yet at the same time, she recalled how cold and angry Vince had been last night, and how he'd scared her. Would he have killed her too, rather than relinquish her to someone else? The image she must retain, she told herself, was of the nicer side of his character. She just couldn't cope with the other. Sally was suffering from a hangover, so Gemma was spared any worrying conversation.

She reached the pantry just as Charlie arrived, carrying a

tray laden with breakfast for them both. As they sat eating their bacon and eggs, he said, 'You look a bit rough this morning.'

'Thanks, Charlie! But you're right – I didn't sleep well last night.'

He asked carefully, 'Gemma, I've got some bad news. Have you heard about Vince Morelli?'

She felt as if someone had spilled a bucket of ice down her back. No words would come.

'I hope this won't be too much of a shock, love, but there's a rumour going around the docks that he was shot last night.'

'It's all right, Charlie. I already know. It's dreadful. It doesn't seem possible, I can hardly believe it.'

'You know?' He looked surprised and suspicious.

'I saw Gus last night when I was with Nick, and he told us. It's hard to take in.'

There was a look of immense relief on his face. 'I was so worried when I heard. I knew you were going to see him.' He gave her a piercing look. 'Are you all right, Gemma?'

She tried her best to behave naturally. 'Yes. I am a bit shaken by the news, of course. I was shocked and sorry to hear about Vince because I liked him, you know I did, and because earlier last night I was with him and told him I wouldn't be seeing him again.'

'You *did* see him then? How did he take it?'

She chose her words carefully. 'He wasn't very pleased and I feel guilty about that. Then I came back to the ship and had a drink with Gus and Nick.' She hadn't actually lied to Charlie, she thought. She just hadn't told him everything. She did feel somewhat disloyal; after all,

Charlie had offered to accompany her when she met Vince, but she remembered Gus's words, to keep everything that had happened to herself.

'You are back with Nick again?'

She sighed. 'It's a long story, Charlie.'

'They say Vince worked for the Mafia,' he said.

'Well, I find that very hard to believe!' she exclaimed angrily. That too was the truth. However she tried, she couldn't see Vince that way . . . and deep down she didn't want to. The terror of the previous night was still raw in her memory and she was finding it very hard to talk about it. Getting up from her stool she said, 'I'd better make a start. Is the clean linen ready?'

'It's all in the cabins. I'll just finish my coffee and then I'll be along.' Charlie sat quietly ruminating. Gemma couldn't lie her way out of a paper bag, he thought. She knew far more about Vince than she was saying, but he wouldn't press her further. As long as she was safe and well, that was all that mattered. As for the revelation about Vince, well . . . Charlie wasn't that surprised somehow. He'd always had a gut feeling about the man.

Until the gong sounded for the visitors to go ashore, Gemma had been on tenterhooks, expecting at any moment to see a New York cop come looking for her. Gus had paid her a short visit, assuring her that all was well, but only when the gangways had been taken away and she felt the ship move from the dockside, did she really begin to relax.

Nick saw her briefly, later, when his watch was over, checking to see if she was all right. Kissing her swiftly on the cheek, he said again that he would meet her after they had docked.

Charlie saw him walk away as he came out of one of the cabins, and smiled. He was pleased to see that the two were back together. That Nick Weston had his head screwed on, and if young Gemma settled down with him, she'd be doing very well for herself.

Vince Morelli's body was lying in the morgue. His apartment had been searched without the police finding any incriminating evidence. Then they started on the car. Under the mat on the floor by the driving seat, a key had been found. With a cry, Lou held it up and said to Gus, 'Hey, Lieutenant, this may be just what we are looking for!'

They read the tag and immediately made their way to Grand Central Station. Gus opened the left luggage box, picked up the wrapped gun with a handkerchief and grinned at his partner. 'This looks very promising,' he said with obvious glee. 'Let's take it to be tested.'

After the ballistics expert had finished his tests, the bullets were found to match those that had been used to kill Gene Bender and in other unsolved murders.

Vito Genovese cleared his organisation of the men who had been behind the plot to eliminate the Anastasio brothers, and the two families held an uneasy truce.

Gus Carter was no nearer breaking the hold the Mafia had on the docks, but as he told Lou, at least two vicious hoodlums were no longer on the streets, so it wasn't a total failure.

As he sat at his desk, he thought over the last few days and thanked his lucky stars that he'd managed to keep young Gemma out of this mess. Nick had called him before the ship sailed and thanked him, saying that all was well between him and Gemma now. If those two got married, maybe he'd be invited to the wedding! Then he could take the opportunity to visit the old country, as he'd always promised himself that he would.

When the ship docked in Southampton, Nick sent a message to Gemma, asking her to meet him at his hotel at six o'clock that evening. She had a bath before she left the ship and changed into her most glamorous underwear, over which she slipped a soft silk dress in the palest green, which showed off her curvaceous figure to perfection. Nick had declared his love for her, and she wanted to look her best, but he had yet to explain about Mrs Van Housen and Sally.

When she arrived at the hotel, she went to the desk and asked for his room number. She knocked on his door, her heart racing.

He opened the door. 'Hello, darling,' he said as he kissed her. 'Come in and sit down. We have a long evening ahead of us, so do you want a drink or shall I ring for some coffee?'

'What I really need is a large pot of tea and a sandwich,' she told him. 'I didn't have much time to eat today.'

Nick phoned for room service, the waiter duly arrived and set a tray before them.

When they were alone, Nick put his arm around her. 'Where shall we begin?' he asked.

'How about with Mrs Van Housen,' she said. 'Who exactly is this woman?'

Nick grinned at her. 'Greta? I've known her for years. We were engaged once.'

335

So what she'd heard about them was true, thought Gemma.

'Yes,' continued Nick, 'but she ended up marrying a friend of mine, an American lawyer.'

'So what was she doing on board the other trip?' she asked, as she poured the tea.

'She'd been handling some business in London. She owns some property there.'

'But you went off with her in New York.'

He gazed into Gemma's eyes. 'That's right, I did. But it was all very straightforward, darling. She and her husband were having a cocktail party and one of the directors of the Furness Withy Lines, whose ships run from the States, wanted to meet me, to offer me a job. Naturally I couldn't tell anyone.'

Gemma's heart sank. Was Nick going to up sticks and move to America? 'Did you accept?'

He gathered her into his arms and kissed the tip of her nose. 'No. I'm happy where I am. I see enough of Americans on board, I have no wish to live among them.'

'That's a bit unkind,' she chided.

'Don't misunderstand me, darling. I love to travel, but I'm an Englishman at heart.'

'There is one more thing,' she said tentatively.

'And what's that?'

'Sally. Sally James, the stewardess.'

He frowned. 'Do I know her?'

'According to her, she knows you very well. She told me she had a meeting with you at the kennels during one trip. She said it was a really private place, unseen by prying eyes.'

'I've only been to the kennels once this year,' he said, with a look of puzzlement. 'I took an elderly lady up to visit her dog. She was a bit upset at being parted from him. Come to think of it, there *was* a stewardess there, looking at the animals, but I don't know her.'

Gemma was furious with Sally for feeding her lies, and even more annoyed with herself for believing them.

He traced his finger along her lips. 'Are there any more questions?' he asked softly.

'No. None.'

'Good,' he said, and pulled her closer. 'I have only one. Were you in love with Vince?'

'Of course not! How can you even think such a thing?'

'I had to ask. I had to be sure. Come here, you little minx,' he said and covered her mouth with his.

His kisses were full of passion, demanding a response, which she willingly gave as she clung to him, her body melting against his. It was as if they had both been starving and were suddenly faced with a luxurious table full of food. They couldn't get enough of each other.

Nick rose from his seat and pulled her to her feet. Then he undid the fine zip at the back of her dress, and she unbuttoned his shirt, peeling it off as quickly as she could. They cast aside the rest of their clothes and he picked her up in his arms and carried her over to the bed, where he proceeded to smother her with kisses.

'Oh, Nick,' she gasped as he buried his head between her breasts. He kissed the small rise of her belly as he caressed her hips and when he spread her legs and ran his sensitive fingers along the inside of her thighs, she thought she would drown in the passion that rose within her.

337

As he kissed her again she whispered, 'Nick, this is my first time.'

He gazed deeply into her eyes and said, 'My darling Gemma, I'll be very gentle and careful.' He reached out for a towel beside the bed and slipped it beneath her buttocks then caressed her, kissed her, teased her, until she was ready for him, before he slipped on a condom.

Never had she realised that sex could be so wonderful. As she felt him move into her she arched her body to meet his, and the sudden short pain she felt as he eventually thrust himself in more deeply, was one of pleasure.

At last they lay damp, breathless and exhausted in each other's arms. He pulled her closer and kissed her eyes. 'Gemma, Gemma,' he murmured. 'You are a wonderful woman.'

'You're only saying that because it's true,' she said softly, and heard him chuckle.

'I wish we had more time together,' he said. 'This sailing schedule is no help at all. I can't see you when we're at sea. It's hell knowing you are so near and I can't even talk to you. But at least we have New York to look forward to. I do have one more thing to ask you,' he said.

Gemma wondered what it could be. 'What is it?'

'Well,' he said softly, 'it seems quite evident to me that you are not safe to be let loose without someone looking out for you, so I think I'd better marry you and keep you out of trouble.' He kissed the palm of her hand. 'Please!'

Gemma looked at him with a startled expression. 'What did you just say?'

He smiled. 'I've just asked you to marry me, you little goose.'

'Oh, Nick.' She felt tears prick her eyes.

He tightened his grip on her hand. 'For goodness sake, darling, there's no need to get upset! I promise to be kind and not beat you . . . well, not very often. I love you, Gemma Barrett. I want to spend the rest of my life with you. Is that so terrible?'

'No, it isn't. But you hardly know me.'

'Wrong. I know a lot about you. I know about the freckles between your breasts, the feel of your bare skin. How your eyes flash when you are angry, and your nostrils flare . . . and I want us to grow old together. Isn't that enough?'

With a deep sigh of contentment she said, 'Oh yes, that's more than enough.'

The corners of his mouth twitched as he tried to smother a smile. 'I take it that's a yes, then?'

Gemma started to laugh. 'Oh, it definitely is a yes.'

The two of them bathed together before dressing, which Gemma thought was just as erotic as being in bed with Nick. Eventually they left the hotel and went to a small exclusive restaurant to celebrate.

Nick looked across the table at her. 'Happy?' he asked.

'Very,' she said. And she was. She didn't feel she had done wrong. She had been with the man she wanted and who wanted her. It had seemed entirely natural. She hid a smile. Eunice would have a fit if she knew!

She gazed into his eyes and said, 'There is just one thing.'

He frowned. 'And what is that?'

She hesitated for a moment and said, 'I long to be your wife, but I do want to see a bit of the world too. For years it was my dream to go to sea and to travel. It was all I lived for – I don't want to give it up before I've been anywhere.'

He looked bemused and pretended to be offended. 'I don't understand you, Miss Barrett. I offer you my everything, only to find it isn't enough.'

'Oh, Nick darling, don't be cross. You of all people can understand how I feel.'

A slow smile crossed his features. 'Of course I do. We don't need to rush into marriage. How about if I applied to go cruising and pulled a few strings to get you on the same ship? Then we could see the world together.'

She threw her arms around his neck and kissed him soundly, to the amusement of some of the other diners. 'You are a darling man. That would be absolutely wonderful. Could you do such a thing?'

'Of course.' He kissed her cheek. 'Restrictions are not quite so rigid on the cruise ships, and we'll be able to spend more time together. It will be as if we are already married. Then in a few years' time, after we are officially married and I get a Captaincy of my own, you will be able to take a few complimentary trips as my wife.'

'Really?'

'Yes, really. But you do realise, darling, that I'll be away from home a lot. I know with your father being a seafarer, you are used to the life, but will you mind terribly?'

Gemma knew she wouldn't be like Eve, discontented with her lot. She had a man she truly loved, and that was enough. 'No, of course I won't.'

'Besides,' he said, with twinkling eyes, 'you'll be busy looking after the children.'

'Will I?'

'Oh, yes, Gemma.' He smothered her cheek. 'You do like kids, I hope?'

As she gazed at his handsome features she wondered what any offspring of theirs would look like. 'Yes, I like children,' she said.

'And another thing,' he added, 'you will have to meet my parents. They will naturally want to meet their future daughter-in-law, and I'll need to meet yours.'

Her heart sank. 'My father left us to live in South Africa,' she said. 'But of course you can meet Eve, my mother.'

'I'll take you home tonight,' he said, 'and we can tell her the good news. Then, after we've done that, we can go back to my hotel. As you know, I've a double room. There, we can have our own private celebration,' he said, with a wicked grin.

Gemma's heart was thudding as she opened the door of the house in Duke Street and walked in with Nick.

Eve was sitting watching the television with Danny when they arrived, but she rose to her feet when she espied the tall elegant figure of the man standing beside Gemma.

He stepped forward. 'Good evening, Mrs Barrett,' he said in his deep, cultured voice.

'Mum, this is Nick Weston, he's the First Officer on my ship. We've just become engaged.'

Nick stepped forward. 'I know I haven't known Gemma for very long, Mrs Barrett, but I love her. We would very much like to have your blessing. You are the first to hear our news.'

'I am?' She was pleased to hear that; it gave her a feeling of importance. She kissed Gemma on the cheek. 'Congratulations,' she said and turned to Nick. She held out her hand. 'Congratulations.'

He took her hand and kissed her cheek. 'I feel I may be allowed such a liberty, Mrs Barrett. After all, you are to be my mother-in-law.'

As Eve looked at the handsome man, with such presence, she felt rather proud. The neighbours would be very impressed with him. She turned and introduced Danny. 'This is a very good friend of mine.'

The two men shook hands, then Danny kissed Gemma's cheek. 'Congratulations, I'm sure you'll be very happy.'

'I'm sorry we have nothing in the house with which to celebrate,' said Eve. 'I don't drink, you see,' she added with some pride. 'But I could make you a cup of coffee.'

The four of them drank their coffee and Nick told Eve and Danny about their plans to travel together before getting married. He chatted to them, charming Eve, making her feel somebody special, until eventually they took their leave.

'I'm staying with Nick tonight,' said Gemma. 'I'll write from New York.'

Eve stepped forward and hugged her. 'I'm so very happy for you,' she said.

In the back of the taxi on the way to the hotel, encircled in the arms of the man she loved, Gemma was content. Her mother had seemed genuinely pleased for her and she was very obviously impressed with Nick. More importantly, she appeared to have pulled herself together, and Danny seemed fond of her, which meant she had a life before her.

Gemma gazed up at Nick with shining eyes. And so, at last, had she.

Now you can buy any of these other bestselling
books from your bookshop or *direct
from the publisher*.

FREE P&P AND UK DELIVERY
(Overseas and Ireland £3.50 per book)

My Sister's Child	Lyn Andrews	£5.99
Liverpool Lies	Anne Baker	£5.99
The Whispering Years	Harry Bowling	£5.99
Ragamuffin Angel	Rita Bradshaw	£5.99
The Stationmaster's Daughter	Maggie Craig	£5.99
Our Kid	Billy Hopkins	£6.99
Dream a Little Dream	Joan Jonker	£5.99
For Love and Glory	Janet MacLeod Trotter	£5.99
In for a Penny	Lynda Page	£5.99
Goodnight Amy	Victor Pemberton	£5.99
My Dark-Eyed Girl	Wendy Robertson	£5.99
For the Love of a Soldier	June Tate	£5.99
Sorrows and Smiles	Dee Williams	£5.99

TO ORDER SIMPLY CALL THIS NUMBER

01235 400 414

or e-mail orders@bookpoint.co.uk

Prices and availability subject to change without notice.